Don't Hunt Werewolves

Jeni Conrad

This book is dedicated to my very supportive and patient beta reader friends. Thank you for all the time and feedback you've given me.

Author's Note

As a teacher who has dealt with teens for many years, not to mention was once one herself, I wanted to bring up an issue in this series that many people struggle with. But for some, reading about it may be uncomfortable or even triggering. This story contains themes of an eating disorder. I am not trying to promote it or glamorize it in any way but rather trying to highlight the struggle a person might have with it and how damaging it can be. The issue does get resolved, but it takes several books to do so. If you or anyone you know struggles with an eating disorder, there is help. https://www.edreferral.com/

Contents

Chapter 1

"I'm not sure this is such a good idea." I frowned and hugged myself against the cold wind.

"Oh, don't be such a stiff. It'll be fun!" Addison nudged me with an elbow as we navigated the rolling grass of the dark cemetery.

Emma giggled. "Stiff, because we're surrounded by dead people. Get it?"

I shot her a look behind Addy's back that I hoped she could interpret. Emma knew about my ghostly problems after I had helped her out with one that had been haunting her attic last month. Mostly, we'd kept away from talking about them, but she had to know that traipsing around dead bodies on Halloween night was not something I should have been doing.

Her smile told me she understood, but she was limited in what she could say since we didn't want Addy to know. "I'm sure everything will be fine. This is just a bit of harmless fun."

Gravestones peeked up out of the gloom, their grey faces watching us as we walked between them. A few trees loomed overhead, and their branches were bare, stretching out with gnarled fingers. The wind sliced through my flimsy costume, and for the millionth time that night, I regretted dressing as a yellow, felt M&M instead of a fur-covered Chewbacca.

Brandon easily traversed the ground next to me, not having to worry about tripping or anything lame like us alivers had to worry about. He chatted continuously even though only I could hear him. I had told him several times to stop talking so much while others were around. It was difficult to tune him out, but instead of getting better at it, I was getting worse.

"Can we talk about how cliche this is? A group of naive girls wandering around in a dark cemetery on Halloween night, planning to set out some candles and have a seance?" He asked, eyeing a nearby ghost who was wandering off in a daze.

I shook my head by way of answer. I didn't dare say anything out loud because I didn't want Addy to think I was weird. Or...well, weirder than she already thought of me.

This was only my second time hanging out with Emma and Addy outside of school. Until a few weeks ago, I'd run with a different crowd of kids, mostly cheerleaders and football players. After I broke ties with Andrea and her crew—which also happened to include Noah, my long-term crush and necromancer friend who also knew about the ghost situation—I'd spent lunches alone in the library and hadn't gone out much at all in the evenings.

Well, at least not with alive people.

So when Addy had invited Emma and me to hang out tonight, I'd readily agreed, even though that meant I had to be the yellow M&M since they'd both picked the other colors earlier. Besides being cold, it was fine. I was just glad they'd thought to include me.

"Emma is right. This is harmless fun. What else could we do on Halloween night? Besides, what's the worst that could happen?"

"Oh, I hate when people ask that question," I muttered, careful not to step on anyone's grave.

For obvious reasons, I usually avoided cemeteries. Ghosts didn't always haunt where they were buried or even where they were killed. However, some still felt drawn to the death, and whatever their ties to the cemetery in life, there were several that haunted it after death.

Wispy blue shadows passed in my periphery, but so long as I didn't acknowledge them, they'd leave us alone. It was a danger having Brandon here since my interactions with him could clue other ghosts in on what I could do, but that gave me more motivation to ignore his comments.

Emma gave me another reassuring smile. "It'll be fine."

"What if we get caught out here? I'm sure the police are all over the cemeteries on Halloween. The sign says it closes at dusk. Isn't this like technically trespassing?" My teeth chattered around my words.

"Why don't you just say why you really don't want to be here? Because you're scared." Addy glanced over her shoulder and gave me a pointed look, her straight pink hair sticking out of the neck of her red M&M costume.

"She's not scared," Brandon said, getting in Addy's face, keeping pace with her so he stayed uncomfortably close. "She's just smarter than you and knows that ghosts actually exist. You do something like this, and you could pull a malicious spirit who could haunt you for the rest of your life. Boo!"

I struggled to suppress a grin at his attempt to startle Addy. The girl had no idea he was wiggling his fingers at her and making spooky noises. Thankfully, the darkness hid my face in shadow.

"I'm not scared of ghosts if that's what you're implying. Well, most of them, anyway. But I am scared we'll get in trouble, and I'll get marks on my record or something. I need to get into a good college, and the last thing my mom needs right now is extra stress in her life."

"I'm sure your grades are good enough. I wouldn't worry too much about having something like sneaking into a cemetery on your file. It'll just give it a bit of color," Emma said while rubbing her arms up and down. "I just wish it were warmer tonight."

Addy shrugged, adjusting the bag strap on her shoulder. The candles and something metallic clinked inside. "I'm sure we'll have plenty of time to worry about college. Right now, we can worry about having a little fun and excitement."

We slowed our pace as we ascended a rather steep hill. My slick flats slipped a few times on the damp grass. Addy and Emma seemed to have no trouble climbing though as both reached the top before me.

Addy put her hands on her hips and surveyed the scene. Her round red costume puckered in at the side as she looked out into the darkness from the highest point of the cemetery. This spot usually gave a peaceful view during the sunlit hours of the day, displaying a solemn place where people went to revere their dead loved ones. However, during night, it showed mostly darkness with the occasional grey of tombstones and the inky blackness of reaching trees.

I finally made it up the hill. "Fine. We're here. Let's just get this over with. I'm thinking Mrs. Nida's warm apple cider would be perfect after this. If she's still handing it out, that is."

"Mmm, cider does sound wonderful right now." Emma rubbed her hands together to build warmth.

"So what do we do first?" I asked, watching Addy plop her bag onto a marble bench and begin to pull out supplies. The bench was probably dedicated to some important dead person, but I wasn't able to make out the name carved into it.

I was grateful there weren't any ghosts hanging out too close to us, yet. Well, except for Brandon, but he didn't count.

"First we set up our circle and light the candles." Addy pulled five candles from her bag and handed three of them to Emma. Together, they placed them in a loose circle that was big enough for three people to sit in.

With a metallic lighter that gleamed in the light, Addy lit the candles. It took her a few tries to get the flame to stay lit with the lighter, but once the wicks on the candles caught, they had no trouble, even in the brisk wind. The flames moved and flickered but stayed lit no matter how hard it blew.

"Then we sit around this one and call to the spirits." Addy placed another candle in the middle.

Emma and I followed her lead, sat on the cold grass, and crossed our legs.

"That's not how this works." Brandon sighed and shook his head. "Kids these days." He sat down between me and Emma. We were so close that his form was halfway between both of us.

I wanted to tell him to move over but didn't know how without looking insane.

Addy put her fingers into "okay" circles and placed them on her knees. Closing her eyes, she turned her face up to the night sky. With a spooky voice, she said, "Oh spirits, hear our cry. We come to you on All Hallows' Eve and entreat your presence."

Brandon rolled his eyes. "What kind of stupid ghost would answer to that?"

Addy and Emma repeated the words both drawing out the syllables in a sing-song rhythm. Emma nudged me through Brandon so I'd join in.

"That tickles." Brandon giggled.

I sighed and came in on the third repetition of the words, but not as loud as the other two. The last thing I wanted was for the ghost that was wandering a few yards away to notice me talking and come over.

At the fourth repetition, my neck hairs prickled, indicating the presence of ghosts was about to increase.

"I think this is working," I whispered, my voice rising in a worried pitch.

"Of course it's working," Addy said in between chants. "Now stop interrupting. You could mess it all up."

"Sorry," I said, peeking my eyes open and unhappy to see we had gained the attention of several nearby ghosts.

On silent feet, they crept toward the circle. At first, it was only three but more joined them soon. Their blue transparent forms shimmered in the dark. Most of them looked sad and haggard with hunched shoulders. They were all wearing whatever they had worn when they'd died. At least that's what I assumed because it seemed to be the rule for ghosts. One girl was in her pajamas—fluffy pants with a faded bunny pattern I could barely see. There was a man in a business suit, an older man in a flannel shirt and saggy jeans, and two girls wearing sundresses and holding hands.

I squeezed my eyes shut, and my heart went out to these lost souls. The two girls reminded me of the pair of sisters we had helped cross over a few weeks ago. It hadn't been easy as one was a poltergeist and had lost most of herself, but thankfully or unfortunately—I still wasn't sure—my powers had given her more energy and allowed her to come back to her sister. They'd crossed over while still hugging each other tightly.

It was, honestly, one of my proudest moments.

Despite my eyes being closed, I could still feel them moving in on us. Thankfully, they paused outside the candle circle, but that didn't stop them from talking. Several moaned and groaned and cried. I winced with each plea for help.

Addy and Emma were oblivious to the heartache that descended upon us, but I could feel myself shaking.

"Tell her I'm sorry."

"She doesn't even know that I love her."

"He's a murderer."

"My mom needs to know how much I love her. I never told her."

"Hanna, this is not good," Brandon whispered into my ear, his voice closer and more familiar than the others.

A few tears escaped my eyelids as I squinted to keep them closed. It was hard not to open my eyes and try to help them. I had only recently accepted that it was my duty to help as many ghosts cross over as I could, but I knew this was not the time nor place to start that. So far, I'd kept it to easy ghosts that I could target by themselves.

In the last few weeks, Brandon and I had helped a kid who had been haunting his mom's car, an older man who haunted my school's library and who had died while walking his dog one day, and a girl hanging out on the baseball field who'd been upset to find she'd died before her team won the state championships.

As we chanted, I had time to think about my new friends versus my previous ones. Even though what we were doing was absurd and scarier to me than they could know, it was nice to feel more included and less annoying than I had usually felt while hanging out with Andrea, Randi, and Stephanie. The change was refreshing.

After several more times repeating the chant, Addy paused and took a deep breath. "I know you're here. I can feel your presence. Show us a sign that you are here."

Barely peeking my eyes open, I saw one of the ghosts peel off from the crowd that encircled us. To my dismay, she stepped into the circle. All the candle flames stood strong and tall, but as the ghost passed over one, it flickered.

Addy and Emma noticed the difference, and both got excited looks on their faces.

I knew my face wasn't showing excitement. I was too busy being shocked. My heart hammered in my chest, and I was struggling just to breathe. This ghost was one I knew and had thought was safe and still alive. She was dressed in a sexy policewoman's costume, complete with fish-net tights and a smart cap. Her hair rolled down her shoulders in waves, and despite her form glowing a soft blue, I knew her hair to be a natural sunny blonde.

"Was that the sign?" Emma asked in hushed tones.

"You can do better than that. Give us a real sign that you are here." Addy sat up straighter and looked around, trying to find any other indications that we weren't alone.

"Where am I? What's happening?" the ghost asked as she took in the scene, not yet recognizing the girls in front of her.

Brandon cursed and backed up towards the edge of the candle circle. "Is that who I think it is?"

It took all I had not to scream and run away. It was one thing to see ghosts all the time. It was quite another to see someone you thought was alive show up dead.

"Show us a sign!" Addy grew more forceful in her commands.

Emma's wide eyes were looking around until she caught sight of my face. "Hanna? What's wrong?"

Addy noticed Emma's distress and began to pay me more attention. "Do you see something?"

"I—I... Yes. No. Yes." Tears trickled out of my eyes, and I was shaking so hard that when Emma wrapped her arms around me, her body shook too.

Stephanie finally saw me after I spoke. "Hanna!" she pleaded, kneeling in front of me. "You have to help me, please! Something happened on the way to the party, and I don't know what to do."

Taking in a trembling breath, I said, "Stephanie, I'm here. It's okay." I wasn't sure if those last words were for her or for me.

Brandon was staring at the dead girl who had been one of my closest friends up until a month ago. We'd hung out at lunch nearly every day for almost two years. It was true that we hadn't ever been super close, but she was still someone I cared about. She had always been much nicer than Andrea.

"What's happening? The last thing I remember is driving in the car with Alex and his friends. We were going to a party and..."

Her eyes widened with the horror of the memory as she placed a hand over her mouth and cursed.

The candles must have had some kind of magical strength to them because no other ghosts entered the circle. Although, after I acknowledged Stephanie, their wails and pleas increased, adding audible chaos to an already terrifying situation.

Addy and Emma were exchanging glances. Addy was confused and slightly freaked out while Emma's lips were pressed together in worry as she put her arms around my shoulders.

"Hanna? What's going on?" Addy asked, abandoning her meditative pose and scooting closer to me. "Is this a joke?"

Emma shook her head, her brown curls wavering around her face. "I don't think this is a joke. I think something real is happening here."

I gently pulled out of Emma's embrace and kneeled as well, trying to get closer to Stephanie's face. "Try to focus, Stephanie. If someone is in trouble, maybe we can help."

Gasping for air she didn't know she didn't need, Stephanie nodded. "Alex and his friends—have you seen them around here? Why am I here?"

Brandon gathered himself and kneeled next to Stephanie, putting his hand on her shoulder. "I hate to break it to you, but you're dead. It's terrible and horrible, and you'll have plenty of time to sort through the feelings later, but right now we need to focus. What happened?"

Stephanie looked away from the kid in 90s clothes and back to me, searching my face. "Is that true? Am I dead?"

"I'm sorry. Yes. Now, are Alex and his friends okay?" I tried to keep my voice even and focused, but it was hard with my chest fluttering.

Ghostly tears welled up in her eyes. "We went over the bridge and into the river. It's all fuzzy after that."

"Where?" I was already pulling out my phone to call the police. Maybe they could get there in time to help. Maybe we could save other lives even at the cost of one of my friends' lives.

"Meadowbrook," she said with a hiccup.

Addy stood and bent down to one of the candles. "This is gone too far. Let's get out of here."

The horde of ghosts moaned and roamed outside the candlelight, seeming to get more excited when Addy had moved as if sensing they were going to be able to flood into the area.

"Wait!" I nearly screamed at her, startling everyone, including the two ghosts kneeling.

Addy froze and stared at me. "What's wrong with you?"

Emma stood and put her hands out in a placating motion towards Addy. "It's fine. Just listen to her for a second. Let's just take a breather."

As Emma tried to help Addy, I dialed 911 and made a feverish call for help at the Meadowbrook bridge. The dispatcher was calm and assured me that they would send people immediately.

I hung up and nodded to Stephanie. "They're sending help. If anyone else is alive, they'll find them."

She deflated, her shoulders slumping and eyes full of pain and tears. "I shouldn't have let Alex drive. I knew I shouldn't have. He was so insistent. I didn't know what to do."

"You can't beat yourself up about it. There's no point," Brandon said, his hand still gripping her shoulder comfortingly. "We all make choices in our lives without knowing the consequences, and then things just happen. Sometimes they are very terrible, horrible things we would have never chosen for us or our loved ones, but they still happen all the same."

This wasn't the time to talk about this, but his words flagged inside my head. I logged them away in my mind to ask him about them later. It felt like a clue to his own death, somehow.

Addy and Emma were standing above me, holding on to each other, their noses red from the cold and giving me mixed looks.

I also stood and made a show to dust off the back of my yellow costume, mostly to stall and figure out what I was going to say to them. Plus, I had the issue of the clamoring ghosts that encircled us. Some had wandered off in despair, but there were still enough to be loud and distracting. "Right. Well, this is going to sound weird to you guys, but once we dissolve this circle, I'm not going to be able to see or hear much until we can get out of this cemetery."

Emma's eyebrows creased with concern, but she nodded. "What do you need us to do?"

Addy wasn't so accepting which I understood. I mean, I was being super weird. "Why? What's going on? Who have you been talking to?"

Brandon was still sitting next to Stephanie in the grass, trying to make comforting noises and patting her back awkwardly as she sobbed into her hands.

"I'm not sure how to say this, but we need to head to Meadowbrook bridge. There's been an accident, and there might be time for them to save the survivors." I looked down at my flats in the grass that were not thick enough to prevent my toes from freezing over. "I have a particular ghost who wants to see who survives. It might be enough to help her cross over, depending."

Brandon shook his head. "If we're lucky. It'll probably be much more complicated than that considering how young she died."

I shrugged. "It doesn't hurt to try."

Addy looked back and forth between me and the place I was talking to. "So there are ghosts here?"

"At least two. There are several more outside the circle right now that seem unable to cross it for some reason. You'll have to let me know what kind of candles these are. They're doing a great job, but once we put them out and head toward the car, I'm sure to be bombarded by them."

I knew somewhere inside of me that I was mourning for Stephanie, or at least I should have been, but I was in too much shock and too focused on the situation in front of me. It was a good thing to have something focus on so I wouldn't collapse into a pile of tears and be useless for several days.

"Okay..." Emma said slowly and looked around as if she'd be able to catch a glimpse of the ghosts.

Addy kept staring at me. "Are you high? This was just a fun seance, not real. Quit being all weird about this."

I sighed and put fingers through my hair, trying to straighten it from where the wind had surely ruffled it. "I'm sorry. I know I'm weird. Just help me get out of here and then you can forget all this even happened. You can even ignore me at school if you want. I understand."

Emma frowned and gave Addy a look. "We're not going to do that. We're your friends, and we're all weird in our own ways. Just tell us how we can help."

Addy studied Emma's determined look and then turned back to me. "Wait. I'm slow. You're saying you can see ghosts?"

"Pretty much."

"That is...so cool!" Addy hopped up a down in excitement a couple of times, causing both Emma's and my eyebrows to raise in surprise. "I've always known there were more things out there than we could see. What's it like? It must be so cool!"

Stephanie sniffed through her sobs while Brandon muttered soothing words, reminding me of the task at hand.

"I can get into all of that later and talk about it so much you'll get bored, but right now we need to get to the bridge," I said, still surprised at her reaction.

"I doubt I'll get bored, but I hear you." Addy nodded firmly.

"What should we do?" Emma asked, letting go of Addy's arm.

"First, we need to get out of here. The ghosts shouldn't be able to follow me out except for those I give permission to. Until then, you'll have to be my eyes and ears and guide me through the tombstones and into the car. There are seriously way too many here for me to even hear my own thoughts, let alone be able to navigate through the headstones without falling to my death several times."

As if on cue or simply from listening to me, the wailing of the outside ghosts grew louder.

Chapter 2

After Emma and Addy had grabbed my arms and steered me through the tombstones, we'd reached the safety of the car and headed out toward the bridge. I had been right about what would happen after we extinguished the candles. So many ghosts had converged on me that it was easier to just keep my eyes closed and rely on my friends to get me through the chaos.

I wasn't used to relying on other humans to help me with ghost issues, but after the night we had, I needed it.

As we pulled up to the scene of the accident, bright police lights bounced around the empty branches of trees and reflected off the sides of cars.

"At least they found the right place," Brandon said from where he sat in the back seat between Stephanie and me.

Usually, ghosts were stuck in their haunts, places tied to their lives somehow, and each haunt was different for every ghost. However, I had a unique ability that no other Seers had that allowed ghosts to travel outside of their haunts, so long as they were near me. I could even summon ghosts to come to me by mere thought, another power that other Seers didn't have, at least according to my grandma who had been my Seer guide for a short time before she'd crossed over.

I still missed her every day.

It was unlikely that the cemetery was Stephanie's haunt. What were the odds of her appearing to me while I was there? It was more likely that my thinking about her and my friends called her spirit to me, and I had accidentally summoned a ghost I hadn't even known existed.

That was new.

Stephanie wiped at her nose, and I wished I could give her a tissue to use, more for comfort than to clean up boogers. "I think this is it. It's hard to tell in the dark."

The area was blocked off by several police cars so we couldn't get very close. After we climbed out of the car, I ran to the side of the bridge and looked down, unsure what I would see and unsure what I wanted to see.

Addy, Emma, Stephanie, and Brandon all came to stand next to me as I peered down. Lights that the police had set up beamed down into the darkness, illuminating the area so the people operating the tow truck that was parked along the banks of the river could see. We'd reached the spot in time to watch them crank the car out by its bumper and haul it onto the grassy ground. Water poured out from everywhere, glistening off the bright lights. The back window had been bashed out with something and, as far as we could see, there weren't any bodies visible.

"Holy Cow," Emma said, her eyes wide and staring. "That's so scary."

"Maybe they got the people out already," Addy said, looking around for signs of life.

Stephanie clutched her hand to her heart as her eyes scanned the area. "I don't see any bodies inside."

She didn't need to say that included her own body, wherever it had gone.

"Maybe we can get some information." I took my gaze away from the car, still seeping out water, and looked towards the policemen. They were trying to keep other bystanders from getting too close to where the bridge wall was broken, and the car had fallen through.

"Excuse me," I said as we approached an officer. "That's my friend's car down there. Did y'all find anyone inside?"

He shook his head. "I'm not supposed to give information out. Only keep the area clear. Please keep back, miss."

"Even if I'm a friend of the victims?"

"Are you family?"

I shook my head slowly.

He shrugged. "Then my hands are tied."

"Couldn't you have lied and said you were his sister?" Addy asked quietly as we walked away from the area.

"I didn't think to do that." I frowned, unable to keep my eyes from continuing to scan the water, looking for bodies or anything unusual.

"I'll see what I can find out." Brandon turned to Stephanie. "Listen, your friends are probably not dead or else we'd see their ghosts too, right?"

I didn't bother to correct him that their ghosts could have easily gone to their haunts without us ever knowing. If it came down to it, I could try summoning them as well, but I was going to keep that as a last step kind of thing.

Stephanie nodded distractedly at him, still staring at the inky water.

Addy sighed and huddled closer to Emma. "You're too honest for your own good I suppose."

"Which isn't a bad thing." Emma gave Addy an amused smile.

"I'll be back in a jiffy," Brandon said.

I nodded at him. "Be careful."

"What? Like I'll get caught or murdered? That ship has sailed, my darling." He walked past me with a grin.

I shook my head with a smile. "Fine. Maybe I should be warning you not to cause any trouble then."

Addy and Emma were looking at me, and my smile changed into an awkward one.

"My ghost friend is going to go see what he can find out. There are advantages to having one around who can go undetected in places I can't."

"That would actually be pretty cool." Addy nodded appreciatively.

"So I suppose we'll just assume you're talking to a ghost when you look off to an empty place and say something that doesn't make sense, shall we?" Emma said with a friendly smile.

Again, it was weird to have girlfriends who weren't constantly trying to put me down. A weirdness I think I could get used to.

"That's probably a good bet." Ordinarily, I would have chuckled at how right she was, but my heart was still too full of pain at losing Steph.

My friend had died that night, and she was standing next to me, sniffing and hiccupping, and there wasn't much I could do about it. Plus, we'd yet to find out if anyone else had died. She'd said Alex and his friends were in the car. I didn't know Alex well, but it would still be sad to see another person die.

Emma's eyebrows creased together. "Didn't you say the ghost who told you about all of this was named Stephanie? Isn't that one of your cheerleader friends?"

"You knew her?" Addy's lips pulled into an empathetic pout. "That's so terrible."

At her name, Stephanie glanced up for a second, and then she looked away, an expression of such loss that sadness sunk deeper into my heart.

"It is terrible."

We stood quietly, looking over the bridge as the tow truck pulled the totaled car onto its flatbed. Water still dripped from its undercarriage and in my sad state, it was easy to imagine it was crying too.

Gravel crunched behind us, and we turned around to see Caleb walking our way. It was kind of him to allow his approach to make sounds so he didn't scare us too badly by popping out of nowhere. Teleportation wasn't on a vampire's list of powers, but they were able to move so quickly that it seemed like they could teleport.

"Hey, Caleb," I said, and turned back to watch the tow truck.

Addy and Emma were slower to get back to our vigil as they looked back and forth between themselves and the newcomer.

Over the last two months, I'd gotten used to seeing him appear at seemingly random times and places. He'd reassured me several times that he was watching over me, and his sudden appearances seemed to confirm that story.

After what we'd both endured at the hand of his former queen, it was an extra comfort to know he was always nearby.

"Nice costumes." He chuckled as he looked all of us up and down amusingly.

"Aren't you going to introduce us?" Addy asked from my left. Emma was standing on my right, and Stephanie was standing cluelessly through both Emma and me.

Caleb came to stand on Addy's other side and flashed her a bright white and charming grin.

"This is Caleb. You might have seen him around school. He's become a family friend of a sort." I vaguely waved in his direction.

"Aren't you on the football team?" Emma peered up at his tall frame with squinted eyes.

"For now. It's been hard to focus on stuff like that recently. There are just more important things in life than football, as hard as that is to believe," Caleb said, still grinning.

"I believe it," Addy said as we watched the tow truck pull onto the main road and take the soggy car somewhere else.

"So how did you hear about the accident?" I asked, remembering that I should probably act surprised to see him.

"Actually, I came here to ask you guys the same thing." Caleb raised an eyebrow at me.

I glanced at Addy and Emma, then once at Stephanie who was still crying quietly, and then back to Caleb. "You're probably going to get upset with me..."

He sighed and shook his head. "Naturally."

"Well, it's just that it was someone I know, you know? Oh, you know her too. Do you remember Stephanie? I used to sit with her at lunch, and you sat next to her that one day and flirted a bit? She's blonde and on the cheerleading squad. You remember her?"

Caleb's dark eyes flashed to the water and back to me. "Of course I remember her. Was she in that car?"

Stephanie's head came up as I mentioned her name, and she sniffed again loudly. She sure wasn't taking this being-dead-and-now-a-ghost thing too well, but it was hard to blame her.

I nodded. "We called the cops so they'd get here as soon as possible and hopefully be able to rescue the others who were in the car. They won't tell us what they found, and we got here too late to see if there were bodies or anything."

"Which there weren't, apparently," Brandon said as he walked back to us. "All the police are stumped because they haven't been able to find any bodies, not even the driver. They've got search parties all up and down the river, but so far, no sign of anyone. It's quite a mystery." He puckered his lips in a scandalous expression.

Unable to hear Brandon talking, Caleb talked over him, and it took me a second to process what each of them was saying.

"No bodies in the car? That's weird. The back window was clearly bashed out. They probably swam out and made for the shore. They could have been carried downstream for quite a while." Caleb's eyes scanned the riverbanks as he spoke.

Stephanie shook her head. "They were way too drunk to be able to swim well."

"The police will find them." Addy nodded confidently.

"Hopefully they'll find them alive," Emma said, craning her neck to look in the direction where the river flowed, now bathed in search-lights as officers scanned the area.

"I know someone who could do a great job at finding them." I gave Caleb a pointed look.

His lips twitched in a smile, but he didn't rush off immediately. "And are you going to tell me why I'm supposed to be upset with you?"

"Well..." I looked at Addy and Emma again, "I had to tell them about the ghosts."

Emma gave him an awkward smile while Addy's eyes lit up.

"Does he know too? Isn't it the coolest thing you've ever heard?" Addy grinned at both of us as if just discovering something amazing.

Caleb's eyebrows pulled together in disappointment. "But I thought we were both in agreement—"

"I know! But it was Stephanie! I had to do something about it." I stared him down despite the height difference.

We probably could have gone on for much longer in our staring contest, which I was sure to lose at some point, but shouts rang out from down the river and pulled our attention away.

All of us dashed across the bridge to the other side as a flurry of activity descended upon the shore to the left. Police officers rushed off the bridge, their flashlights bobbing in the darkness as the search party hollered for more help.

"Brandon, can you—" I started to say.

"On it." He ran off to follow and go where we couldn't go.

"Maybe I better go see too," Caleb said and spared a glance for Addy and Emma.

They both looked confused, but I wasn't about to explain how Caleb could also get around without being seen. Instead, I nodded. "Be careful."

He chuckled at my advice and jogged away, going the same direction as everyone else.

"But won't the police just stop him? He's not invisible like your ghost friends are," Emma said, her eyebrows creased in confusion.

"I wouldn't worry about him. What do you think they found?" I tried to peer into the darkness where the commotion was, but my eyes were too human to make out anything other than the occasional flashlight and shadow.

"I hope it's not a dead body," Emma said, linking arms with Addy for support.

Stephanie was still standing next to me as if walking any further than two feet away would be scary, but her attention was fixated on the shore just the same as the rest of us.

It wasn't long before Brandon came jogging back. "They've found them! Three boys, all water-logged, but all alive."

"Oh, thank goodness." I pressed my hand to my chest.

Stephanie fell to her knees in a sob.

"They've found three boys," I said for Addy and Emma's benefit. "Stephanie, was that everyone who was in the car?"

"Yes, there were three...plus me," she said between sobs.

Brandon sunk onto the pavement next to her. "It's alright. You're not down there anymore. You're here with us. Besides, do you really want to see your dead body?"

She only kept sobbing, and Brandon looked up at me with helpless eyes.

"Stephanie, it's going to be okay. I promise." I kneeled next to her and would have put a comforting hand on her shoulder, but of course, I couldn't.

Several figures emerged from the darkness and into the searchlights. Officers were helping the three boys climb up the bank and onto the road. An ambulance stood nearby and EMTs rushed about trying to help the boys sit down.

We couldn't see much from where we stood, but I'd seen Alex's pale face shine in the gleam of a flashlight, and the other boy was one of his friends I vaguely recognized.

Addy, Emma, and I all exchanged worried glances, but there wasn't much else we could do.

Splashing echoed from underneath the bridge and tore my attention away from the mass of authorities trying to warm the boys up and wring information from them.

"Hold on. I'll be right back. Stay here in case Caleb comes back," I said to Emma and Addy, who were still clinging to each other, and to Brandon who was still trying to comfort Steph.

I didn't know what I was running into as I went down the length of the bridge and then onto the side of the riverbank, but my legs were eager to do something.

I arrived in time to see a dark silhouette rise from the water and step onto the bank. He was huge, easily above six feet, and carried another with him, cradled securely in his arms. From the still roaming search-lights, the blue and white lights of the police cars, and the random bobbling flashlights officers were using to look through the woods, I caught glimpses of his awe-inspiring features and his wet muscles gleaming through his ripped jacket.

Without stopping, as if merely walking down a paved street on a warm Sunday afternoon instead of climbing a muddy bank while holding another person's body, he headed towards the road, which also happened to be in my direction.

I didn't know whether to run toward him to help or run away and scream for others to help. Deciding he looked capable enough, I scampered out of his way. I was not nearly as graceful as he was. As he neared where I was standing, the mud slipped beneath my feet, and I would have taken a tumble, probably all the way down the hill and into the water, if he hadn't caught me.

Somehow, quicker than my eye could follow, he'd placed the person he'd been carrying onto a safe place near the road and had made it back in time to grab me by my flailing wrist. My body changed the direction of the momentum, and I fell back into his arms like the fair lady I was.

"Careful, there," he said, his voice deep and husky.

"Thank you." I was breathless, and it came out a little airier and more girly than I wanted it to.

He smiled as an errant light shone brightly onto his face. The stunning smile with perfect teeth was only slightly overshadowed by the feral, yellow gleam in his eyes as they glinted with reflection like an animal's in the dark. The surreal sight, combined with his secure embrace, despite being soaking wet, made for an odd mixture of sensations.

My expression must have put his thoughts in focus because he glanced back at the person laying in the grass beside us. "I'm afraid this one didn't make it. Can you alert the authorities as to her position? No need to get me involved in all of this."

I nodded as he helped pull me up the bank and onto the flat road. "I'll let them know. How did you... I mean, where did you come from?"

We stared down at Stephanie's water-logged body. Her blonde hair fanned out around her face in a wet halo. She was indeed wearing a policewoman Halloween costume that had made her muscular legs look amazing. It was the same outfit her ghost was now stuck in until we could figure out what her unfinished business was. There was hope that it was only helping the boys get found and that she would easily cross over once she saw everyone was safe.

If we were lucky.

I was relieved that her eyes were closed, either done by the thoughtful stranger or they had been closed in death. I knew that the image of her body lying in the slick grass was going to be seared into my mind forever, and I was grateful that her unseeing, dead eyes weren't going to be there when I tried to go to sleep at night.

"I was driving behind the car and saw it weaving all over the place. I knew they were drunk." The stranger sighed and shook his head. "And this poor girl paid the price."

"She was my friend," I said, letting a few tears escape as the reality of seeing her lifeless body somehow felt more real than having seen her ghost sob miserably.

"Oh, I'm sorry." He glanced back towards the bridge where shouts and footsteps were headed in our direction. "I should be going. Make sure your friend gets the care she deserves."

I pinched my eyebrows in confusion, but he was gone before I could say anything. The way he melted into the darkness creeped me out, even though I'd been hanging out with a vampire quite a bit lately.

Alone, I looked down at Stephanie, unsure what to do. Even if I could lift her body, it probably wouldn't have been in a respectful way. I would have to drag her heels or hands and that wasn't what I wanted for my friend.

Instead, I took a breath to holler over for some help, but before I could get so much as a squeak out, a cold hand clamped over my mouth.

"Wait. I have an idea." Caleb's deep voice purred into my ear.

He let go of my mouth once he was satisfied that I wasn't going to yell for help. Instead, I smacked him on his marble-hard bicep. "Hey!"

Usually, he probably would have given me that vampire grin, but our eyes were drawn to Stephanie again.

"She didn't deserve this," he said.

"No, she didn't."

Silently, not even needing to grunt, Caleb bent over and picked her up like she weighed no more than a wet blanket. "Don't tell anyone you found her body here."

"I didn't—"

"Oh, give me some credit. I know you were talking to a feral dog who had pulled her out of the water."

"He wasn't a—"

He finally grinned again. "Wasn't he?"

I frowned. "What are you going to do?"

"I know some people. The problem is I have to leave you for a little bit. Will you promise to go straight back home? You know you're safer there than anywhere else, and as fun as it is to watch over you every second, I've got an errand to run."

I nodded, not wanting to be kidnapped by vampires again. A few weeks ago, Caleb had brought one of his friends over to put a protection spell around my house. I hadn't even known there was such a thing, but I shouldn't have been surprised after all the crazy stuff I'd seen recently. His friend had been a super cool witch with rainbow hair, a leather skirt, and tattoos all over her arms and legs. She was confident and smart, and if that's what all witches were like, I wouldn't have minded becoming one.

Too bad I was stuck as a different creature of the night.

"Okay. I'll get Emma to drive me right home. We might only stop for a coffee or something."

He gave me a stern look.

"Okay, not even that, but what are you going to do with her body? What do I tell her ghost? What about her family? Shouldn't they know about this?"

"We'll get to that when we need to. For right now, just keep this secret between the two of us. If my idea doesn't pan out, we'll find a way to reveal her body later. At this point, do you really still not trust me?"

It was an old argument between us so I didn't feel bad rolling my eyes. "Fine. I'll do as you say, even if you're being a cryptic old man."

His chuckle rumbled deep inside his chest, and he left me alone next to the muddy bank.

This time I didn't hesitate. Memories of being entranced by an evil vampire—as opposed to the mostly good one who was now my friend—popped into my mind and had me jogging back to the bridge.

"There you are!" Addy said as I found my way back.

"We were worried. We almost gathered a search party to go after you." Emma looked me up and down, probably assessing to see if I had gotten hurt.

Stephanie's ghost was sitting on the edge of the bridge, looking into the water. Had she been alive, I would have freaked out and dragged her back from the side, but as it was, I let her be.

Brandon leaned on the bridge next to Steph and frowned as he looked at her.

"It's okay." I shrugged, trying to convey relaxed confidence even though my hands were shaking slightly. "I just thought I heard something. No big deal. Are you guys ready to go?"

They looked at each other, back toward the police officers and bright cars, and then back at me.

"Are *you* ready?" Addy asked.

I nodded. "I think we've done everything we can do here. We called the police and got the boys taken to safety, and we just need to leave everything to the authorities now. It's late and we still have school tomorrow."

Emma nodded and unlatched herself from Addy's arm only to link her elbow through mine. Our round costumes bent oddly to accommodate our closeness. "You're right. Let's go."

Addy looked around again and shrugged.

"Stephanie, we're not done yet, okay?" I called out to her blue form. "We'll talk later, and I promise I'll help you, okay?"

She glanced at me once so I knew she had heard me, but her eyes were so full of sadness I felt my chest rip open a little more.

"I promise I'll take care of you!"

Emma frowned and pulled me away.

As we walked back toward her car, Brandon came to walk next to me. "This is a sad day."

"It is a sad day."

Emma nodded as if I were talking to her. "One of the saddest yet."

"I can't believe you found out about the accident from a ghost. It might be because of you that they found those boys so quickly," Addy said and rubbed her hands up and down her arms again, trying to get some warmth.

"Maybe." I didn't feel like telling them about the strong stranger even if he hadn't told me to keep him a secret.

"It's sad that she's going to be stuck in that outfit until we can help her cross over," Brandon said as we reached the car.

"Yes," I gave him a flat look, "that's what's sad about it. At least she's not stuck in some old 90s clothes with pants so big you could fit two other people in them."

Emma gave me a confused look and then smiled and shook her head. Unlatching her arm from mine, she opened the car door.

Cold ebbed into my arms when her warmth was gone, and I hurried to climb into the back seat.

"You can fit three, actually. We tried it one day with my little sister and her friend."

"Wow. Your poor sister."

Addy got into the passenger front seat, and she hugged herself while jiggling her legs. "Next year I'm going as bigfoot with fur and a full mask and wearing longjohns underneath it."

"Sexy." Emma chuckled as she started the car.

"How about we just don't spend the whole night in a cold cemetery and then go to a bridge where our friends drove off and killed one of the cheerleaders?" I hadn't meant to sound so bitter when I'd first started my statement, but it evolved quickly.

Addy looked at me from the front seat with a sad frown. "That sounds like a good idea."

Brandon had climbed in the backseat next to me and was staring out the window at Stephanie's blue body. "Guess we know which ghost we're going to help next."

Chapter 3

T he next day was Thursday and, even though it had been Halloween the night before, we were still expected to go to school. At least we hadn't been drinking which was not something I could say for some of the other high schoolers. Most of the more popular kids were mysteriously missing for the first two periods of classes, and when they did show up, they looked worse than I felt.

Must have been some fun party I didn't get invited to.

A month ago, I would have minded. I guess I was growing as a person. Or something.

Word had gotten around about Alex's accident the night before. Of course, someone had to post about it, and then share the juicy gossip about how the boys survived while Stephanie's body was still missing.

Neither Alex nor his friend was at school that day. If I were their parents, I would have made them stay in the hospital as long as they needed and then stay home after that. Maybe even stay home forever and never let them drive or hang out with friends again.

Whatever had happened, I hoped he wouldn't get away without being punished. Surely, there would at least be a mark on his record, and he wouldn't be able to get behind the wheel of a car any time soon, if ever.

Noah wasn't in history class, but Mr. Tyler did stop me on my way out of the classroom.

"Hey, Hanna. Can I talk to you for a second?" he asked, standing behind his desk at the back of the room while all the students filed out.

"Sure." I stopped and stood next to the desk, giving awkward smiles to the last two students leaving the classroom. "Have you found any-thing else about Rose...or Ann, I mean?"

We'd learned from the vampire queen which had been possessed by my grandma's ghost at the time, that the psychic who I was looking for wasn't who she had claimed to be. Her real name was Ann Good, and she was older than Caleb, as hard as that was to believe. She'd been around during the Salem witch trials. She was also a super-powerful witch who stalked Seers and was often somehow involved in their deaths.

Mr. Tyler pinched his lips and shook his head. "No. I'm sorry. Obviously, I started with the internet and haven't found anything there, despite my mad interneting skills."

"Of course."

"So I've got several...you might call them "friends", who are helping to find out what they can. But that's not why I need to talk to you."

"Oh, okay." I sighed. "After last night, it's hard to focus on much else, even things that are as important as helping free those ghosts."

Mr. Tyler nodded slowly, and we shared a small second of silence in Stephanie's honor. A student from the next period came into the classroom and made his way to his seat, shaking us into the present.

"Right," Mr. Tyler's voice was more hushed, "can you meet me here after school? I have someone I want to introduce you to, and maybe...ask you for another favor?"

"Oh, yay."

Mr. Tyler gave me a half-smile. "Yeah, sorry."

"It's fine. It's my life now. I'll be here."

He chuckled. "Don't sound so defeated. Many would die to be in your position."

I rolled my eyes at his joke and hurried off to get to my next class in time.

At lunch, I avoided the crowded cafeteria. To my surprise, Emma showed up in the library maybe twenty minutes after lunch had started. I waved her over when I saw her pause at the door and look around. She smiled and sat down at my table which had been empty except for me.

"I figured I'd find you here."

I smiled and leaned in closer so we could talk without being too loud. It was a library after all. "What about your other friends? Won't they be wondering where you are?"

She shrugged and put her bag on the table. "It's fine. I told them I had some work to do here. Spending one lunch with you won't kill me."

I laughed quietly and shook my head. "Oh, the puns today."

"Sorry?"

"Oh, nothing. Do you want to come with me to check in on Stephanie's ghost today?"

We both glanced around just to double-check there wasn't anyone listening. There was another group of students sitting at a similar table nearby, but they were all busy playing a card game.

"I would love to, but I'm so sorry I can't. I have debate club after school." She frowned like she meant what she said.

Her acceptance of my quirks made me think of Andrea again. Why had I hung out with her for so long?

"Oh, that's okay!" I smiled reassuringly, hoping she wouldn't feel bad about living a totally normal life and not having to go visit a ghost after school. "I'm not even sure the bridge is her haunt, honestly. If it isn't, I might go somewhere else, less..."

"Like the scene of a terrible accident that killed her?"

"Yes! Less that."

We shared a smile and then I sobered quickly. "I still can't believe what happened. As far as I can tell, everyone thinks she's missing, hoping that she isn't dead since they haven't been able to find the body yet."

I felt a shard of guilt stab into my chest for holding back more of the facts from the night before after I'd been able to be so open and honest with Emma, but Caleb and that stranger had wanted secrecy. If there was one thing I'd learned since working with the occult, it was that secrets were there for a reason. They might not have been necessarily good to keep but letting them free would have been worse.

After an enjoyable lunch with Emma, I slogged through the rest of school. I caught glimpses of Caleb, but he was always busy—probably on purpose—so I didn't feel the need to bother him too much. Yes, I was desperate to learn what he'd done with Stephanie's body, but I highly doubted he would tell me his plan until it was important for me to know.

Vampires were cagey like that. Maybe it came with the old age.

Trina and I had gotten closer in the last month since she'd revealed she could also see ghosts, but she always wore a necklace that kept her powers from working. She'd taken it off to help rescue me from the vampire seethe, but then put it right back on. I was still working up the nerve to ask her why, but a part of me completely understood that she would want to avoid any and all ghosts.

I saw her in the hallways a few times too, but mostly we went about our daily routine, pretending to be normal high school girls who only worried about boys and grades.

When I walked back into Mr. Tyler's classroom after stopping at my locker and grabbing the things I'd need for homework that night, I was relieved to see it was empty, except for Mr. Tyler, of course.

"Ah, Miss Sanchez. I see you've remembered our meeting today." Mr. Tyler looked up from a workbook and gave me a personable smile.

"Was there doubt?" I put my bag onto a desk in the back row and sat sideways in the chair so I could still face Mr. Tyler.

"I'm a high school teacher. I'm always doubting. It's part of my survival skills." His tone told me he wasn't completely bitter and was somewhat kidding.

"So what did you want to talk about?" I glanced at the hallway where students still milled about after the initial bustle of the after-school rush had died down. "Is this really the best place to talk about...things?"

"Oh, yes. After our fun adventure last month, I hired a witch to help put up a protection spell and ward my classroom. It's a good thing Caleb doesn't need to take my classes anymore." He chuckled. "Anyway, when I close the door, no one can hear what's being said in here unless they're in here, you know?"

I nodded appreciatively. "Well, look at us getting smart. Caleb had a friend do the same thing to my house. Maybe it was the same witch who helped us out."

"Could be. Could be. I just hope she didn't charge Caleb as much as she charged me. The amount of money we pay for security, am I right?"

"I wouldn't know about that, but I'd also say that Caleb probably has enough to spare. If he hasn't saved up lots of money by being three hundred years old yet, I'd say he's doing this vampire thing wrong." I kept my voice quiet since the door was still open and didn't want to be overheard joking about vampires like they were real or something.

We shared a chuckle.

"True that."

"So what did you want to talk about?"

He glanced at the doorway, still sitting in his chair. "Actually, I wanted to introduce you to someone...ah, and here he is."

My heart skipped a few beats inside my chest and then pounded erratically as I saw who walked into the room as if on cue.

Mr. Tyler stood up and went to shake his hand. "I wasn't sure if you'd have a hard time finding this classroom."

The stranger from last night chuckled. "No worries. I just followed my nose. You have a distinct smell that might get better if you'd shower more."

Mr. Tyler laughed good-naturedly and clapped the young man on the back. It had been dark the night before, but it was easy to see this was the same guy who had pulled Stephanie's body out of the water. He towered over Mr. Tyler, and, even though he wasn't wearing a ripped jacket and t-shirt, I could see his toned muscles move easily beneath his polo shirt. His hair was a surprising silver-grey color, short on the sides and back but long on top with a curl that swirled onto his forehead. He was cleanshaven but there was darkness around his cheeks and jaw that indicated he could grow a decent beard in a matter of minutes.

I was starting to think the supernatural beings were all gorgeous simply because it was a survival mechanism to draw in hapless humans.

And it was working.

"C'mon in." Mr. Tyler gestured for the guy to enter more into the room as he went to close the door behind him. "This is the young lady I was talking to you about."

As the stranger's eyes connected with mine, I took a breath to explain that I had already met him the night before. As if knowing what I was about to say, he shook his head subtly and put a long finger over his lips.

"Gryphin, meet Hanna. Hanna, this is my nephew, Gryphin." Mr. Tyler puffed his chest out and beamed at the stranger, who I suppose now wasn't a stranger anymore. If there was a nephew show like there were dog shows, Mr. Tyler would proudly display this fine specimen to the judges.

I stood, feeling silly for being the only one sitting, and nodded. "Nice to meet you."

"The pleasure is mine." Gryphin's deep voice purred in his chest, and I couldn't help but remember being enclosed in his secure embrace the night before.

Mr. Tyler gestured for us to sit and made his way back to the desk chair. It creaked when he sat down and the wheels squeaked as he scooted it toward the desks we sat in.

A student's desk wasn't made for tall guys like Gryphin and especially not for him to sit in sideways as he faced Mr. Tyler. His long legs stretched out across the aisle, which explained why he'd chosen a seat two aisles away from mine.

"Alright, now that we're acquainted, let's talk about why we're really here." Mr. Tyler's grin faded somewhat. "I'm afraid, dear Hanna, that we need your help. I'm well aware that the pack already owes you for that unfortunate...curse situation, but we're going to need your help again."

I took a breath and shrugged. "Such is the role of the Seer, I'm beginning to see."

"So it's true, then? You're really a Seer?" Gryphin sat up slightly in his chair and leaned closer toward me.

"Guilty."

"Wow." He glanced at Mr. Tyler and then back to me. "I've met all kinds—vampires, witches, even the odd necromancer or two, but I've never met a Seer before."

"Yeah, well, now you have." I didn't want to sound completely rude so I punctuated my sentence with a smile in hopes of seeming more kind than sarcastic.

"I hope you can also see that it's not just being needed to clean up ghost messes all the time and that it's honestly really cool," Mr. Tyler said with an encouraging nod in my direction.

I thought of Brandon and how I had been able to connect more with my Gran after she'd died and eventually helped her cross over. Then I thought of how Stephanie had helped the boys who'd gone over the bridge.

"Okay." I nodded slowly. "I'll try to think of it more like that. It's hard, though, when you're being kidnapped by vampires or used by a witch to enslave ghosts inside a crystal."

"You did what?" Gryphin's eyes widened in excitement.

I cringed. "Well, I didn't know what I was doing. I was still new to all of this and was honestly thinking we were helping them go beyond or wherever the next place they needed to go was, not sending them to serve a deranged witch who would then disappear before I could confront her."

He chuckled and sat back into the desk. "I'm getting the sense there's a good story there."

"I'm afraid we're about to start another one, right Gryphin?" Mr. Tyler turned to his nephew with upraised eyebrows in a pointed look.

"Oh, right. So here's the thing. My dad is the alpha of our pack and my stepmom, his mate, has been dead for a few months now."

"I'm sorry for your loss," I muttered, hoping I didn't have to face the death of my own mother for many decades.

"Yeah, it's been hard. Thank you." He glanced at Mr. Tyler who nodded with a sympathetic press of his lips.

"The whole pack has had a hard time. It's not easy to lose a high-ranking member like that, and it's even worse on the alpha, which also affects the pack even more," Mr. Tyler said.

"Oh," was all I said because I didn't know a single thing about werewolf packs. I was finding it quite surreal to be casually talking about them while sitting in my history classroom after school hours.

"Yes, and even though the death is terrible by itself, there's another issue that's been complicating the whole thing and making everything worse." Gryphin frowned.

"Let me guess. It has something to do with someone being haunted?" I said, trying to piece together what they needed me for.

"Actually, quite the opposite, I'm afraid." Mr. Tyler leaned forward in his squeaky chair. "We have no idea where her ghost is or where her haunt might be, and we were hoping you could locate it for us, for the pack."

I pulled my eyebrows together. "Er... I've never had to do that before. I don't even know how or if I can do something like that."

Mr. Tyler and Gryphin shared a look that seemed to say my reaction was something they had been expecting.

"Well, we clearly would have a much harder time doing it than a Seer," Gryphin said with hopeful eyes.

"I suppose that's true."

"I've seen you do some amazing things that Seers aren't supposed to be able to do. I mean, you did command that teacher ghost to get into the witch's circle, did you not?" Mr. Tyler said.

I nodded slowly. "Unfortunately."

"Putting that sullied situation aside, the fact that you can command a ghost to do anything is amazing. Have you heard of a Seer doing that before? Because I sure haven't."

Gryphin nodded appreciatively. "That's a pretty neat trick."

"I can also summon a ghost to be near me, but so far, I've only tried it with ghosts I've already met. Plus, I knew where their haunts were and was able to easily picture the ghost in my mind and call their names. It takes longer with some ghosts than others, but I've been able to do it a few times." I felt my cheeks heat up as I talked. It felt really weird bragging about my powers in this way, but it seemed like something they should know.

"Oh, that could work. Does that mean you'll help?" Gryphin's slumped shoulders lifted a little.

His eagerness alone was almost enough to spur me into action, but I also didn't want to give them any false hope. If the summoning trick didn't work, how was I supposed to find a haunt for a specific ghost? It seemed like the exact opposite of how I usually found a ghost to help. It was easy to imagine Brandon shaking his head and saying something snarky, along the lines of, "Did these guys just ask us to track down their lost ghost doggy?"

I pushed the thought of Brandon out of my head just in case I accidentally called him to the room. It was way too easy to summon *him* these days, even if it wasn't so easy to summon other ghosts.

"I'm not sure. This sounds difficult, and I would feel bad letting you guys down." I looked mostly at Mr. Tyler when I talked, but honestly, I was probably more worried about disappointing his muscular nephew over there.

Mr. Tyler nodded. "I get you, but hey, if you try, you can't disappoint us more than if you merely say no."

His sly grin earned a flat look from me. "I mean, I guess when you put it that way, but I've learned, recently, to dig deeper into something before I agree to help. Why do you need to find this ghost so badly? Are you sure she's even a ghost? Maybe she has already crossed over to the other side quite peacefully."

"Obviously that could be a possibility." Mr. Tyler nodded again. "But we have good reason to think she would stick around to finish some business."

Gryphin shifted in his seat and crossed one long leg over the other at the shin. "The circumstances surrounding her death suggest she wouldn't have peacefully passed over. She'd either want revenge or answers or maybe both."

"I suspect at the very least, she'd want her pack to have closure." Mr. Tyler looked down at the school-issued brown carpet with a thoughtful gaze. "She was considerate like that and wouldn't want us to be so lost and in the dark about her death."

"Okay. That makes sense." I glanced at Gryphin and then back to Mr. Tyler. "I hate to be insensitive, but can I ask how she died? I think having the most information I can get about everything, the better I can help you guys out."

They exchanged glances again, but Mr. Tyler gave a subtle nod to Gryphin as if giving him permission to delve into more pack secrets.

Gryphin sighed, looked at the ceiling and popped his neck first to the left, then to the right. Still staring upwards, he spoke, "The details aren't super clear, but from what we've been able to piece together, she went looking for a magic user to help her with something. We're not sure what, exactly, but we found the information on her phone. Without telling anyone, she packed a bag and left our house. We know this because the stuff was missing from her room—several shirts, pairs of pants, socks, most of her toiletries, stuff like that. She didn't even leave a note or tell anyone she was going anywhere."

He stopped talking for a minute and his jaw clenched, his mouth pressing together as if holding back emotions.

"I'm sure this is hard to talk about. I'm really sorry to bring up bad memories, but I'm just wanting to understand as much as possible," I said, resisting the urge to move chairs so I could be closer to Gryphin and rub his shoulder in a comforting way.

"Of course. We get it," Mr. Tyler said with an encouraging smile. "It doesn't mean it'll be easier to talk about, but we get it."

Gryphin's eyes finally left the ceiling and looked straight at me. "If more information will help us get closer to the truth, then it's worth any painful memories I may have to talk about."

I merely nodded, lost in his forest-brown eyes. If I stared too long, I could almost hear the calls of birds over treetops as the wind ruffled my hair.

"So then, of course, we tracked her scent as far as we could. She knew how to throw us off the trail, though. Even our best trackers couldn't find her after she crossed the river," Gryphin continued to explain. "She'd left her phone behind so we couldn't track her that way, either. Luckily, we were able to find where she'd been researching about the magic user, and as we had no other lead, we had to follow that one."

"Did you find them?" I blinked a few times, trying to clear my head from what I could swear was the rushing of a clear waterfall.

"No. One of the biggest problems is they're a member of the biggest and most powerful coven in the states."

"What's a coven? I'm sorry if that's a stupid question, but all of this is so new to me. Plus, it's not like my history teacher teaches me pertinent information I might actually need in daily life." I shot Mr. Tyler a teasing grin which he returned.

"Well, there are rules about that kind of thing," Mr. Tyler said. "A coven is a family of witches, similar to a werewolf pack or a vampire seethe. Each group has its own culture and rules and stuff, but the concepts are the same. I'd say a vampire seethe was the most brutal of all, but a witch coven isn't far behind."

"Spooky. So they're hiding behind their coven and they're refusing to help or give you information about your missing pack mate? Isn't that bad for pack and coven relationships? Are there politics going on with the different groups as well as inside the groups? Ugh. My brain hurts." I closed my eyes and shook my head quickly to clear out the cobwebs.

"Of course." Mr. Tyler chuckled. "We might be supernatural creatures, but we're also part human. Just as there are all kinds of history with human countries and groups, there is history and relationships with all of us occult folk. In general, we try to hold an uneasy peace to keep our secrets as best we can. It seems clear to all of us that if one of our identities gets confirmed, it's only a matter of time before the others get hunted out. Unfortunately for us, our pack is relatively small and the witch coven we're dealing with is a national group with the most powerful witches. They couldn't care less about a pack as small as ours. We wouldn't be able to leverage them enough to get cooperation unless we had somehow united all the werewolf packs throughout the states, and I can tell you right now that will never happen."

Gryphin shrugged. "Maybe if all the vampires united and started hunting us, it could be possible?"

"Let's hope that never happens." Mr. Tyler shook his head. "Anywho, we're hoping to go a different route with this issue and find her ghost. If we can talk to her at least we can get some answers, maybe even closure for the pack."

"And if we're lucky, something we can use to avenge her." A flicker of anger flashed in Gryphin's eyes that made me sit up straighter.

"*If* there's something to avenge for," Mr. Tyler said, giving his nephew a look.

"Wow, this is a lot." I took a deep breath and stared at my shoes, trying to get my thoughts arranged.

It was Gryphin's turn to comfort me. He must have been braver than I was because he did switch seats, taking the one across from me. His legs were so long that his knees rested on the outside of my thighs while his callused hands enclosed my own and rested on my lap. "I'm sorry to drop this all on you the day after your friend...was hurt. I'm sure this is a lot to process. Please believe me that we wouldn't be dropping this all onto you if it weren't important."

The intensity of his gaze bore into me, and it felt like he could really see me and what was inside. It made it hard to hide, hard to pretend to be strong. Tears prickled at the sides of my vision. "The worst part is that everyone else thinks she's missing or something, but I saw her ghost. I saw her sobbing on that bridge all alone as we drove away. She was too young to go."

Mr. Tyler's chair squeaked as he wheeled it closer to me and put a warm hand on my back. "That's got to be difficult. I'm sorry, Hanna."

I nodded, not trusting my voice right then. I also pulled my eyes away from Gryphin's, afraid of falling into the wildness and intimacy I saw there.

"If you need time to think and process things, we understand." Gryphin squeezed my hands before letting them go.

The air was cold on my skin as he removed their warm contact.

Mr. Tyler's chair squeaked again as he sat back. "Wait. How did you know about the missing girl?"

Gryphin glanced at me and then back to his uncle. "Oh. People were just talking about it all over the school as I walked in. Werewolf hearing and all that."

"Except how did you know the girl was a close friend of Hanna's?" Mr. Tyler peered over the top of his spectacles.

Gryphin shrugged. "I just figured she might be. This is a small school and all."

Mr. Tyler grunted his response, sounding not quite convinced.

"Thank you for being considerate about my feelings after Stephanie's...disappearance. I suppose it's because your mom died recently, and you're more in tune with how that pain can feel?" I said because I was thinking it, but also because I wanted to steer the conversation back to the point. If Gryphin wanted to keep it secret that he'd been part of the events of last night, I figured it wouldn't hurt to back him up.

Gratitude and amusement crossed Gryphin's features. "Perhaps I am more in tune with that right now, but she wasn't my mom. Werewolves can't have children unless the woman is human, and even then, it's risky. No, she was my stepmom. My real mom is a human."

"Oh, sorry." My cheeks probably reddened with the flush of embarrassment.

Gryphin waved it off. "It's fine. I don't expect people who don't interact with wolves all the time to know much about us. Although, as a Seer, I imagine you've seen all kinds of things."

I laughed a little, the sadness still too close to my heart to feel more levity. "Not really. I mean, yes, kind of? The last month has been crazy, including seeing your uncle here partially change into a werewolf. It was insane."

Mr. Tyler's lips twitched between a smile and a cringe.

"Then I got kidnapped by a crazy vampire queen. That was intense. But aside from that, I feel totally lost in this occult stuff. I feel like I don't even know everything about ghosts yet, and I'm supposed to be this amazing expert on them."

"I'm sure it's been a shock to see what's really out there." Gryphin's grin got a bit feral.

I nodded. "Understatement. I'm still not able to say the word…" I changed to a hushed tone, "vampire out loud very well."

"I don't blame you there. Talking about the devil will do no one any good." Gryphin said.

I glanced at Mr. Tyler, thinking about how he knew Caleb and how Caleb had been close to snapping his neck, yet after that Mr. Tyler still hadn't seemed too angry with him. "Surely there might be good vampires out there?"

Gryphin shrugged. "Maybe somewhere."

"So sorry again if this is a hard question, but how do you know she's dead and not just missing or something?" I asked, checking the time on my phone. This meeting had taken a lot longer than I'd expected, and I hadn't told my mom or Trina where I would be. They were probably going to be mad. During the last few weeks, they'd been vigilant about keeping track of me.

Mr. Tyler answered, "No, that's a good question. We know she's dead because of the pack bonds. If a pack member dies, we can all feel it. I suppose it's hard to explain if you haven't experienced it, but it's like we have this deep connection where we can vaguely feel each other all the time."

Gryphin nodded. "It is pretty neat when it's helpful, but it can make keeping anything private a hard thing to do."

I smiled slightly imagining having a bunch of people in my head all the time.

"So when someone dies, the whole pack is affected. The best way I can explain it is like losing a limb. Well, that might not be fair because I don't know how that feels, but it's kind of like that? A piece of us is ripped away. The emptiness is raw and pulsing for a long time. It's quite painful," Mr. Tyler explained in his teacher-lecture voice.

"I can only imagine what Dad is going through, feeling the pack bonds and the mate bonds broken at the same time." Gryphin sighed and turned his intense gaze back onto me. "That's why we need you. My dad won't ask for any help, but we know he's struggling, and we thought that getting some closure for him would be good. Please say you'll help us."

"Well, after that plea, I'm not sure how I could say no," I said, hoping my smile was less wobbly than it felt.

Chapter 4

Mom had texted me a few times throughout the evening, but she wasn't home when I finally got there. She'd been working extra hard to get her photography business going. It had been hard on her to leave us alone so much, but she figured it would be harder on us if we didn't have electricity or a place to live.

I was grateful for her absence so she hadn't been home to panic when I hadn't shown up right after school. Trina had sent me a few questioning texts and rushed out of her bedroom when I finally opened the door.

"Hey, like I texted, just spent a few minutes after school with Mr. Tyler. No biggie," I said before she could give me a painful interrogation.

The vampire kidnapping had made Mom and Trina double their watch on me, and I hated the feeling of needing to be babysat almost as much as I hated the random panic attacks I would sometimes get at night when my imagination ran a little wild.

It had helped our peace of mind a lot when Caleb had gotten the witch to bless our house, but I couldn't help but think about other creatures besides vampires trying to sneak in and kidnap me or something worse.

"Why did you have to do that? Have you been late on homework or something?" Trina asked, her arms folded across her chest and her eyes narrow as I walked past to her toward my own bedroom.

"No. He had some questions about being a Seer and wondered if I could help him and his pack talk to a ghost. It's no big deal. Really."

She grunted, and I could feel her eyes on me until I shut my bedroom door.

There was one thing I found that had helped ease the anxiety at night, but it was something I also felt guilty about. If my gran's ghost was still around, I was sure she'd lecture me until she was blue in the face, pun intended.

Brandon kept me company almost every night these days. I know, the irony of having a ghost for comfort instead of a teddy bear sounds just as ridiculous as it was. My only defense is that his dumb jokes kept the spiders of fear from invading my mind.

But, as a bad side effect, it also kept me from being very productive with homework.

"Do you have to keep humming?" I frowned as I stared at my French worksheet. The letters seemed to blur and dance on the page as I sat at the desk in my room.

"Oh, was I humming? Sorry." Brandon was sitting on my bed, fiddling with the ghostly pocketknife he'd had in his pocket when he'd died. Apparently, the stuff in your pockets dies and travels with you when you become a ghost. No, I didn't know why or how it worked.

Like I said, lots of stuff about the ghostly world still confused me.

"I hope you didn't think I'd forgotten what you said yesterday." I turned away from my homework to look at him.

He paused to look at me. "About what? Pretty sure I said lots of stuff. It seems to be a problem of mine, talking too much. I mean, I don't get what the big deal is. If you don't want to hear me, don't listen? I'm not sure who wouldn't want to hear my amazing jokes though, as cool as I am."

"Don't think your attempts to chatter and distract me will make me forget what I'm trying to point out."

"Fine." He sighed dramatically.

"You said something about your personal life and about your sister. I know you hoped I hadn't caught it or that I'd not notice, but I did."

He shrugged.

"You just talk so little about your life before you died that I feel like I'm starving to learn more about you."

"Starving?" His grin told me he was teasing, but I also knew it was another attempt to throw me off the scent.

It did cause me to roll my eyes, though. I found I did that a lot when he was around. "Is it so bad that I want to get to know you more? I mean, we do sleep together every night."

"Be careful. You'll make me blush."

It was my turn to grin. "Just saying. Anyway, maybe we can start small. Can you tell me about your family? It doesn't seem fair that you know all about mine, maybe even things I don't know about with your sneaky ghostly ways."

"I'm too busy worrying about you to spy on your family members."

I shrugged. "Fine. So tell me about your family. Surely you can talk about some of it?"

"I guess. I've told you my dad left when I was eight, and my mom raised us on her own after that."

I nodded, afraid to say anything or else he'd get distracted and stop.

"I had two younger sisters and one younger brother. As the oldest, it was my job to help my mom which meant getting them ready in the mornings and on the school bus as my mom worked graveyard shifts and usually wasn't home by the time we needed to get ready and leave."

"Wow, that's a lot."

"Yeah, well, I learned how to do the girls' hair pretty good though."

"Maybe you can give me some tips sometime."

"Maybe, but as far as I can see, you're always beautiful, even when your hair is messed up or there is drool on your face or even when you're snoring."

I slapped at the air in his direction. "What! Oh my gosh! Why would you say that? If it's so terrible, you don't have to stick around. In fact, why don't you go back to sleeping in the skatepark? It seems like a lively place at night in the dark."

"Hey! I was trying to compliment you."

I threw my pen. It sailed through his chest and clattered onto my nightstand behind him. "Get better at compliments!"

We grinned at each other for a second. "Alright, so you had two sisters and a brother. What were the age differences? Would you be brave enough to tell me their names or have you already forgotten them?"

I meant it as a joke, but his grin faded a bit. "I'll never forget them. The girls were twins and two years younger than me, and Justin was five years younger. The twins' names were Shannon and Savannah."

"Why do you keep saying 'were'? You're not that old. They could still be around living normal, happy lives."

"They could be, but they're not."

I got up from the chair and climbed onto the bed next to him. "Oh, Brandon. I'm so sorry. What happened?"

I wanted him to steal some energy from me and solidify so I could at least hold his hand or rub his shoulder, but I was too shy to ask him to do it, so I sat as close to him as I could and stared sadly at his face.

He shook his head with his eyes closed and then kept his gaze averted from mine. I knew that was the most I was going to get out of him at the moment, and while I was disappointed, I was glad he'd at least shared something with me.

"I can see why you wouldn't want to talk about it if something happened to them. It must be very painful."

The silence stretched between us as Brandon looked down at the ghostly knife and rolled the handle between his fingers.

"So I see you *can* be quiet. Why aren't you like this when I need you to be and more talkative other times?"

He gave me a look.

"Have you thought about the fact that they might be ghosts too?"

His fingers stilled and his whole body froze for a second. Then he looked right into my eyes. "Don't tell me you've seen them? Wait, how would you know it was them? Did they talk to you? Who is it?"

I raised my hands in surrender. "Woah. No, sorry. I didn't mean it like that. No ghost has come up to me claiming to know you, no. Just that I was thinking that it was possible they were ghosts maybe? You won't tell me what happened, but I can guess that they probably had unfinished business with whatever happened."

He sighed and looked back down. "I'm not sure. Maybe. I haven't wanted to think about the whole thing. I've been hiding from it."

"Even though I don't know what happened, I'm sure whatever it was couldn't have been good for all three of your siblings to be gone. It must have been traumatic, no matter what it was."

He turned to me and used energy to make his forehead solid enough to rest on my shoulder.

My heart melted for his pain while also speeding up with the closeness and contact. I wrapped my arm around his head, and with soft fingers, played with the tips of his spikey hair. Since we'd met, I had wondered how it stuck up so well but based on the touch, it felt like his hair naturally poked out all over his head. It was easy to put my fingers in and brush them through softly.

"I'm sorry. I didn't mean to make you sad. I just wanted to learn more about you."

He shrugged as his shoulders became more solid and the transformation seeped down his body. As far as I could tell, once he started changing one part into realness or whatever it was called, the change slowly worked through his whole body.

"I'm the one that should be sorry. I'm sorry to have dragged you into this whole thing. You'd be better off if I weren't around."

I backed up so his forehead had nothing to rest on and he'd lift his head. Angrily, I stared into his dazzling green eyes. "Don't you ever for a second think that my life is worse for having you in it. In fact, it's a million times better. You've helped calm my anxiety every night for weeks. You helped me accept my powers and have been there this whole time for support and companionship. As odd as it sounds, you're my best friend, and I honestly don't know how I lived before we met."

His eyes still held skepticism, so I wanted to prove my words with a physical gesture. Grabbing him by the back of his soft, spikey head, I pushed him into a kiss. It was the most passionate one we'd ever shared. At first, he was hesitant, but I kept steady pressure, and I guess he finally believed that I wanted to kiss him.

That he was worth kissing.

He leaned into me and placed a cool hand on my cheek, the tips of his fingers digging firmly into my hair.

A warm heat rose from deep inside my chest, and I suddenly couldn't get enough. I wanted to feel as much as him as I could while he was still physical. Clutching at the back of his hair, I pulled him closer into our kiss, and he let out a soft moan low in his throat. His hand in my hair moved deeper while his other hand encircled my waist. I got as close to him on the bed as I could, and I must have pushed too hard because we toppled over amid shared giggles.

We laid side-by-side on the bed and shared a few more kisses, but the spell had been broken.

Thankfully.

Desire coursed through my body, but I knew we shouldn't stoke the flames too much. He must have seen the thoughts in my eyes because he let go of the energy and the outsides of him started fading back to blue.

Before he was gone completely, he gave me another kiss. This one was softer and more tender, full of feelings neither of us were willing to say out loud.

"So you like having me around, do you?" His teasing grin was back, and it warmed me, even if he was once again untouchable.

"Of course!" I could have gone with the usual banter, but after he'd shown such a depth of emotion, I wanted to reassure him again.

The banter was fun, but sometimes it was important to be honest.

The grateful smile told me I'd chosen the right response.

Chapter 5

As I was climbing into bed beside Brandon who was sitting on the other side, leaning against the wall, someone knocked on my bedroom door. I'd gone back to doing homework for a few more hours, but it was late, and I needed to get to sleep.

"Yes?"

My mom peeked her head in. "Sorry, honey. Just got home and wanted to check in with you about your birthday."

"Uh oh, you're busted." Brandon gave me a teasing wide-eye look. "No boys allowed in your bedroom!" He said the last bit in a girly voice that must have been his effort to impersonate my mom.

I smiled and my mom probably thought I was super eager to see her and talk about my birthday.

"Oh." I sat back and turned on the bedside lamp. "It's nice to see you've been able to get so much work lately, even if you're not home as much."

She smiled and came into my room. The bed squeaked as she sat down near my feet. Her usually smooth chestnut brown hair was piled on top of her head in a messy bun while the circles under her eyes were a bit dark. The dress shirt she wore was wrinkled in the back as if she'd been sitting with it against a chair for a long time.

"I feel the same way, sweetie. I'm so grateful for everyone who has booked shoots and all the extra bookkeeping and social media stuff I've had to do, but yes, I miss you girls very much. Hopefully, we'll be able to spend some time together next weekend. I've made sure not to book any shoots for Saturday, so I'll be free all day."

My birthday was on the tenth of November which also just happened to be on a Saturday this year. Mom had been talking about it for weeks, and I was certain she was more excited about it than I was.

"Really? It'd be nice to spend some time together."

"I need to have sixteen birthdays to catch up to my real age. Do you think we could fit all of that into one day?" Brandon said while I kept focusing on my mom's face.

Sometimes I wasn't sure if he was actually talking to me or if he just liked hearing the sound of his own voice.

Mom nodded. "I've told Trina to keep that day free, as well. I thought we could start by having breakfast at your favorite pancake place with just us girls. Then hit the salon and get mani-pedis and then maybe some shopping. I've managed to save a little bit of money for the day, and your dad even pitched in."

"He did?" It wasn't like he was neglecting us or anything but since he'd found his own apartment, he'd been busy settling himself in and getting used to his new life. Without us. We'd gone on a few dinner dates with him, and one time he dropped off some groceries for us, but we hadn't seen him much besides that.

"And he even said he might be able to make it to the party." She was strong to put on a happy face, but if I were her, I didn't think I'd want my ex to be hanging around.

"Oh, do we want him to be at the party?" I gave her a knowing look.

Her smile faded slightly. "It's going to be hard, yes, but it's up to me to get used to being around him for family events. We can't shut him out of our lives, and even though it might seem easier to do that right now, in the long run, it's easier to get used to it as fast as we can."

I grabbed her hand that was resting on the bed and squeezed it. "You're really strong, you know that? Gran was right that you can handle all of this. I'm glad you're my mom, and I can see how a strong woman works through stuff like this."

I didn't know if it was because I invoked Gran's name or because she was touched by my words, but tears prickled at the corner of her eyes. "Oh, sweetie. I feel like the lucky one. You and Trina are such good girls. The teenage years are hard with bodies changing and life changing, and you guys have had to put up with more than the average person."

"I would argue with you, but it's kind of hard to pretend we haven't taken down a vampire seethe with the help of ghosts and necromancers and zombies. That is something that most kids can't say they've done."

"Not to mention hang out with handsome ghosts," Brandon added helpfully.

If I were to give any indication at all about Brandon's presence, I really would be in trouble. There was one thing to have a boy ghost hang out with you all the time, but it was quite another to have him share your bed at night.

She smiled despite the few tears that dribbled down her cheeks. "That they can't. Thank goodness for Caleb and the spell on this house or else I don't think I would be able to sleep at all. I'd probably sit outside your bedroom all night with a baseball bat just waiting for some vampire to slink down the hall and try to kidnap you again."

Brandon smirked. "Yeah, because that's how they'd do it."

I didn't bother to tell her that as far as a I knew, vampires preferred to use the windows when they wanted to sneak into a bedroom and could do it so quietly you'd never have known one was in the same room with you. And yes, I knew all of this by experience.

"Yes, I'm glad he was able to do that."

"Which brings me to the party bit. I know you wanted to have it at the party room in the bowling alley, but I'm sorry, honey, I just can't let you do that. For one, it's quite expensive. For the other, I'd be so worried about you and Trina the whole time, I'd be the worst helicopter mom in the world."

"So we'll have to have the party here? Isn't that going to be kind of...cramped?" My heart fell as the dreams of a fun party full of bowling and jukebox music flitted out of my mind.

Her shoulders fell and she sighed. "I'm sorry. I really am. There's only so much worrying a mom can do before she gets unsightly wrinkles and more grey hair."

"And we can't have that, darling." Brandon flicked his wrist like the fancy lady he was.

Logic battled emotion, and I closed my eyes to calm myself down before I said anything I was going to regret. Last year Trina had had her birthday party at the bowling alley, and, even though I mostly hung out on the sidelines, it looked like her friends and her had had so much fun. Ever since then, I'd wanted my own party there, and now that I was finally in high school, I had hoped it'd be even more fun.

Mom squeezed my hand before letting go. "Again, I'm so sorry, Hanna. If I could, I would. It's just not possible right now."

I kept my eyes closed, holding in my anger and disappointment, but I did nod so she knew I had heard her.

"We can talk about it later if you'd like. Don't forget to invite your friends." The bed squeaked as she stood, and the door clicked shut behind her.

I let out a breath and stared sullenly at the *Harry Potter* poster on my wall.

Brandon gave me a few seconds before talking, which was pretty decent of him. "Well, that's a bummer. I know how much you were looking forward to it."

Still not trusting my voice, I shrugged.

"I mean, she's right, though. If it helps? It would be pretty easy for a vampire, necromancer, witch, whatever, to snatch you or Trina away during the chaos of a party like that. I mean, if I were a bad guy trying to catch myself a Seer but knew there was a protection spell on her house and she was well protected at school by others, I'd look for a perfect time like a birthday party at night to steal her away."

I grunted, still staring.

"I guess we could always get into a wild set of shenanigans to raise the money for it and somehow convince Caleb and Noah to stand as bodyguards. That would probably cost extra though. Too bad your rich vampire friend doesn't need any favors done for him right now."

Finally, I sighed and rolled over. I punched my pillow into submission a few times before resting my head on it and giving Brandon an icy look. "It's fine. It's not like I have lots of friends to invite to it, anyway."

Brandon laid on his side, facing me. "You do if you count all your haunting friends."

I smacked him with my pillow, but it just hit the blanket harmlessly.

Friday morning came with bright sunshine and happy weekend vibes, even if it was a bit dampened from the news I'd gotten the night before. Brandon didn't need to sleep so he'd usually disappear sometime during the night after he was sure I wasn't waking again. Sometimes I had bad dreams, and I'd wake to find him gone, but it was easy enough to summon him back.

It was nice to have someone to talk to whenever I needed it.

As I walked around school that day and overheard people talking about Stephanie, I felt a stab of guilt for not going to see her yesterday. I should have taken time out of my evening, no matter how much homework or clandestine meetings with werewolves I'd had. She was newly dead and deserved any type of comfort I could give her. One complication was that the bridge wasn't somewhere I could just walk to. I'd need to get a ride there. I considered summoning her to a quiet place where we could talk, but I didn't want to scare her too much without first explaining what was happening.

Noah found me at lunch, and I had mixed reactions at seeing him come in through the library doors. I was grateful he was alone, that was certain, but I wasn't sure I wanted to talk to him. It had been easy to avoid him for the last few weeks as he'd been busy hanging out with Andrea, making out with Andrea, flexing on the football field for the cheerleader Andrea, and then probably doing weird creepy things like raising zombies to scare innocent vampires with his necromancer buddies.

However, he'd been my crush for two years, and he had recruited his necromancer order to rescue me from a vampire queen.

Oh, and I might add that I suspected him of possessing a vampire just to dance with me at Homecoming. I mean, what was a girl supposed to do with that?

Wordlessly, I moved my bag off the table so he could sit down next to me. My preferred table was further back by the wall with a little privacy, but we still needed to talk quietly.

"So, this is where you've been hiding." Noah tried to catch my eye with a smile, but I kept my focus on the book in front of me.

"Not that good of a hiding spot. You could have found me if you wanted."

"Ouch. That's fair, but ouch."

I gave him a side-eye and went back to my book. It was too hard to concentrate on actually reading the words in front of me, but it was better to stare at the dancing letters than to fall into Noah's hazel eyes.

"What do you want?"

"Look, I—I just want to clear the air between us. I feel like you've been avoiding me since...well, since you know." He took a breath, probably waiting for me to correct or agree with him. "Are you weirded out now...by me?"

I laughed into my book and used it to quickly cover my face and hide from the librarian's eagle eyes.

Noah's face reddened slightly, and he looked around to see if anyone had taken notice of our odd, hushed conversation. "It's that most girls don't like seeing zombies, and now that you know what I can do and everything, I figured you'd think I was gross."

"Uhm, no. I don't think you're gross. Okay, I mean, maybe it is gross to raise zombies like that, but I don't think *you're* gross," I whispered behind my book, finally looking him in the eyes so he'd have a better chance at believing my words.

He sat back into his chair with a relieved sigh. "Okay. That's good."

I went back to pretending to read.

After a few seconds, he spoke again. "So why are you avoiding me?"

Finally feeling bad, I put the book down and turned to him. There were lots of ways I could have taken the conversation, and I wasn't sure what would be best. I needed to both keep my distance from him to protect my heart and keep him close in case I needed help from a bunch of necromancers again.

Which in my line of work was entirely possible.

"I'm sorry, Noah. You're right. I have been avoiding you, but before I can answer that question, can you answer one of mine?"

"Uhm, sure?"'

"Can you explain why one of the vampires who kidnapped me at the dance decided to dance with me first and acted completely different afterward, almost like he was a different person? And then after that, he claimed there were necromancers around. Do you happen to know anything about that?"

His face went red again. "Er, I..." Biting his upper lip awkwardly, he looked around the room once more, but this time it was probably for an escape.

"The funny thing is when I asked him his name he stuttered with an 'n'. I didn't think about it at first, but I do happen to know a necromancer whose name starts with 'n'."

I blinked at him expectantly until he was able to figure out this wasn't going to go away.

"Okay, fine." He let out a deep breath. "It was me. I noticed a new vampire enter the school, and I figured I could have a little fun."

"I get that. If I could possess a vampire just for the fun of it, I would too. I'd do all kinds of things, but I don't think dancing with a friend would be on the top of my list. Why did you make him dance with me? It felt like he entranced me, and the world fell away and it was just us dancing. He was sweet and friendly and dare I say...charming? Why did you do that?"

Noah looked everywhere but at me while I talked, and his knee was bouncing up and down so much it was jiggling the table. "It just seemed fun?"

I kept staring at him. It was entertaining to see him struggle so much, but I also really wanted to know the reason. If he was just having fun, it seemed like a cruel trick to play, especially if he realized I'd had a crush on him for forever.

"Alright!" He threw his arms up into the air in surrender. "I really wanted to dance with you and that seemed like the easiest way, considering everything."

I burst out laughing. "I'm sorry. I just can't imagine how possessing a strange vampire would be the easiest way to get a dance with me while we're standing in the same gym a mere ten feet apart."

A smile twitched on his lips. "Well, when you put it that way... It's just there are lots of things going on that you don't know about."

"Like the fact that you and Andrea are so close these days I wouldn't be surprised to see a marriage announcement in the mail?"

"Oh, well it's not like that. We're definitely not getting married anytime soon."

I nodded and sat back into the metal chair. "That didn't sound reassuring."

He frowned. "I'm sorry. It's really hard to explain. I have to be with Andrea, even if I don't want to be."

I rolled my eyes. "Oh, please. It's not 1670, and you're not a prince who is being forced into marriage with a princess of a neighboring kingdom to strengthen the ties between countries."

"Right. Well…"

"And Andrea is no princess," I said with a scoff.

"I mean, it's complicated like that."

I furrowed my eyebrows and crossed my arms over my chest. "So what's it like, then? Do you even like her?"

"If I would have known how this conversation was going to turn, I'm not sure I would have come to find you." He started to stand up, but I grabbed his arm.

"Wait. I'm sorry. I don't mean to be so pushy, but I feel like I'm constantly behind and have no idea what's really going on around me. All this occult stuff is so above my head while everyone else seems to be experts in it. All I want are answers."

He sat slowly back into the chair and pushed his brown hair out of his eyes.

"Besides, you can't do what you did and not expect me to at least ask questions."

Shaking his head, he took another deep breath. "You're right. I shouldn't have done it. I had a moment of weakness, and you just looked so beautiful standing there without anyone to dance with, and

Andrea was just going on and on about some girl on the cheer squad, and I was going out of my mind."

"All I'm hearing are excuses, not truths." A month ago, I would have been so thrilled to be talking to Noah alone that I wouldn't have dared confront him about these things, but time and experience had made me braver.

"Fine. The truth is that I like you. I've liked you for...well, a while, but it doesn't matter what I want, or what I think. I've got to be with Andrea, like I said." As he spoke, he finally looked me in the eyes as if wanting to convey to me the honesty of his words.

I had to admit, it was thrilling to look into his eyes. Despite not knowing how I felt about him these days, my heart picked up the pace, and I found myself feeling a bit warm.

"Oh." It was my turn to look away, thinking.

"You're right, though. It does sound archaic. The fact remains that it's basically an assignment from the order. They haven't told me we have to get married yet, but I've got to at least be with her for a while."

"But you don't get a say in this? Andrea doesn't get a say in this? Does she even know or are you supposed to just woo her over? And again, why?"

The bell rang, signaling the end of lunch. We both glanced up, and relief washed over his face.

"I'm sorry that you got mixed up in this." He stood and slung his backpack over one shoulder. "No, she doesn't know. Yes, it's a crappy thing to do, but it still has to be done. At least two lives depend on it."

I stood as he turned away from the table and gave me a small wave. Half-heartedly, I returned the wave and began to gather my stuff. It had been nice to speak freely with him, but at the end of it all, I felt more confused than before.

Chapter 6

After school, I walked out the usual side doors to head home. I was so lost in thought that I walked right by Gryphin without really seeing him. He was leaning against a tree with one foot propped up on the trunk. Fall had fully arrived, and brown leaves skittered around his blue Converse shoes.

"Hey!" he called as I walked past.

Vaguely, the image processed in my mind, and I turned to find him walking toward me. "Oh, hi."

"Billy said he'd let me get back with you on helping us." Gryphin glanced around, probably checking that nobody else was close enough to overhear a conversation that wasn't meant for human ears.

"Who's Billy?"

"Oh," Gryphin chuckled and shook his head, "right. You call him Mr. Tyler."

I was momentarily distracted by the alluring corners of his mouth when he laughed and how the sound was almost like a purring growl.

"Hanna?"

Shaking my head to clear the boy-crazed thoughts, I forced myself to focus. "Sorry. Yeah. It's just so weird to think of Mr. Tyler as a

"Billy". I wouldn't have pegged that as his first name. He's more like a Scott or Randy or something."

Gryphin chuckled again, and I found myself wanting to make him laugh more. "I guess. I don't know. I've only known him as Uncle Billy my whole life. Are you headed home? Should we walk together?"

I nodded. "Sure, if you want."

Before I could get my foot off the curb, I bumped into a solid chest. Startled, I looked up to find Caleb's smoldering, dark scrutinizing eyes on me. He must have been on his way to football practice because he wore the school's uniform and clutched a helmet in his hand. "Who's the stranger?"

"Oh, hey," I said breathlessly, trying to recover from bumping into him. Backing up a few steps, I gestured to Gryphin who was standing beside me. "This is Gryphin. He's Mr. Tyler's nephew, a member of his...family."

Caleb's eyes narrowed as he appraised Gryphin. I was surprised to see that Gryphin was a few inches taller than Caleb. For so long, the vampire had seemed larger than life. They were both about the same build though—big muscles, thick chests. How anyone believed they were normal high school kids was beyond me. Even Gryphin's fuzzy darkness around his jaw suggested he was more man than boy.

Gryphin's shoulders were relaxed, and he wore a friendly smile as if sensing the situation may need de-escalation. "Of course, I'm a member of his family. That's how nephews and uncles work." He added an easy laugh.

"Right. Silly me." I pushed out my own chuckle. "Gryphin, this is Caleb. He's a friend, kind of an old family friend. He watches out for me and makes sure I don't get abducted or anything crazy."

"He definitely looks like an *old* family friend," Gryphin said, and then eyed Caleb's outfit. "Probably way too old to be enrolled in high school and playing football. Are your kind even allowed to play sports? Isn't that cheating?"

Caleb's face remained forcedly neutral, and he moved his eyes away from Gryphin and toward mine. "You're supposed to walk straight home where you're safe, and I can attend practice without having to worry about you. That was the deal, remember?"

I nodded, trying not to feel like I had gotten into trouble.

"Yesterday was bad enough with you staying after school so long. I had to pretend to run to the bathroom while watching over you as you walked home. It was quite an inconvenience."

"She was only—"

I cut Gryphin off with a wave of my hand. "It's okay. I can stand up for myself. I'm sorry you think of me as an inconvenience. Was I so inconvenient when I helped your vampire queen find her niece and stopped her from searching everyone's houses and causing lots of destruction?"

Caleb's eyes narrowed. "That's not what I meant."

"Isn't it? I'm sorry you have to keep tabs on me. It's not like I asked for this."

Gryphin stepped in between us and held his hands up in a peaceful gesture. "Okay, let's just take a breath. We all want the same thing here, Hanna's safety. It's so nice that you have someone as strong as he is to look out for you, isn't it?"

His forest-brown eyes peered down at me, and I swore a fresh breeze smelling like a clear stream drifted past us at that exact second.

I nodded, more out of automation than conscious thought.

He turned his gaze to Caleb's dark eyes. "And do you think Mr. Tyler would introduce her to me if he thought she was in danger from me?"

Caleb's eyes didn't leave my face, but he shook his head slowly, eventually.

"Great!" Gryphin clapped his hands together cheerfully. "So now that we're all friends, Caleb can get to practice, and I'll walk Hanna home to where she's safe. I'll keep a good eye on her, I promise."

"I'm fast enough and close enough that you just let out one call, just one, and I'll be there before you can blink." Caleb backed off a few steps toward the football field, giving space between him and Gryphin.

I managed to scrounge up a grateful smile. "I know. Thank you, but I'm pretty sure we'll be fine."

Caleb glanced at Gryphin one last time before nodding curtly and jogging toward the field in what was probably a very slow and forced human-looking jog. I had to admit that the uniform made his calves look fluid and powerful.

"Why is he so worried about playing football, anyway? I don't think I'll ever understand vampires," Gryphin said as we watched him leave.

"Me neither, but I don't understand many other people so that's not saying much. I know he can still hear us, so I cringe to say this out loud, but I am grateful for his protection. I'm sure there is more than one time I would have died without his help."

Gryphin shrugged. "Maybe, but I wonder how many times you were in danger because of him too."

I pulled the corners of my lips into an appreciative frown and nodded. "Fair point."

Caleb turned just as he entered the gate for the field and even though it was far enough away, I couldn't see his expression clearly, I knew he was giving me a flat look.

I waved prettily and set off.

"So I'm sure you're here for more than just walking me home," I said as we stepped away from the school grounds and into the neighborhood.

"That's true, although I'm more than happy to provide you with an escort. It's nice to feel useful for once." Gryphin kept a sharp eye on the usually innocent street, but just based off his scrutiny, one might have inferred the suburban houses were packed with nasty monsters who were going to jump out and devour my soul at any second.

"Do you not feel useful in your life?"

He shrugged. "Not really. Especially not since my stepmom died. The pack has been so consumed with it that everything else has been pushed to the side. That's one reason why I was eager to help Uncle Billy, Mr. Tyler, whatever you want to call him."

I adjusted the backpack strap on my shoulder so the heavy weight wasn't digging into me. "What's the other reason?"

A mischievous glint in his eye twinkled. "I hoped to also find a bit of adventure. It's so boring staying at the commune all the time...and it helps that the Seer is a girl."

I rolled my eyes and shook my head. "I should have known. You boys are all the same."

A corner of his mouth perked up, revealing a large canine tooth. "Surely we're not *all* the same."

Shaking my head again, I said, "Tell me more about the commune. I'm assuming you go to school there? I've never met anyone who lived in a commune."

"Oh," he waved his hand around nonchalantly as he explained, "it's not that different. It's just like a small city on some private land my pack owns. The alpha acts like the mayor. We're able to govern ourselves and make the rules and use pack laws to uphold structure. You'll find that while it seems a bit more chaotic than this quiet neighborhood, there is a lot deeper social structure among us wolves. We always know who is higher or lower than ourselves in seniority, and there are important ways we should act, or fights break out. It's not usual to have a full werewolf child like me, so a few of us have grown up together, roaming about the hillsides in freedom while occasionally being corralled into a math lesson or two."

"Wow. For a wolf, that sounds like paradise. I'm not sure I'd be into it too much, though. I'm not much of an outdoors type."

"You'd probably adjust to it if you needed to. Have you thought any more about helping us? Where do you think we should start looking for Sarah's ghost? Maybe you'll end up spending a lot of time on our lands after all. There's a special place where we bury our dead. Maybe her ghost is there?"

"Sarah? Is that your stepmom's name?"

He nodded.

"Okay, wow, for some reason knowing her name makes the whole thing a little more real."

"It wasn't real before?" His eyebrows perked up and he tilted his head to the side in such a puppy-like expression that it made me smile.

"I mean, yes, but no. I don't know. Of course, I'll help you guys. Mr. Tyler has been a good teacher to me. He helped my mom and sister when they were panicked about me being kidnapped. Even though your pack already owes me a favor for saving his life, apparently, it might be good to have you guys more in my debt."

Gryphin narrowed his eyes while still maintaining an amused smile. "I see you have quite the scheming mind."

My cheeks flushed. "I suppose I'm learning to survive in all this occult stuff while still being a weakling human."

"I can respect that."

We rounded the corner of my street and were only about a block away from my house. "I suppose it wouldn't hurt to look first at Sarah's favorite places. I wish my Gran were here so I could ask her more about ghost haunts. As far as I can see, there are a million different reasons why a ghost has a particular place to haunt. There is one problem, though."

"What's that?"

"Okay, maybe two problems. I'm not sure how far this commune is but I doubt it's within walking distance for an average human such as me without taking several hours to get there."

He thought for a second and nodded. "Perhaps. What's the other one?"

"How are we going to get away from my family? My mom and sister are even more overprotective of me than that vampire back there if you can imagine that."

My neck prickled, and a shiver went down my spine, clueing me in to what was about to happen. Guilt washed through me as Brandon appeared on the sidewalk. I had somehow forgotten to summon him for our usual walk home together.

"I see you've managed to find yet *another* boyfriend." Brandon looked Gryphin up and down like a farmer appraising a cow before purchasing it.

"It sounds like they love you very much. You might not be in a pack, but you've got a good support system set up. Seems pretty cool to me," Gryphin said, clueless about our newcomer.

"Uhm, yes. Well, remember how I'm a Seer?" I said to Gryphin with a pleasant smile on my face.

Confusion flitted across his features. "Of course."

"Well, things are about to get weird, and I'll ask you to hold out on some judgement as it looks like I'll be talking to myself. It might even get confusing as you won't be quite sure if I'm talking to you or a ghost."

Gryphin's eyes widened, and he grinned in excitement. "There's a ghost here with us? Right now?"

Brandon rolled his eyes. "Where did you find this kid? Is he even a kid? He seems like a puppy inside the body of a full-grown male."

"I'm so sorry, Brandon. I didn't mean to forget about our walks together. It's just that Mr. Tyler needs help with a ghost issue, and he sent his nephew to help me figure out how to help. This is Gryphin."

I gestured toward the wolf who was doing the usual looking around pointlessly that people did when I told them there was a ghost nearby. We'd stopped walking at that point, still about five or so houses from my own. Cars drove on the street periodically, but thankfully there weren't many people walking about in the late afternoon.

"Is that his real name or is he part of a boy band or something?" Brandon kept looking him up and down.

I held in a smirking giggle. "That's a fair question. Gryphin, even though you can't see him, I still feel like I should introduce you to Brandon. He's a ghost from the 90s, and he's kind of like my ghost-helping-crossing-over partner person."

"Don't forget to tell him that you also sleep with me every night and sometimes we even kiss."

I gave him a flat look.

"Oh, that's sick. Nice to meet you, er, wherever you are." Gryphin stuck out his hand for a handshake and moved it around in random directions.

Brandon kept his arms crossed and eyed his hand disdainfully. "So, what do you say we ditch the lapdog and go help Mr. Tyler with whatever ghostly issues he has this time?"

"I can't. I need his help to show me the different places around the commune that Sarah enjoyed. I doubt they'd let me in alone. Plus, we don't know where it is, and it'd be nice to have another person around to protect me from potential kidnapping vampires, don't you think?"

Brandon didn't have an answer for that, so he just stared at me in disapproval.

Gryphin finally put his hand down but didn't seem too worried about the fact that he'd apparently been left hanging. "You definitely need me. There are lots of places Sarah could be."

"I'm sorry. Brandon can be a bit..." my mouth twitched up with the word, "territorial."

Gryphin nodded. The grey curl on his forehead bounced slightly with the movement. "I know all about that. Still, that's funny coming from a ghost, isn't it?"

With a knowing smile on his lips, Gryphin placed a warm hand on my shoulder and gazed down into my eyes. "I mean, it would be a shame for someone to encroach upon his territory."

Blushing, I stepped back and removed my shoulder from under his warmer-than-normal hand. "Yeah, that would be weird for a ghost to be upset about that."

Brandon, to his credit, merely stood and fumed. His eyes were steady as steel as he stared.

"Uhm, he probably doesn't care about any of that. He's just a good guy who wants to help other ghosts cross over, that's all."

I could tell from Brandon's expression that that had been the wrong thing to say. My intention wasn't to hurt his feelings or belittle him. I was only trying to get Gryphin to back off and not feel like he was in a competition or that there was even any kind of competition to be had. Apparently, I should have claimed that Brandon and I had plans to get married in the near future, and it didn't matter that we couldn't actually touch each other or that anyone else could even see him. Our love would conquer all.

"Is that all I am?" The anger seemed to deflate out of Brandon's chest. "Yeah, I suppose that makes sense. Right. Well, I'll leave you to it."

With that, he winked out and my heart went with him.

I cursed, earning a surprised eyebrow from Gryphin.

"What? What's wrong?"

Huffing a sigh, I put my hands on my hips and stared up at the clouds. It seemed unfair to summon him back when he didn't want to be here. As far as exits go, he was one of the best at making a good one and leaving with the last word.

"Nothing. It's fine." I blew out another frustrated sigh. "It's good to be reminded of reality sometimes, as painful as it can be."

"I kind of feel like whatever just happened was my fault. Did Brandon leave? I'm sorry. I was just teasing."

I was pretty sure that if Gryphin's tail had been out, it would have been tucked between his legs.

Shaking my head, I took off down the sidewalk, and thought about how I was going to get away from Trina and my mom without having them worry. The last thing I wanted was another person I cared about being upset with me.

Chapter 7

The house was quiet as we walked inside. Afternoon sunlight filtered in through the blinds of the kitchen, giving the place a dim peacefulness that made me want to take a long nap.

"Nice place." Gryphin stopped at the display case of knick-knacks my mom had collected over the years. It reminded me of Brandon because that had been the first thing he'd done when he'd visited the house for the first time.

A lump formed in my throat, and I pushed a small hope into the world that Brandon would forgive me, and we'd be fine.

"Thanks. I guess my mom isn't home. She's been pretty busy lately. Trina should be here, though."

I walked down the hallway toward Trina's bedroom but found the door open and the room empty, albeit every bit as messy as a teenage girl's room should be.

"Looks like we have the place to ourselves," Gryphin said while leaning on the doorframe beside me.

I didn't bother to respond but went back to the kitchen and grabbed a soda. "Do you want anything to drink?"

"Nah. I'm good. So I guess we're free to go with no one here to stop you? I mean, you technically came straight home like you told that bloodsucker. Now you've held up your bargain, we can get to work, right?"

Grabbing a quick swig, I thought about what to do next. There was a risk leaving my house, but it was probably less risky leaving during daylight hours and being in the company of a werewolf. Plus, there was one other thing I needed to do.

"We're still stuck with the problem of transportation. I don't suppose you want to shift, and I could ride on your back all through town?"

His lips twitched with a smile. "How do you think I got to the school in the first place? My car is in the parking lot as we speak. Well, it's not my car. It belongs to the commune, but they let me take it out sometimes."

I glared at him as I took another drink. My stomach felt empty and my whole body felt light, which I took to be a good sign I was keeping my weight down. Drinking the soda helped with the shaking fingers and the low energy that often came with watching what I ate.

"Why didn't you say so in the first place?"

He shrugged. "A ghost showed up. Things got dramatic. What can I say?"

Shaking my head, I tossed the empty bottle into the recycling. "Alright. Guess you earned a walk back to the school. Grab your car. We can head to the commune, find Sarah's ghost, and get the answers your pack needs before anyone will notice I'm gone."

"Sounds like a plan. I'll be back before you notice I'm gone." He grinned as he opened the front door.

"I doubt that."

As I waited, I changed into clothes that were more suited for walking around in the woods than sitting primly in a classroom.

It didn't take him long, probably after jogging quickly through the neighborhood. I was sitting on the porch as he pulled up in a silver minivan. He jumped out of the car and darted around to open the passenger door for me.

His eagerness earned a small smile despite my gloomy feelings.

As we pulled out of the neighborhood, I said, "Can we stop by the Meadowbrook Bridge first? I've got a small errand to make."

"Are you sure your vampire friend will like that?" He grinned a wide smile that revealed too many sharp teeth.

"I'm sure I have nothing to worry about. I haven't been back to visit Stephanie, and I told her I would. I can't just not show up. Plus, I've got to start working on her unfinished business, so we can help her cross over. It's kind of what I do, and Stephanie was a good friend to me while others around weren't so good."

Gryphin nodded, the smile gone. "I get it. I'm sorry. I didn't realize you meant to check on your friend's ghost."

I let his comment rest, and we sat in silence until we made it to the bridge. The road was open and working as usual, but there was warning tape and orange cones around the spot where the car had bent the guardrail and gone over. We parked on the side of the road before getting to the bridge, so there was still plenty of space for the traffic to pass by as responsible adult people got off from work.

There was no sign of Stephanie's ghost as we got out of the car and walked onto the sidewalk. My eyes zipped around the area quickly several times until I started to feel dizzy.

"Do you see her?" Gryphin walked beside me, making sure to stay on the outside near the traffic like the gentleman he was. He also looked around with sharp eyes.

"Not yet. Sometimes it takes a minute for the ghost to grab onto my energy. As far as I can tell, it takes a lot of energy just to exist as a ghost, and without my added energy around, they don't hang out as much or as long. Not to mention, I'm not even sure this is her haunt."

"I wish I could see ghosts. It sounds so cool. Have you seen a lot of dead confederate soldiers hanging around town?" Gryphin put a little hop into his step, and I wondered where he got all *his* energy.

"Some. I wouldn't say a lot. Most of them probably went back to their hometowns and stuff where their haunt would be. I certainly wouldn't want to hang out in the place I died for the rest of eternity."

"You mean like your friend here?"

I sighed, stopping in the middle of the bridge and looking out into the water that flowed downstream with an innocent rushing sound. "Yeah, I guess just like that."

The usual neck prickles announced Stephanie's presence on the other side of me. She sat on the guardrail and stared at the water with us. "Where did my body go?"

I glanced at Gryphin and gave a subtle nod in her direction, so he'd understand she'd appeared and that I wasn't talking to him. Then I turned to face Stephanie directly. "My friend took it...somewhere? I don't really know, actually. I'm sorry. He's got an idea for something, and honestly, I have no clue what he's up to, but I do know I trust him to have your best interest at heart."

She furrowed her finely sculpted eyebrows and finally looked at me. "You're saying that he took the body of a teenage girl somewhere and you don't know where, what, or why he did that?"

I frowned. "Right. Well, when you put it that way, it sounds pretty creepy."

Gryphin stood quietly and let me do my thing, but I had to admit it was nice to have a solid presence at my back, even if I would have enjoyed hearing some snippy comments from a certain ghost every once in a while. The world seemed so much quieter without him.

"And ugh, look at me!" Stephanie waved her arms up and down her body. "I'm stuck in this horrible costume! I didn't even want to be a sexy policewoman, but Andrea talked me into it because she was going as the sexy nurse this year. I've tried everything to get rid of these terrible fishnets, and nothing works!"

I laughed way harder than I should have, but once I started it was like I couldn't stop letting it out until my body was ready.

Gryphin watched me with an amused expression on his face but kept his mouth closed. Stephanie hopped off the rail and glared at me while putting her hands on her hips.

"What, may I ask, is so funny?"

"I'm sorry. I didn't mean to laugh." I used a finger to wipe away a tear. "But I really needed that. I should be thanking you. It's just so nice to see you back to your old self."

"Oh." She dropped her hands and stood up straight. "Well, I guess that's true. Am I really that shallow?"

"Oh, honey. You're not shallow. Well... I mean, not too shallow, anyway. You've just always been careful about how you look. That's not bad, is it?"

She frowned. "It sounds bad after everything that's happened. Oh, Hanna. You were always so nice to me. I'm sorry I didn't stand up for you in front of Andrea! I feel like my life was pointless and full of useless things now that it's over." Blue tears formed on her blue face.

"I'm sorry. I wish I could hug you. It might feel like that right now, but you've only just died. You're probably still so shocked that it's hard to remember the good things you did in life. I'm sure you helped others. Oh, and don't worry about me. I'm glad I finally woke up from Andrea's spell. I have no idea why I tried to be her friend for so long, but I am glad I was able to be your friend. And Randi's. You guys were always so much nicer than Andrea."

A faint smile spread over Stephanie's lips. "It does feel a little better to hear that."

"I'm glad. That's actually one reason I'm here. Haven't you wondered why it seems like only I can see and hear you?"

"Uhm, I guess." She peered around me to look at Gryphin who was still dutifully watching the road and area around us in case the boogeyman jumped out or something. "Can he not see me? Who is that hot hunk, anyway? I've never seen him at school."

I smiled, relieved he wasn't able to hear her call him "hot". "He's Mr. Tyler's nephew. You know that history teacher at school?"

"Okay. That's a shame he doesn't go to our school. I'd love to look at him all day long." She swept her eyes all over his broad shoulders and tight-fitting jeans.

I shook my head and chuckled. "Oh, I'm so glad he can't hear you right now."

Gryphin glanced at me with a bemused expression.

"It is pretty fun to be able to talk about whatever and whoever I want without them knowing I'm talking about them. This would have come in handy a few times at cheer practice." She grinned brightly, but it faded quickly. "So how come you're the only one who can see and hear me?"

"It's a weird gift, power, however you want to say it, that I inherited from my gran. I'm a Seer, and it's my curse, or privilege, again however you want to look at it, to help ghosts cross over."

"What do you mean cross over?"

"Ghosts are only left here on earth because they have some kind of unfinished business. Once we complete it, you can cross over and go to the next phase of existence, whatever that is."

She shuddered. "I still can't believe this is happening to me."

I nodded in agreement. "Me neither, but here we are. Let's try to make the best of it. Now, I've got to go help Gryphin here find another ghost, but I'm going to leave you with some homework so we can start working on your unfinished business. I get the feeling you don't want to be hanging out on a bridge in a skimpy skirt and fishnet stockings for the rest of existence."

We shared a small smile.

"No, I don't want to be. So, what's my homework?"

"Just try to think about your life and figure out what your unfinished business is. It's easier for some to figure out than others, but just kinda search your mind for anything that sticks out from what you wanted to do before you died. Can you do that?"

"Wait, what if it's being a virgin? How can we fix that?"

I stifled another laugh. "You're still a virgin? I wouldn't have expected that... I mean, of course you are!"

She glared for a second, but it dissolved into a laugh. "Yeah, I talk a big game. Too bad your friend over there couldn't help me work on that issue."

"Right," I glanced at him again and laughed. "Try to work past that and focus on other stuff. As far as I know, that's not really a thing I'm equipped to help out with."

"Bummer. Okay, I'll see what I can come up with. It'll give me something to do at least with all this time by myself. One can only watch the traffic pass by for so long."

I gave her an empathetic side-smile. "I'm sorry. I'll try to help as much as I can so you can pass over."

"Pretty sure anything will be better than sitting in this mini-skirt and watching cars drive by."

"Probably."

We both smiled and waved at each other as Gryphin and I walked back to his car.

"That seemed to have gone well," he said after a few seconds.

"I think so. I still feel sad and worried for her, but overall, I do feel a tiny bit better. She's acting more like herself and that was nice to see, although she's still dead and went long before her time."

Gryphin nodded. "It's sad. Death is sad."

I studied his side profile for a second. His nose was so straight I imagined tiny people skiing down it like a snowy slope. Pain lingered in his eyes. I wondered how close he was to his stepmom or perhaps some of the pain he was feeling was combined with the grief of the whole pack. It must have been weird to be that close to several people who weren't blood related.

"It doesn't always have to be sad," I said, turning my eyes back to the sidewalk so I didn't trip and fall. "Without it, I wouldn't have been able to meet Brandon, or if I did for some reason while he was alive, he'd be this creepy middle-aged guy with kids or something."

As we reached the car, Gryphin opened the passenger side door, keeping himself between me and the traffic whizzing by. "You really like that guy, don't you?"

I shrugged, suddenly embarrassed. "Well, you know, I've kind of gotten used to having him around."

"You might want to tell him that."

As I slid into the seat, I was close enough to get a whiff of his scent. It was fresh and free as the breeze, bringing the smells of burbling streams, earthy grass, and towering pine trees. I'm not sure how one got all of that from one whiff, but it seemed like everything about Gryphin made me think of being outside in the forest.

It almost made me want to go running through the woods.

"What should I tell him?" I asked as Gryphin climbed in on the other side and started his car.

"You should tell him that you enjoy his company and are glad he's your friend. Of course, I could only hear one side of the conversation, but if I had to guess, I'd say he's feeling insecure. It would be good for him to hear how much you like him."

I laughed softly and shook my head. "I don't know. He always seems pretty confident to me. I'm afraid if I give him compliments, he'll get more insufferable."

"Sometimes guys use those types of comments to hide insecurities they actually have. He might be hurting more than you realize."

I frowned and watched as the scenery zipped by. He didn't head back into town, but instead took the highway that led out of it. Buildings became sparse as trees and fields flew by us.

"I guess that could be true. Maybe I'll have to ask him. I know he's been through some tough things. He hates talking about his life before he died, and from the little I know about it, I can't blame him."

Silence descended on us for several minutes. I didn't mind it, though. It wasn't awkward or filled with tension. It was merely time to think and to observe the world around us and that was perfectly fine and peaceful.

My thoughts swirled with Brandon for a bit, and then I thought about where we were going and what we were supposed to be doing. "So where do you want to start first? What were Sarah's favorite places to hang out when she was alive? I have no idea what the rules are for haunts or why a certain place is picked, but we might as well start somewhere."

Gryphin nodded, keeping his eyes on the road as the dutiful driver. "Sounds good to me. I can think of a few places she and her wolf form enjoyed, but," he glanced at me with a grin, "it might take a bit of running to get there. How do you feel about going for a jog in the woods?"

Normally, I probably would have said no with a disgusted pout on my face, but after spending time with him and getting impressions of the woods as he saw them, I wanted to go out and experience it for myself. Not to mention, running was good exercise, and exercise was always a good idea when one was trying to lose fat and look toned.

"I'd say I'm glad I changed into better clothes. Probably won't be able to keep up with you, though."

"I don't think you'll need to worry about that," he said with a cheeky grin.

After a few more minutes, he turned the clunky van onto a road I hadn't noticed before. It started paved but after a mile or so, it turned to gravel. The bumping and crunching of the drive made me clench my teeth. Finally, after taking several turns and enduring several potholes, I was thoroughly lost. Gryphin took one more right turn and the trees parted, revealing a long driveway that went straight into the heart of a small collection of buildings. Thick forest surrounded the area and, in the distance, a few mountains peeked up over the trees.

"Wow, this beautiful and exactly the kind of place I'd picture werewolves would flourish in. Does Mr. Tyler drive all this way to school and back?" I asked, staring out of the window in wonder.

"Yes. He could live outside of the commune if he wanted to, but he prefers to come home every evening. I haven't lived outside myself, but I'd wager the pull to be closer to the pack would be powerful and distracting." Gryphin took the van up the driveway and pulled into a parking lot of sorts.

Several cars were lined up but there wasn't cement or pavement, it was just more gravel. It was probably easier to get gravel up here than a cement truck. Most of the vehicles were kind of old and beat-up looking, similar to the van we'd arrived in. There were a few sports cars, but even those were older models.

"That sounds intense. I still can't decide if being a werewolf and part of a pack would be cool or terrible."

He chuckled. "It can be a bit of both. Everything here belongs to the pack as a whole, and we view property differently than most people do. We share everything and everyone gets the things they need, and sometimes even silly things they want if there is enough money to go around. Like last year Mrs. Jensen wanted a swimming pool, and my dad agreed to it as long as everyone could take a dip whenever they wanted. Actually, we all pitched in to build it, and it was kind of fun to see it come together."

"Oh, I can see how that could be good, but it could also be bad if you had a selfish person or something."

"We've had a few of those from time to time, but the alpha can usually get them to play along."

We got out of the van. I opened my door before Gryphin could rush around to do it for me, so we met face-to-face as soon as I stepped out.

"Hi," I said with an awkward smile.

He grinned and turned away.

The clear air filled my lungs as I took a deep breath. Yes, there was something nice about being in the wild, even if Caleb was probably cursing my name right now. He'd been trying to drill into my head that I needed to be smarter about where I went and who I hung out with. A little swirl of guilt stirred in my stomach as I realized I'd taken another risk.

It was one thing to be hanging out with Mr. Tyler inside the school while he brought in his nephew. It was quite another thing to be driving off to the countryside alone with said nephew. Maybe I really was as thick-headed as Caleb thought I was, but my instincts told me I was safe with the wolf.

We walked up the rest of the gravel road into the werewolf village. The houses looked modern enough. Most of them were well-kept trailers that were common to see around the hills of Virginia. In the center, there was a large cabin, or maybe it was more like a lodge of some kind. It was built all from wood and was an impressive three stories high with two decks overlooking the area. People milled around doing various activities, but almost all of them stopped to at least check us out and see who was walking into the place.

A few children played on a swing set in a patch of grass that looked like it had been set aside for a park. It even had a few picnic tables underneath a large pavilion. I caught a glimpse behind an older-looking small cabin and saw a navy-blue cover stretched tight over a rectangular shape of concrete that could have only been a pool.

Before we'd made it too far in, a tall man came jogging toward us. He was as well built as Gryphin, and I was beginning to think that it was a common thing for a wolf's human form to be strong and fit. Even Mr. Tyler looked toned, although he wasn't nearly as big as Gryphin or the stranger coming toward us.

"Gryphin! I see your mission was successful," the man said as he came within a few paces of us.

"Yes, she was graceful enough to come. Hanna, this is Kage Aikawa, second in command of the Blue Ridge pack. He's the one who has helped us back here while Mr. Tyler and I were..." Gryphin trailed off as if unsure how much to say out in the open like this.

There wasn't anyone too close to us at the moment, but if werewolves were anything like real wolves, or even vampires, they probably all had amazing hearing.

Kage smiled, and the skin around his eyes crinkled warmly. It was hard to place his age, but not in the way that had been hard to place a necromancer's age. Instead, it was like he'd found a really good brand of moisturizer and had been able to keep the effects of aging at bay. His dark hair only had a few strands of grey, and it grew down to his shoulders like a sleek, black waterfall. Standing at a few inches shorter than Gryphin, he was about a foot taller than me. He wore a plain white t-shirt that showed off his lithe build and cargo pants that had more than a little dirt on them.

"Yes, let's go inside my house so you can debrief me and introduce your new friend," Kage said with a nudging nod to the side.

Chapter 8

We followed Kage past a few different trailers and cabins. I enjoyed looking at each place as they were all so different. The trailers were from all different time periods and had many shapes and styles. Some were even RVs. All of them were kept up with, and even though some looked old, they didn't look run-down.

One cabin was tiny, like probably had one room and maybe a bathroom and kitchenette tiny. There was a meticulous little garden, a lovely fern wreath hung from the door, and a birdhouse on one of those wire stands was implanted into the grass.

There was one trailer with orange siding that had a giant set of antlers above the door and a pair of old boots sitting out front.

It was kind of cool to see that while these people lived together in a shared space, they were also allowed individual expression.

Kage's place was another small cabin. It was back a few rows of houses and close to the main lodge building. Despite it being smaller than an average house, it was much bigger than the tiny cabin I had spotted earlier. A statue sat out front that I wasn't familiar with, but it looked like a little house with a four-pointed roof that curved upwards at the corners. Instead of a dirt pathway like most of the other places had, this one had a series of stone steps leading toward the door. There were several tiny bushes around the cabin that I could tell had been trimmed meticulously.

As he led us inside, he pointed to a small shelf next to the door where several shoes were already stored. "If you would, please."

We followed Kage's example and took our shoes off, placing them in empty slots on the shelf. It took Gryphin a few extra minutes to pull at his laces and shimmy out of his tennis shoes, but it was only a second for me to pull off the running shoes that I'd had for a while yet looked nearly brand new.

"Welcome to my home. Have a seat," Kage gestured to the couch on the right where an area had been designated as a front room of sorts. Most of the cabin was an open space with the kitchen and front room and laundry room all in one area, but there were a few closed doors off to the left where I assumed a more private bedroom and bathroom were.

If I had to guess, I would have said he lived with a feminine touch since gauzy white curtains framed the windows and a pot of flowers sat on the coffee table.

"You have a lovely place," I said, sitting on the couch next to Gryphin.

It had seating enough for three, but Gryphin was so big that he took up nearly two spots. There was only an inch between us, and I made sure to sit as close to the armrest as I could.

Kage sat in an armchair and steepled his fingers together while giving me an intense look. "Thank you. I have to say it's an honor to have a Seer visit our little village. It's been quite a while since we've had one."

"Oh, thank you. It's nice to be here. It seems like quite a lovely place to grow up." It felt weird being praised like that, but I figured I could at least play along enough to seem gracious.

Gryphin leaned back into his seat and draped his arms on the back of the couch. I tried not to notice as his arm rested right behind my shoulders and neck. I wasn't sure if I should move away from his almost-touch or not since that movement would certainly be noticed.

"We work hard to keep ourselves protected. It's difficult to keep a pack close these days. Not all wolves choose to live so close together, but it suits us well." Kage glanced at Gryphin for a second. "For now, anyway."

"That sounds ominous." I also glanced at Gryphin, hoping they didn't have such good hearing as to pick up on the sound of my quickly beating heart.

I would like to say that being so close to him didn't affect me at all, but unfortunately, I didn't have that strong of a constitution. He smelled so good, like a bonfire on a chilly night.

Kage shrugged. "There are no immediate threats, but we're also aware of how quickly things can change. It doesn't help when our alpha is so distracted. He's not at his full strength, and it's only a matter of time before someone tries to challenge his rank."

"Which for werewolves means a fight to the death," Gryphin said with a tense press to his lips. "Before my stepmom died, my dad was easily the strongest wolf in our pack, but if someone wanted to cross him now, I'm not sure how he would fare."

Kage nodded. "The wolves can feel it, and some are getting restless. We need to help him work through this and recover before there are deadly consequences."

"Alright. I'm willing to help, but my mom and sister are super protective of me right now due to...a situation with some vampires a few weeks ago. I can help, but I should be home before dark." I glanced to the window where early evening sunlight lit up the room.

"Of course. Gryphin will give you access to whatever place you think she might be. He knew her as well as the rest of us. It's my job to make sure no one gets suspicious or tries to stop you from your quest, although I don't really see this as a problem. Gryphin hasn't brought anyone in from the outside before, but it's not so uncommon for our youth to want to show friends around. Of course, most of the newcomers don't know what we really are and figure we're a bunch of weird family members who want to live together or a crazy religious group of people, which is what we want them to think."

"Right, because that's much easier to deal with than the truth," I said, and we all shared an amused smile.

"So let's get to it. Shall we?" Gryphin stood up and held his hand out to me.

Gingerly I placed my small hand inside his large one and let him pull me up from the couch. Normally, I would have preferred to get up on my own, but I didn't want to be rude. His calloused hand wrapped around mine warmly, and his grip felt secure and reliable.

After we'd gotten our shoes back on, both of us having to take a moment to lace and tie them securely, we headed out into the evening air.

"Have a nice tour," Kage said loudly as he waved to us from his front step.

"Thank you." I waved back.

"Let's start with the lodge." Gryphin gestured to the nearby building and took the lead. His long legs covered distances easily, and I had to almost jog to keep up with him. "This was the first thing built here on our land. It dates back to 1850, or so, if I remember correctly."

"Wow. It's impressive."

We both played the parts of tour guide and tourist where the others could see and hear us easily. There were a few who passed by on the main thoroughfare who politely nodded but didn't interfere with the presence of an outsider.

If I hadn't known what they were, I probably would have been suspicious of their acceptance to allowing an outsider to take a tour simply because they felt like it, but it made more sense when you knew they werewolves. It was unlikely one or two outsiders would be able to cause much harm to anyone here. It also made sense that as long as the wolves cooperated with the community and didn't seem too secretive and suspicious, they were more likely to coexist peacefully.

At least, that's what my thoughts on it were. For all I really knew, the wolves actually ate the human visitors and most of them found the end of the tour more than they had been expecting.

Gryphin held the heavy wooden door open for me, and as I stepped inside the lodge, I had to pause a moment for my eyes to adjust to the dimness. The first floor was a large community area with several chairs and couches placed around the room. A group of ladies was sitting around a table playing cards. They looked up at us when we came in, and a few gave Gryphin appraising looks, but most went back to the card game.

Vending machines lined the wall on one side. There were a few pool tables toward the back where huge glass doors overlooked a vast field stretching out to meet a sizeable lake, which must have been loads of fun in the summer months.

"Here we have the main floor. This is where most of our family meetings happen. It's also where we gather in the evenings to tell stories or maybe have a birthday party or two." Gryphin lifted his arm in a gesture as if revealing a grand place.

As we ascended the stairs to the second floor, Gryphin leaned in close to my ear and whispered, presumably so that the others wouldn't hear and not as an excuse to get close to me. "The lodge is where the alpha and his family live. We're going to the third floor so we can look around."

"It would be too easy for her haunt to be the place she lived in, but it would also be dumb not to check it out," I whispered back, hoping my breath wasn't too bad.

Gryphin nodded, leading me up to the second floor. In a normal voice, he said, "The second floor is for offices and where the administration does the boring work of keeping the budget and planning for everyone's needs and all that jazz."

"Oh, those sound like important things, even if they might be boring," I said, noting that the two desks were tidied neatly with papers and supplies.

The second floor wasn't as open as the first. There were several closed doors running along the wall that I guessed were probably for supplies and smaller offices.

"And the third floor is the private quarters of our mayor and his family. I'm sorry to say I won't be able to take you up there, but if you please will continue this way..." Gryphin walked loudly down the hallway, letting his shoes clomp on the wood.

When we got halfway down, he stopped and held a finger to his lips. In the barest of whispers, he said, "We'll sneak upstairs, but they'll hear your footsteps. I'll have to carry you. Is that okay?"

Alarm washed across my face, earning a grinning smile from him. I made sure to keep my voice down still, though. "Is that really necessary?"

"I'm sorry. I know how to avoid all the creaks in the stairs, and no offense, but humans are just so loud."

I glared and he laughed silently.

"Hey, it's fine. I promise to behave myself and keep my hands in respectful places."

Finally, I nodded, trying to focus on the job of finding Sarah's ghost and not on the fact that even though I was outwardly protesting, inwardly I did want to feel the touch of his hands again.

Still grinning, he swooped me up as easily as if lifting a bag of groceries. His hands and arms went underneath my knees and behind my shoulders. I had to lean into his chest and place one of my arms around his neck for balance. It was impossible to ignore his woodsy scent and feel the warmth from his muscled body.

Blushing, I made sure not to look into his eyes and kept my gaze on the stairs in front of us, lest I give him any indications that he could lean in for a kiss or something.

I blushed more while thinking about his lips.

He had been right about being silent though. My human ears couldn't detect a sound from his feet as he ascended the broad wooden stairs. I could hear, loudly I might add, my breathing and heart rate. I was afraid they were so loud, the ladies downstairs would be able to hear them.

I'd never been so close to a handsome man...or werewolf male in this case, for so long, and it was all I could do to focus on keeping my breathing steady as if I were the one carrying another person up the stairs.

As for Gryphin, he seemed perfectly comfortable and at ease. Almost as if he did this kind of thing every day. It got me wondering about girls his age living here. Were there many? Was he so used to flirting with others that carrying me like a newlywed bride was no big deal?

Thinking about all the many girls he was used to and how I was probably just one more helped me calm my racing heart. Only a little.

At the top of the stairs, there was a small landing and then an ornate wooden door. Gryphin had no trouble opening it with the hand underneath my knees. As we entered the room, he set me down gently and turned to shut the door carefully behind us.

Leaning in close and still whispering, he said, "This loft has been the alpha's domain for decades, at least for several wolves before my dad."

I nodded, a bit breathless still and focused on keeping quiet.

The first area was a cozy front room. There was a large fireplace with a set of giant antlers over the mantle. They were so large that I had trouble imagining the beast they'd come from. Three couches spread out in a semi-circle, and a big TV was mounted on one wall. I don't know why, but that kind of surprised me.

Putting a finger to his lips again, Gryphin motioned for me to follow him. He was trying to tell me to be quiet, but all it did was bring my attention back to his soft, alluring mouth.

Carefully as I could, I followed him through a doorway and into the kitchen. It was decently modern for being in a lodge in the middle of nowhere. I imagined many homecooked meals made here and lots of laughter shared.

We went down a hallway, which was carpeted and easier to walk quietly on. After passing a bathroom, four other doors turned out to be bedrooms. Gryphin led me to the furthest room away and opened the door to reveal a stately master bedroom.

"This is where they slept, and coincidently, where my dad spent lots of his time after she'd disappeared. Sometimes he didn't get out of bed all day." His voice was still low and the lighting was dim, but I could still see pain flicker in his forest-brown eyes.

I stepped into the room and tried to push away the feeling that I was intruding into someone's private life. So far, I hadn't seen one ghost in the lodge, which honestly surprised me. Even if it wasn't Sarah, there were bound to be werewolves roaming through the halls of a place they'd spent many days of their lives.

And yet not a ghostly blue swirl in sight.

The room had been tastefully decorated, at least from what I could see underneath the clutter. Clothes were scattered on the floor, heaped in piles on the dresser, and the closet door was propped halfway open, revealing a series of empty hangers with a few straggling jackets still hanging. I assumed the bright pictures of daisies on the walls had once been straight. For now, they contrasted heavily with the gloomy miasma that seemed to permeate the place. There was a large king-sized bed with several pillows in a chaotic spread while the blankets were twisted and wrapped around each other.

"Where is your dad now? He's not here, is he?" Worry spiked through me at the thought of stumbling upon an angry werewolf in his own territory.

"Oh, don't worry. Kage made sure he was busy with pack business. It's not hard to set up some kind of problem for him to solve." Gryphin's friendly smile was back, but the pain kept to the shadows in his eyes. "There is always drama inside the pack, and if it's quiet, that usually means something big is coming. We might be wolves, but we're humans, too."

"And we know how humans like to cause trouble." We shared a smile, and I went back to looking around the room, hoping my presence would give any nearby ghost the energy it needed to appear.

"It's been a while since I've been in here. I didn't realize it'd gotten so bad. Otherwise, I would have asked Kage to get someone to clean it up." Gryphin frowned as he nudged a large sneaker that was turned on its side near the doorway.

I shrugged. "It's fine. Kinda gives us a look at what's going on inside of him. I can't imagine losing my significant other, best friend, and lover. His soul must be hurting so badly."

After a few seconds of quiet, Gryphin spoke. "It's even worse when it's a mate. Werewolves have strong bonds with the pack and their mates. It's difficult to explain to someone who hasn't felt it, but I can promise you his soul looks much worse than this."

"And all of you can feel the pain through the pack bonds plus your own grief. I'm sorry you have all had to go through this. I wish I had better news, but I haven't seen a ghost this whole time I've been here."

His shoulders slumped, but he kept the disappointment out of his face. "It's okay. We have lots of places to search for her. Too many, in fact."

We stepped back out of the room, and I chewed on my lip in thought. "That's the weird thing, though. Even if we didn't find Sarah, we should have found at least one other ghost wandering around somewhere. There's got to be people who would at least haunt the village, if not the lodge."

Gryphin's eyebrows creased in consideration. "Huh. Odd."

We walked back down the hallway, but Gryphin stopped me as we passed another door. "Want to see my room?"

He was already opening the door before I could respond. If my Gran were still around, she would have scolded me for going into a boy's room to be alone with the boy, but she would have been way past angry at this point. I had traveled with someone I didn't know well to a remote place and then followed him into an empty loft where there was no one to make sure we made good choices.

Thinking about Gran reminded me of what she'd said to me right before she crossed over. I logged the memory inside my head so I could pull it out when I had more room to work on *that* mystery. Whatever she'd put underneath the rock in her garden could wait. It'd waited all this time.

"Welcome to my sanctuary." Gryphin stepped back into the hallway to let me enter.

"Well, it's cleaner than the last one, at least."

I'd meant it as a joke, and he smiled, but I felt bad the moment the words left my mouth.

He had his own giant bed, and it was actually neatly made. His dresser had various pictures sitting on the top and only a thin layer of dust had settled on the happy faces. All the dirty clothes had made it into the dirty clothes bin, and the shoes were piled inside the closet. The messiest part was his desk where papers were scattered about, with a pencil and a calculator only half-covered.

I took a few steps inside and approached the pictures on his dresser. "Is this Sarah?"

He leaned in over my shoulder to see what I was looking at. Since it was his bedroom, he probably didn't need to look so closely. He'd probably looked at million times, yet there he was, his chin almost resting on my shoulder while his cheek was easily less than an inch away from my own.

"It is."

The picture was taken on a sunny day at a park or in the woods somewhere. Trees stood sturdily behind the trio of Gryphin, Sarah, and what had to have been his dad. Gryphin appeared to be a few years younger than he was now, but he still had a solid, lithe build. It was obvious where he'd gotten his looks from as his dad stood proudly behind him with a hand clamped onto his shoulder. The alpha had the same grey-silver hair but kept it shorter and slicked back while Gryphin's had a bit of a wild curl going on. Father and son shared the same deep brown eyes, and I had a feeling that if I were to look into them too long, I'd hear the birds chirping and the clear stream of the forest gurgling down the hill.

Sarah was tiny compared to her husband. Her red hair was cut short in an A-line bob that rested at her chin. Her clothes were neat and fashionable, and her eyes looked full of love and confidence. It was her smile, though, that drew my eyes.

"She was very beautiful. How come I didn't see any pictures of her in your dad's room?"

Carefully, I put the picture down and stepped to the side. My heart thundered in my chest, and I didn't know if it was from eagerness to be close to Gryphin or an instinctual warning.

"Not sure. I imagine it's hard enough to be in the bed they had once shared, let alone have a picture to stare at." Gryphin sighed and led me back out of the room.

As we walked outside, talking loudly for the benefit of the ladies still playing cards, I couldn't help but notice how low the sun was in the sky.

"I should probably be getting home," I said, stepping down the stairs.

Gryphin followed my gaze upwards. "Yeah. Too bad you can't sleep over. My bed is plenty big enough."

I knew it was a joke, but a blush rushed my cheeks all the same. "Oh, I'm sure my mom would love that."

"At least it would give those old ladies something interesting to talk about." Gryphin grinned but before I could look into his eyes and fall for him like a silly girl, I spun on my heel and headed back toward the van.

Chapter 9

As soon as we drove back into a place with cell service, my phone started going crazy.

"Oh, crap." I frowned as I scrolled through the list of messages, most of them from my mom and Trina.

"Guess you were missed," Gryphin said, a teasing smile on his face while he kept his eyes on the road.

"You could say that. I don't know how I'm going to get out again to keep looking for Sarah. We might have to come up with a good lie." I hastily texted Mom that I was fine, on the way home, and should be there before the sun had fully set.

"It's a shame we didn't find her today." His knuckles were white as he gripped the steering wheel.

Telling myself I was brave, I put my hand comfortingly on his shoulder. It looked small in comparison. "I'm sorry. I wish these things were easier. To be honest, even if we did find her, it might take more time to get answers. Ghosts can be fickle and confused, so in all fairness, we'd have to go back again, anyway."

He nodded and pressed his lips together firmly in resolution while I chided myself for paying so much attention to his mouth.

A few minutes passed between us, and I watched as the familiar landmarks of town went by.

"Maybe you could invite your ghost friend to come with us next time? I get the feeling he'd want to be included."

I sighed and rubbed my forehead. "Yes, maybe. At the very least I owe him an apology. Again."

Gryphin chuckled. "Yeah, friendships can be like that. Or relationships. Whatever y'all are to each other."

I shook my head. "I don't even know."

As I got out of Gryphin's car, I waved to my new friend and turned to see Trina and my mom rushing out of the house.

"Where have you been?" Mom basically yelled as she pulled me into a hug.

"And who was *that*?" Trina asked, watching the van drive away.

"There you are!" Caleb appeared out of nowhere, startling all three of us.

Later, we were sitting around the kitchen table with various drinks, me with a diet soda of course, and I filled them all in on the story of Gryphin. I felt relieved coming clean.

"I don't know if this sounds weird, but it's actually kind of nice to be able to tell you guys about all the insane stuff I'm dealing with. I mean, I'm not happy that y'all had to get mixed up with the vampires and necromancers last month, but in a way I am, if that makes any sense."

Mom patted my hand that was resting on the table. "As scared as I am for you almost all the time, I'm glad you can tell us too. I'd rather know what was going on than not."

Trina nodded. "Yes, it's definitely hard to hear all this stuff, and sometimes it's just downright unbelievable, but it's good to know it."

"I don't like it." Caleb was leaning back in his chair, and the front two legs of it were several inches off the ground. I could tell by my mom's eye twitches that she was working very hard not to say anything about it. Whenever I sat like that, she always told me I'd fall, but vampires probably didn't have to worry about that with their quick reflexes and all.

Personally, I wished he would fall, just because it would be funny to see a vampire surprised and maybe a little embarrassed.

"Of course you don't." I sighed. "But what else can I do? That's my whole reason for existing, right? Helping the ghosts cross over?"

Mom nodded. "It is, but does it have to be right now? You've got your whole life ahead of you to help them. Can't you just live your life right now and enjoy growing up still?"

I shook my head. "I tried that. It didn't work."

"Would this happen to have something to do with a certain skater kid who can't seem to keep his mouth shut?" Trina asked with a teasing smile.

Of course, all of us were avoiding the elephant sitting smack dab in the middle of the table. Trina had revealed to us—to save me so it had been pretty gallant—that she was also able to see ghosts. Gran had given her a golden necklace that looked like a creepy eye to keep Trina from having to see the ghosts at all. Unfortunately, or maybe fortunately, I still wasn't sure, there was only one necklace so I couldn't have that luxury. After everything, though, Trina had chosen to put the necklace back on, and we were all ignoring the fact that all these issues could be her issues too. I mean, I could have used her help, but I figured it was her choice to come out when she was ready.

If she ever got that way.

I shook my head. "It's not just him." Yes, it probably was. "It's all the other ghosts who need help. I feel bad to see them so sad, and you know I can't ignore Stephanie. I *have* to help her at least cross over. Did I tell you guys she's stuck in a sexy policewoman's costume since that's what she died in?"

Mom and Trina giggled, and their exchanged glances told me they knew they probably shouldn't have been laughing at the poor girl, but at least that bit was pretty funny.

"And that's the only reason you want to help her?"

Leave it to Caleb to bring us all down.

"Of course not. She was my friend, and I feel terrible about everything that happened. It's the least I can do. Oh, and that reminds me, what about your idea with her body? What did you do with it?"

Caleb swatted my question out of the air with a flick of his hand. "Don't worry about that. It's in the works. You might just want to hold back on trying to get her to cross over yet though."

I scrunched up my nose. "Why?"

"Just trust me."

Rolling my eyes, I said, "I swear you make up stuff just to sound mysterious sometimes."

"Or maybe he can't help it," Trina said with a slight glance in his direction, confirming my suspicions that despite everything she knew about Caleb, including a possible previous romance with our own grandmother, she still had a crush on him.

Part of me thought it was absurd, but then the other part reminded that I'd stolen kisses I knew weren't good for me. Perhaps feelings weren't that controllable.

"So we trust this werewolf kid? I'm upset that you went today without telling us, but I do have to say I'm grateful you came back before dark, at least." Mom took a sip of her sweet tea.

"I don't know. I don't know anything about this werewolf pack except they keep to themselves and hunt sweet innocent bunnies down in the forest." Caleb's dark eyes simmered as he talked, making me wonder how real the feud between vampires and werewolves was.

When Mr. Tyler had been cursed, Caleb sure had been ready to take him out, but other than that, I didn't know about other interactions between Caleb and wolves. Of course, there were several hundred some odd years that I didn't know a thing about from his life.

"Not the bunnies," Trina said with a pout.

"Better than humans, I guess." I shrugged with an awkward smile. "My instincts tell me he's trustworthy. The whole village seemed like such a peaceful and happy place."

Caleb barked out a laugh he didn't bother to try and conceal.

"What? It seemed good. I didn't actually meet the alpha, Gryphin's dad, but I saw his room. The depression in there was so thick, I can't imagine what he and the pack are going through. I want to help. Plus, Gryphin said something about her trying to track down a witch who is in a powerful coven. What if this helps us learn more about Rose?"

Mom's eyebrows crinkled together. "Why would they be connected?"

"Maybe they're not, but it wouldn't hurt to try."

"Until you get kidnapped again," Trina said brightly.

I glared at her.

"And there's no way that Caleb could come with you on these trips?" Mom glanced at the dark stranger who enjoyed a good pint of blood every now and then but had an open invitation inside our house and to follow me around wherever I went.

These were weird times.

"Oh no, vampires should not step foot on werewolf lands." Caleb shook his head and threw his large hands upwards as if pushing away the very thought.

"Why does that feel cliché?" Trina grinned and nudged Caleb with her shoulder.

I forced myself not to give her a look for her too-obvious flirting. If she kept this up, Mom would start freaking out that she was going to have a vampire son-in-law that could have easily been her stepfather at some point.

Ew.

"I guess it is, but clichés come from somewhere." Caleb shrugged.

"And there's no cell service at the werewolf village place?" Mom chewed on her lip. "I'm not sure I like this at all. I don't know how I can let you go out there again. It just doesn't seem safe."

I sighed. "I know it doesn't, and I wish I could give you more reassurances, but this is something I need to do. What if I make sure to never be there at night?"

"Why? Caleb just said there wouldn't ever be vampires up there. Everything else that wants you as their personal servant can come get you during the day. What about those necromancers? What's stopping them from doing the same thing the vampires did? Or any other creepy monster out there?" Trina glanced at Caleb with a flush to her cheeks. "No offense."

Caleb grinned and shook his head.

I frowned at my sister. "Thanks. Now I'm sure Mom will let me go."

Mom rubbed her forehead and eyes. The dark circles and tightness clued me in that she must have been pretty tired. Then I felt bad for putting all of this on her. Maybe it would have been better had she not known.

"Hanna, you're only fifteen," she said and stared at her drink. "At your age, I was worried about wearing the exact right pants and using the right brand of makeup, not looking over my shoulder every second for vampires or necromancers to take me away from my family."

I leaned over and wrapped an arm around her shoulders. "I know, Mom. I'm sorry. Honestly, it's probably harder on you than me."

Of course, I didn't tell her about the panic attacks I probably would have had nightly if it weren't for Brandon.

Mom patted my arm and leaned into my hug. "You're so strong to deal with this."

Trina's eyes dropped to her glass of sweet tea, and she chewed on her lip.

"So does that mean you'll let me go help the wolves?"

With a deep sigh, Mom finally nodded. "If you think it's safe. I have to learn to let you go, I guess."

Tears sparkled in her eyes. While relief rushed through me, I also felt a twinge of guilt.

"Thank you, Mom."

"Not really my choice, but you're welcome. At least even if Caleb can't go, you can bring your ghost friend so that if something goes wrong, we know where to find him and talk to him."

"That sounds like a reasonable deal. Now I just have to convince Brandon that it is." I pulled away from Mom and gave her a grateful smile.

It was late when I finally crawled into bed. As I snuggled into the blankets, I smiled in gratitude that it was Friday night. Hopefully, I could sleep in and catch up on the rest I hadn't gotten from the mess on Halloween night and the last two days of insanity.

I didn't even have time to think about Brandon before I fell asleep.

Chapter 10

After a lovely morning of sleeping in, I allowed myself to eat a banana and felt good enough to go for a jog. Honestly, I didn't think of myself as the type of person to go jogging as it wasn't something I did like...ever, but I wanted to try to exercise more. If eating less food was good for losing weight, so was exercising. I owed it to myself to do as much as I could to be fit and thin, even if it wasn't for Noah anymore.

I wanted to keep up my fitness for myself.

Trina was still in her room, and Mom had left for a fun photoshoot at a baby gender reveal party. Neither of them would probably like the idea of me going out for a run alone, but I had a feeling Caleb kept good tabs on me all the time.

Poor guy. I know he didn't need sleep, but it was still probably annoying to have to keep a constant eye on a teenage girl who literally ran around all over the place. Maybe we should have set up a tent for him in the backyard or something.

After gearing up with some athletic leggings, an old t-shirt, a light jacket, and my running shoes, I stretched a little and jogged right out the front door. It was a cool day with dark clouds rolling into the skies.

The wind brought the smell of rain, and I took deep breaths of it, relishing the freshness.

At first, I hadn't decided exactly where I should go or how far, but in what shouldn't have been a surprise at all, I found myself going by the skatepark. By the time I reached it, I was out of breath and my calves were burning. It wasn't hard to slow down and take a break.

Apparently, there were some very committed skaters around because a few of them zipped and zoomed over the concrete even when rain was threatening on the horizon. I would have preferred to be there alone, of course, since it would be easier to talk to Brandon, but I could still work with it.

I made my way over to the tables, sitting at our usual one in the back, and pulled out my phone. Pretending to talk on it, I said as loudly as I dared, "Brandon? Can you hear me?"

The wind rustled through the grass. Kids chatted and yelled at each other while they skated and watched others skate. Cars drove by on the street, but there was no sign of Brandon.

My heart sank.

"Brandon? I know you're here. Where else could you go? I hope you can hear me. I'm really sorry about saying you were just being my ghost helper. You're more than that and we both know it, even if we don't want to admit it."

A few more cars drove by. The grass swished.

"Oh, please don't ghost me," I said with a slightly unhinged giggle. "I'm trying to apologize."

I waited a few more minutes, watching the kids practice jumps before I gave up and put my phone back into my pocket.

Sighing, I stood and decided this was as good a place as any to stretch out my muscles. Propping my foot onto the bench, I reached over and grabbed my toes. The stretch pulled at the whole length of my leg and while it kind of hurt, it also felt kind of good.

"It's not fun to have someone ignore you, is it?" Brandon said, appearing on the other side of the table. He had his back to me while he sat on the bench facing the chain link fence around the park. Someone had planted a whole row of thick bushes on the other side of that fence, probably hoping to keep the chaos of the park from being a distraction in their private backyard.

"I wasn't ignoring you." I sighed and switched legs to stretch.

"First you act like all we are is business partners in front of this stranger, nobody guy, and then you don't bother to talk to me all day, not even at night." His shoulders had been set back with angry tension, but then they slumped in defeat. "I thought that was our thing, you know? Comforting each other at night. At least, it seems like you've needed it as much as I have."

Frowning, I pulled my leg off the bench and walked around until I could see his face. He didn't bother to look at me, keeping his gaze on the grass.

"I thought you might get mad if I summoned you against your will after you left so angrily like that. It didn't seem right. I wanted to apologize to you first."

He was quiet for a few moments. It was long enough for me to realize I probably looked weird standing next to a table and staring at the bench without doing anything, so I started my stretches again, this time working on my thighs.

"I missed you if that helps."

"Really?" He finally looked up at me, and the hope and pain in his eyes tore at my heart.

"Yes, of course!" I sat down next to him. "I miss you any time you're not around. It's infuriating, actually. Even if you're not there, I can hear your sassy comments in my head as I imagine how you'd react to whatever insane things are happening around me. I can't even have peace from you if I wanted it."

A twitch of a smile worked at the corner of his lip. "That's actually kind of funny. Maybe I should apologize for being so predictable you can figure out what I would say without me even being there."

"I don't think that's necessary. You manage to surprise me all the time."

We shared a small smile, and then he went back to staring into the grass. "It is nice to hear that you miss me. I have to admit I miss you too. If it were up to me, I'd be around you all the time."

Warmth spread into my heart, repairing some of the damage it had gotten from seeing him so pained. "All the time? Don't you think that might get a bit...much?"

"Only if you start farting or something."

Laughing, I swatted through his shoulder. "Oh my gosh!"

He grinned and chuckled.

Despite being totally embarrassed, I wanted nothing less than to keep the memory of his roguish smile and the sound of his amused laughter inside my mind forever. Other boys could still make my pulse quicken and even take away my breath, but none of them had ever made me feel as seen and accepted as Brandon had. There was an ease I felt around him, and even though he didn't (usually) have a body, I also felt a sense of solidarity.

After a few seconds of laughing, Brandon sobered and took a breath. Something seemed to flash across his face, and he let the breath out slowly without actually saying anything. I mean, I wasn't sure he was actually taking in the air but that's what it looked like he was doing.

I glanced around the park, hoping no one noticed I had been laughing to myself. "What? Is there something you want to say?"

"I'm sorry. Yes and no. Kind of. Even if we were both normal kids with a totally normal situation, it would be hard for me to ask this, but as we're not...it's probably pointless to even think like this. In fact, it would probably be better if we just stopped hanging out at all. I'm holding you back, aren't I?" The words poured out of him in a rush as if he was afraid he'd lose the nerve to say them.

"Wait. What? How could you think like that?" I could feel my heart thumping in apprehension of what he was going to say next.

He fiddled with the wallet chain that always hung from his belt loop. "It's just that...well, what can the future be for us? I can't keep stealing energy to grab kisses from you. I can't have you help me with my unfinished business because I'm certain I'm not going to a good place. Even if we were somehow madly in love, which I'm not saying we are so don't freak out, but even if we were, there's no future for us. We can't be together. There's just no way."

"So...what? You're like breaking up with me?" My heart pounded in my ears, and my fingers started to tremble as if they had accepted defeat before I did.

"No, I mean, maybe. I guess? How can we break up if we're not really in a relationship?" He kept his eyes on the chain, probably scared to look up at me.

I thought for a second, letting the sadness of what he was saying sink into me. "Alright, so we're not in a relationship like that. I get it. I wouldn't want to date someone like me, either."

Concern made him glance at me. "Excuse me? Are you insane? I'd date you in a millisecond if I had hands that you could actually hold. In fact, I'd find a stake in case that vampire kid got any ideas about touching you, and I'd pack silver bullets all the time so that werewolf would leave you alone, and we all know that Noah would be super easy to scare off. I can't even tell you how many times I've thought about what I could and would do if I were only alive. Hanna, I've never wished so hard in my whole life to be alive."

Emotion welled up inside my chest and into my eyes. Pressing my lips together, I looked up at the cloudy sky and blinked several times.

"What? What did I say? I'm not trying to make you cry here. I'm trying to get you to realize how awesome you are." Brandon's eyes roamed over my face in urgency and near-panic.

A small smile spread over my face despite a few tears that were working hard to escape. Trying to keep myself together, I looked back at him. "That's just probably the nicest thing anyone has ever said to me, ever."

Relief washed over his face, and a half-smile perked up the corner of his lip. "Oh good. I was freaking out for a second there. I never want to hurt you, Hanna. Never."

"I know." I looked back down at my worn sneakers. "But you're trying to push me away and *that* hurts."

The wind pushed through the almost-bare branches above us as brown leaves skittered around the pavement and swirled in the air. Chatter from the kids behind us became loud for a few minutes as we sat together in silence. It wasn't awkward, just heavy with thoughts and feelings.

A leaf landed on my lap, and I picked it up. It was brown and brittle like I knew my heart would be if I let Brandon go, regardless of how much he thought he was holding me back or whatever nonsense he was thinking. "At least stick around to help me with other ghosts. You might mess stuff up worse sometimes, but overall, you can be helpful. Plus, my mom is relying on you to keep watch over me when I go back to help Gryphin look for his stepmom. Now that I'm thinking about it, you can get into places I can't while at the commune and may even be able to help me find her faster."

He glanced at me for a second with another small smile and then went back to watching the leaves. "I guess I can do that. I mean, I have a super busy schedule here sitting and doing nothing. It's really important work that someone has to do, but I suppose I can put it off. For you."

"Oh, only if you're sure. I would never want to deprive this bench of having a ghostly butt sit on it and do nothing."

"I'm sure the bench thanks you, but I have a feeling it'll be fine. In fact, it might not even notice my absence at all."

We looked at each other, and I was full of so much relief that even his small smile and the prospect of hanging out with him, even if only to catch ghosts, was thrilling.

Brandon's smile was slightly giddy, so I wondered if he were feeling the same. "Can we backtrack a bit? Your mom is relying on me? What do you mean by that?"

I told him more details about the wolf situation, about how Caleb couldn't be there to protect me, and how Mom was going to let me go as long as Brandon could pop back to inform Trina if something had gone wrong.

Neither of us had discussed how Trina wouldn't be able to hear him unless she took that funky necklace off, but if I came up missing, that would hopefully be the first thing she did.

"Aha, so I am good for something!" He said triumphantly and posed like a superhero with hands on his hips. The effect was slightly marred by the fact that he was still sitting.

"Of course you are."

Chapter 11

Later that afternoon, I found Trina outside in the backyard. I'd gotten home and taken a shower, while Brandon had hopefully stayed dutifully in the kitchen and not been spying on me.

"Hey, sis. How's it going?" I sat down next to her on the other patio chair while Brandon followed me outside.

Sunlight highlighted the golden strands in Trina's silky, chestnut-colored hair, but it was still chilly enough to need a jacket. She was curled up with a blanket and doing homework.

Looking up from her work, she smiled. "Hey. Just thought I'd soak up some rays before the weather really turned yucky."

"I hear ya. So, listen, there's something I haven't told anyone something Gran said to me before she...left."

"That's one way to put it." Brandon stopped in front of my chair and slowly bent over as if he was going to sit on my lap.

"Hey! You sit over there!" I pointed to the last free patio chair.

Cackling with laughter, he hopped up and went to where I had dictated. "What? It's not like you'll feel anything. I'm as light as a feather."

I gave him a stern look while Trina watched my side of the exchange with a bemused expression. "I take it Brandon is visiting today."

"What can I say? Ghosts love me."

"Well, at least one does." Trina's smile told me she somehow knew more than I wanted her to, maybe even more than I knew myself...or maybe it was more than I was willing to admit to myself, anyway.

"Right, well, anyway, before Gran left, she said something about needing to check under the rock in her garden at her old house. Do you know anything about that?"

Trina closed the book she was working on and sat up in the chair, putting her stocking feet onto the ground. "Not unless you're going fishing and needing to dig up some earthworms or something. Why are you just now telling me about this? Gran has been gone for a month."

I shrugged. "It took me time to process and figure out that I had no idea what it meant, and then I wasn't sure I really wanted to figure it out. But it was something she urgently told me right before crossing over. I have a feeling it might be important if not now, then later."

"Interesting."

"Since Gran made sure to tell me about it before she died, this has got to be really important."

"That must mean it's really important." Brandon nodded as if an expert on all things of importance.

"Wow. Have you told Mom this? What did she say?"

"No." I sighed. "She doesn't need more things to worry or think about, and it's always hard to bring up Gran's death. I figured I could work this bit out myself and not bother her unless I need to."

"So by working this out yourself you've come to me for help?" Trina's smile told me she was teasing, mostly.

"Exactly. Since the house is on the other side of town, I was hoping you could drive me there?"

She checked her phone and pursed her lips. "I'm supposed to meet my friends in an hour at Bri's house so we can do some studying, but they probably won't care if I'm a little late."

I jumped up. "Then we have no time to lose."

After we had piled into Trina's car, with Brandon in the backseat enjoying the fact that he didn't ever have to wear a seatbelt again, Trina asked some very good questions. "What if there are people living at Gran's old house, and they're home? What if there's a giant dog in the backyard, and they've fenced it all around, and we can't get back there without disturbing them?"

"What we need," Brandon sat up close and peeked his head between the seats, "is a good lie."

I glanced at him before looking back at Trina. "Oh yes, that's a great plan. Two teenage girls, not in any uniform, showing up, claiming to be from the gas company and needing to check the meter in the backyard. I'm sure they'll believe us."

Trina chuckled. "I had almost forgotten how mouthy Brandon is."

I gave her an awkward smile, thinking if she'd just take off that weird necklace, she'd be able to hear him all the time. Then again maybe he was the only reason she kept the necklace on at all. As cute as he was, sometimes he got a tad bit annoying.

"It's impossible to stifle genius," Brandon said with a false and terrible British accent.

I rolled my eyes. "Yes. He can be too much at times, especially if I'm trying to ignore him. So, let's just get there and see if anyone is home. Hopefully, they're out on a Saturday afternoon with important things to do or are too nearsighted to be looking too much out the windows into their own backyards."

"Oh, here we go with Hanna's terrible planning skills." Brandon's smile lessened the blow of his truthful comment a tiny bit.

We pulled up to the house several minutes later and parked across the street. We had sold the property several years ago. I had been too young to really remember most of the outside details but seeing it again brought back lots of memories. It was almost the same except the trees out front had grown and thickened over the years. The blue siding had faded some, but whoever owned it now was still working to keep the place up. The bushes were neatly trimmed, awaiting the cold of winter, and the garden had been freshly raked out.

Trina must have been feeling some of the same nostalgia because we were quiet for a second as we studied the place where we'd shared many warm memories of Gran. It was the only house she'd ever lived in my lifetime, and while that hadn't been too long before she'd died, it was still a steady place in my heart.

"Alright, well, let's see if we can sneak into the backyard and dig under the rock. Hopefully, we'll be able to lift it, at least. Pretty sure I know which one she meant," I said as we climbed out the car.

"There is a truck out front, so someone is probably home." Trina followed behind me as I walked toward the one-story ranch-style house. "What do we say if we get caught digging out there?"

"Maybe the truth would be nice, for once?" Brandon walked behind Trina with his hands in his pockets and the wallet chain swinging back and forth.

"Hey, if I went around telling the truth of what I was doing all the time, I'd be thrust into an insane asylum. I try to tell the truth as often as I can, but that doesn't seem to be very often," I said with a pout in his direction.

He put his hands up in surrender. "Woah. Sorry. Didn't mean to hit a sore spot. Just trying to make a little joke is all. You don't have to tell me why keeping secrets is important."

Trina must have been getting used to my odd outbursts because she didn't bother to give me an odd look. "Well, we could just explain we lived here before, and we're looking for a time capsule thing. They might buy that."

"Let's just not get caught. How about that?" I said, tempted to duck behind the truck and do some covert maneuvers before sneaking to their backyard. However, since more people in the neighborhood could see me behind the truck than could see me from the house, that probably would have been a stupid thing to do.

Acting like I was supposed to be there, I walked down the driveway and into the backyard. Thankfully no one had put a fence up, and there weren't any dogs trying to use the bathroom on the thick grass.

That's where my luck ended because the whole area had been completely redone, at least from what I remembered. Instead of the back garden where Gran had grown her lovely flowers and had kept a small stone fountain, there was only grass. Whoever owned the house now must not have wanted to keep up with such a large garden and turned it all into yard. It was a simple square area with no garden and no indications as to where the rock might have once sat.

Trina stood next to me and kept glancing at the windows of the house. "This is not good. There was a garden here, right? Where is the rock? I was young, but I still remember a garden and a rock."

"Me too." I frowned. "If they've moved the rock, whatever was under there was probably moved too, especially if they had to do any digging or anything to flatten the area."

"Looks like we're in between a rock and a hard place," Brandon said, standing on my other side.

"I might be able to guess where the rock was, but it doesn't feel right to dig into their grass. It looks so nice, and they're bound to notice the disturbance." Trina glanced at the windows again.

I followed her eyes, hoping not to see a face peering out at us. My heart was beating loudly in my chest, and I decided that sneaking around other people's property was not something I enjoyed.

"Let's just get out of here."

No one bothered us as we walked back to Trina's old Honda, less enthusiastically than when we had left it.

"How important did we say that object was?" Trina asked as she slid into the seat and put the keys into the ignition.

"Important enough to tell me about with her last breaths." I stared out the window at the house that now looked more foreign than familiar.

"Right." Trina exhaled and also stared ahead without turning her car back on yet.

"So, what do we do about it?"

Brandon sat forward in the back middle seat, his face popping between us again. "Don't we know a wolf? Don't they dig pretty well?"

I turned to look at him with a furrowed brow. "I don't know much about werewolves, but I doubt they'd want to come and dig a hole for me. That seems beneath them. They're not household pets."

Trina gave me an appraising look and finally started her car.

Brandon shrugged. "He might help if it was important?"

All the way home, my thoughts were churning with what could have possibly been so important that Gran had hidden and protected it. My memories were still fuzzy of that night, but hadn't that lady said something about needing it to talk to someone?

Chapter 12

Gryphin came to pick us up at about two o'clock that same afternoon. The days were getting dark faster, so we had to get out to the commune earlier in the day to keep my mom happy...or as happy as she could be considering everything.

"Good afternoon!" Gryphin grinned as he opened the passenger-side door.

"Hi. You know you don't have to open the door for me. I could get it myself and then you wouldn't have to walk all the way around the car." I smiled so he would know I wasn't trying to be rude.

He shrugged. "It's the nice thing to do."

"Oh, man. I can tell this is going to be a super fun guy to hang around," Brandon grumbled as he fazed through the sliding van door and climbed into one of the middle seats.

"Well, thank you." I slid into the front seat and made sure all my limbs were in before he shut the door.

"You better tell him I'm here, so I don't have to witness any surprise kissing or flirting or whatever. I'm not sure I could keep my breakfast down if that was to happen," Brandon said as Gryphin made his way back to the driver's side.

"I will. Don't worry."

Gryphin opened his door and sat down. The air from outside brushed past him and brought his scent into the car. I couldn't help but close my eyes for a second as the smell held the now-familiar images of the forest—water thundered down a cliff as flowers bloomed along the banks of the rushing river. The wind brushed through the treetops, and they fluttered their leaves in response.

He must have seen something in my expression because he laughed. "Are you smelling me?"

"That's rich coming from a wolf." I grinned to chase away my embarrassment.

"Ugh, no flirting!" Brandon covered his ears with his hands.

I did the usual eye roll Brandon seemed to bring out of me nearly every day.

"Fair enough. So, I figured we'd venture into the woods today and see if we can visit her favorite places." Gryphin turned the keys and started the van.

"I figured it was something like that when you texted me to wear comfortable hiking gear. Listen, I ought to tell you that my friend is coming with us today."

"Oh? Do I need to go pick them up?" Gryphin glanced at me as he pulled onto the road.

"Nope. Brandon's already in the car with us, and you should be grateful you can't hear his constant peanut gallery comments," I said while giving the ghost another pointed look.

Thankfully, Brandon took it as the joke it was and didn't get offended again. "You just wish you were as witty as I am."

Gryphin glanced at me again and then back towards the seat I had been glaring at with an amused smile. "Actually, I wish I could hear him. I'm sure he'd liven up my day quite a lot."

"I'll show you liven up your day!" Brandon waggled his head in a sassy way.

I stifled a giggle. "Yeah, I'm sure he would. Anyway, he's going to help us find your stepmom." I was careful to choose my words since the topic was heavy between Brandon and me. He'd gotten so angry when I'd said he was my partner with helping ghosts and not anything else, but then we'd had that conversation this morning where we'd agreed it would be best to keep things focused only on helping ghosts cross over instead of any secret kisses or whatever.

Yes, it was a fair bit of confusion.

"Brandon can get into places I can't, and, while he's not quite dressed for an excursion into the woods, I have a feeling he'll be able to keep up," I said with a nod.

"We'll see." Gryphin's mouth quirked into a side smile as he drove out of the neighborhood and pulled onto the main road.

"That was creepy," Brandon said, giving the wolf an odd look.

"What do you mean by that?" I asked Gryphin.

He shrugged his muscled shoulders. "Sarah was a wolf. We'll have to go far distances to reach her favorite places to run and play. We won't be able to take any vehicles where we're going, so it only makes sense that we'll need to run as the wolves do."

I blinked, looked back at Brandon who shrugged, and blinked again. "So..."

"Yup, you'll have to ride on my back like a blonde Princess Mononoke." Gryphin chuckled. "Think you'll be up for that?"

"Hey! I know that movie. It came out a year before I...well, anyway, it's cool they have anime in the commune." Brandon nodded appreciatively.

"Really? That's what you're going with when he set you up for a perfectly good ride joke?" I said to Brandon, feeling the beat of my heart increase at the notion of riding on top of Gryphin's back while he dashed through the woods. It was scary and exciting.

It was in these kinds of moments that I often wondered what was wrong with me.

"What? What did he say?" Gryphin glanced behind him again as if he'd be able to see him that time somehow.

"He gave you props for knowing an anime reference. Are you sure you'll be able to carry my weight like that? I'm sure you don't have a wolf saddle thing, so I'll probably be pulling your hair...or fur, pretty hard to keep from falling off. That doesn't sound very comfortable."

"I'm sure I'll be able to manage." Gryphin's amused grin appeared again, and I felt bad for enjoying it so much.

"I can't believe this is happening." Brandon looked up at the van's roof as if appealing to a greater being.

When we finally arrived at the commune, Gryphin parked the van in the same place as last time and zipped around to open the door for me before I could even pop the handle.

Brandon groaned and fazed through the van's side door. "I'm not sure which is worse to hang around. Caleb is freaky and makes outlandish insinuations while this guy is overeager and polite and ugh. Seriously, Hanna, can we talk about your choice of friends? Let's go hang out with Emma and Addy again. They were nice."

"I bet you'd like that. You probably thought those girls were cute." I stepped out of the way so Gryphin could close the van door and took a deep breath of the clean air. "I could get used to hanging out here. It really is beautiful."

Gryphin nodded. "I'm partial to it myself. Uhm, I'm sorry if this is a weird question, but I'm unsure as to what the etiquette here is. Growing up in a commune, I haven't had a lot of socialization, and I often feel like I'm doing it wrong, but should I just ignore it when you're talking to your friend, Brandon, was it? Or should I try to figure out what you're talking about and join in on the conversation?"

My heart warmed towards his awkwardness, and I smiled. "No, that's not a weird question. In fact, I should be apologizing. I'm sure it's not very nice to be talking to an invisible person and not explain what is going on. Truth is, I'm not sure there is a correct way to handle this odd situation. It's not like society has to deal with things like this all the time."

"Oh, don't apologize!" Gryphin held his hands up, palms toward me earnestly. "I don't want to intrude on your friendship. I'm just not sure what I should be doing with myself."

"I could tell you what to do. Get lost, that's what," Brandon muttered.

Shooting Brandon a sharp look that I hoped would get him to be nicer, I turned my smile back on Gryphin. "No worries. I'll try to explain more of what he's saying if I talk back to him. If I ignore his comments, just figure they're worth ignoring."

"How rude." Brandon folded his arms across his chest like the little girl from *Full House*, some TV show that was popular back in his day. He'd had to explain it to me a few times.

"Okay," Gryphin said with a nod. "That works. Are you ready to go? I'll just go on the other side of the van here and change and then we'll be off into the woods. Isn't it a beautiful day for a run? Oh, by the way, you'll probably hear some weird bone-crunching sounds and maybe a howl or two. I'll try to keep quiet, but the changes aren't the most pleasant thing to endure."

"Ew." Brandon raised an eyebrow.

"Are you sure you have to change? Mr. Tyler said that changing without a full moon is harder. Maybe we could just jog? I feel bad that you have to do that just to take me there."

Gryphin's left shoulder lifted in a shrug, and the thin t-shirt he wore did nothing to disguise the toned muscles underneath. "It's fine. Oh, and the other thing is I won't be able to talk in wolf form so that might cause us some confusion. Basically, we're going to run out to a few spots she likes. You guys can look around and see if you can find her. If she's not there, give me a signal, and we'll run to the next place. When we're done, we'll head back here, and I'll change back into human form. Does that sound okay to you?"

I nodded. "I guess, but what if I do find her? I might need your help to ask her questions and stuff. It always helps a ghost if we can start with the familiar."

"Good point." Gryphin turned back to the car and pulled out an athletic backpack. "Wear this in case I need to change back. There are clothes inside. We wouldn't want me to be walking around naked in the trees, would we?"

His grin told me that maybe he wouldn't mind, but my ghost and I sure did. "No, we wouldn't."

"Again. Ew." Brandon shook his head. "Listen, I'm not hitching a ride on this wolf. Just summon me when you get to the places or need help or something. Enjoy your furry horse."

"Right. Er...okay. See you in a bit then," I said, unsure if I wanted him to leave me alone. I turned back to Gryphin's puzzled eyebrows. "Brandon said he'll join us when we get to the spot. He isn't up for a run this afternoon apparently."

"Okay. Whatever works. You ready to go?" Gryphin didn't wait for an answer before taking off his shirt.

Despite the sun shining in the sky, there was still a chilly wind, but it didn't seem to bother him at all. His defined chest showed no signs of goosebumps, and I feel confident in saying so since my eyes inspected the area carefully.

"Oh no, that's my cue. Please don't let him deflower you." Brandon's alarmed eyes were wide as he shook his head and disappeared.

Blushing, I nodded at Gryphin. "Yup, sure. Ready. I'll just hang out over here, shall I?"

Turning around, I took a few steps away from the van and tried to focus on the gravel path leading toward the village.

With laughter rumbling in his chest, I heard Gryphin walk around to the other side of the van. After a few seconds, probably taking off the rest of his clothes so they didn't rip or whatever as he changed, I heard an alarming series of sounds that are quite hard to describe unless one has already heard a human morphing into a werewolf. Pretty much it was crunching bones, grunts, snarls, and more crunching bones. It took several minutes for the change to occur, and I remembered seeing Mr. Tyler's half-wolf form when Caleb had been threatening to snap his neck. Wincing, I couldn't imagine the pain of having claws and sharp teeth sprout out of one's body, not to mention growing all that fur in such a short amount of time and having one's insides nearly completely rearranged.

Yup, I was good staying a human.

It was quiet for a time as he probably gathered his bearings and prepared to go on a run. I was just about to gather enough courage to go check on him when a loud howl poured out from around the van, and Gryphin's wolf trotted past the front.

Now, I had been to the zoo a few times and have seen some wolves. They were larger than most dogs with thick muscles and long legs, but those had not prepared me at all for what I saw. Werewolves were huge. I mean, maybe Gryphin's wolf was like extra huge, but I assumed most werewolves were just as large.

Let me put it this way, he was easily as tall as the van. His paws were bigger than my whole torso and the teeth...

"My what big teeth you have," I said, feeling my muscles freeze so tightly I could only take in short spurts of air.

I don't know if real wolves can laugh or do laugh, but this one seemed to bob his head up and down in a kind of wheezing chuckle. His fur was the same silvery grey as his human hair, and there was even that little curl over his forehead. His eyes were the familiar warm, forest brown that I'd grown to know, and they studied me more intelligently than any wolf's eyes would.

Logically, I knew it was Gryphin, but my instincts were screaming that if I made one wrong move, this thing was going to gobble me up in one bite. He must have sensed my paralyzed fear because he moved toward me slowly, put his head down, and rubbed the side of his forehead gently across my arms and chest, almost like a cat.

The motion made me smile. Fingers trembling, I put them into the fur around his ears. He leaned into the touch, and I swear he would have started purring if he had been a cat. It took a minute for my lungs to thaw, but a few more soft head butts had me giggling.

Gryphin backed up and nodded his head in the direction of the woods, indicating we should get going.

"So do I just like climb onto your back or something? Where do I put my feet? I don't want to hurt you." I reached out a hand and then pulled it back, unsure what to do.

Shaking his head, he lowered himself to the ground so that I could climb onto his back. It still took some doing, and I apologized several times for pulling on his fur. He only laughed his weird wolf chuckle.

After I was settled, he slowly rose, letting me feel where I was going to need to hold on. I couldn't sit upright like I was on a horse because I'd fly right off. I leaned down, kept my legs squeezed tight, and wrapped my arms around as far as I could reach, clinging to his back, again apologizing for having such a tight grip on his fur.

He started to jog slowly at first toward the trees, probably giving me time to adjust to the movements. It was disorienting being so far off the ground while having fur tickle my arms and chin. His muscles moved beneath me, feeling strong and solid even underneath all the soft fur. At first, I was overwhelmed by the powerful potential this wolf form had, but soon I grew used to it, and the rhythmic movements became comforting. Thank goodness he kept his fresh forest smell and didn't stink like a wild animal.

It didn't take long before we hit the trees, and he glanced up at me as if asking if I was okay.

"I'm good. I think I've got the hang of it. Again, sorry if I'm pulling your fur. There isn't much else to hold onto."

Gryphin loosed a rumbling snarl I didn't know how to interpret and then began his real running. I might have screamed like the little girl I was and clung even tighter to his back. It was impossible to see straight ahead without rising and losing my grip, so I kept my head down, my gaze to the side, and stared in wonder as the trees whizzed by.

The wind rushed past my face, and my hair was going crazy. I couldn't let go to hold it back, so it just thrashed around. I couldn't even find the dread for all the tangles I'd have to sort through later because the run was thrilling. Adrenaline raced through my body as I fought to hold on, experiencing a kind of freedom I'd never felt before. Sure, a car could go just as fast, but not through the woods on giant bounding paws, jumping and dodging obstacles so easily it felt like a kind of dance. I found myself breathing heavily even though I wasn't the one doing the running.

I have no idea how far we traveled when he finally slowed to a stop, and the woods opened to reveal a meadow. There was a glittering pond in the center, probably about as big as a modest house. Wild grasses waved a greeting as Gryphin padded into the clearing on silent paws.

He lowered himself to the earth again, and I climbed off, immediately adjusting my socks so they wrapped around the outside of my pants in case any ticks were still around in November. As pretty as the high grass was, ticks terrified me.

The second thing I did was try to tame my hair with my fingers. There were snarls and knots all over the place. Thankfully, I'd thought to bring a hair tie with me and pulled it off my wrist, wrapped it around the hair to hold it tightly in place, and hoped Brandon wouldn't make too much fun of it when I summoned him back to help.

Gryphin pranced in front of me a few times as if he was showing off the meadow or maybe proud of his fast dash through the woods. Either way, his excited feet were cute to watch.

Then something caught his attention, and he started sniffing around and exploring the place, probably on the trail of a rabbit or something.

Taking a deep breath to calm myself, I called to Brandon. "Yo, we're here. Want to come case the joint for a missing ghost?"

Immediately, he popped in, not even giving the neck prickles time to warn me. I could summon other ghosts as well, but none of them ever appeared as quickly as Brandon did. I wasn't sure what that meant, but I figured it was either because he was lonely and waiting for the summon, or there was a kind of deeper connection between us.

"Oh, this is a nice place." Brandon surveyed the meadow before us with his hands on his hips. Then his eyes landed on me, and he tried to stifle a laugh.

At least he was nice enough to try and stifle it.

"What happened to *you*? Did you pee on an electrical socket?"

Pressing my lips into a straight line, I gave him an annoyed look. "The ride was lovely, thanks for asking. Not all of us coat our hair in inches of pomade."

He grinned as he brushed a hand over his blond spikes. "It takes talent to look so good."

"I'm sure. Okay, so we're looking for a ghost. Do you see one?" I looked around, trying to focus on the task at hand and not the memory of putting my fingers through his hair. The strands hadn't been sticky with product at all, but actually soft to the touch, a feeling I'd probably never get to feel again. My heart dropped an inch inside my chest with the sad thought.

"Do *you* see one?" Brandon gave me a cheeky grin and then put his attention to the meadow. "If he hitches up a leg to pee on a tree, I'm out of here."

Gryphin was still investigating the area, sniffing around and digging at the ground a few times.

Sighing, I shook my head and walked further in. I could easily see why Sarah had enjoyed this place. The sun was still high enough that light came into the clearing and fell onto the pond, glittering off of the ripples. The ground was spongey as I got closer, but I wanted to look into the water and see if there were any visible fish or frogs.

"This place is beautiful," I said, peering into the water.

Gryphin huffed an agreement nearby while Brandon stared into the water next to me.

"There are worse places to haunt," Brandon said.

"Yeah, like a noisy skatepark."

"I'd rather have that place than a bridge with heavy traffic."

"Poor Stephanie." I sighed. "We need to help her cross over. Caleb told me I could put it off for a bit as he was working on some crazy idea, but I feel bad just letting her hang out and watch traffic go by."

Brandon nodded. "We'll get there." Spinning around, he looked over the grass. "Doesn't look like this is the place. Surely, she would have appeared by now?"

"Yeah, I guess not."

As I was turning to Gryphin, an eerie howl echoed through the trees, and then a deeper one answered the first. Goosebumps perked up all over my arms.

Gryphin's head popped up immediately, his ears standing at attention and listening. Then he glanced back at me as if unsure what to do.

Before either of us could decide, the eerie sounds flooded into the clearing, and I was startled see several ghost wolves prowl past the trees. I spun in a circle, amazed to see we'd become surrounded by what looked to be werewolf ghosts. These wolves were much larger than their animal counterparts and stared at me with intent.

"Wow, I thought all dogs went to heaven." Brandon spun around as I had done.

Gryphin's attention was still further out in the woods as the deeper howl sounded again, much closer than before. Then he whined and pressed his ears flat onto his head. He kept glancing at me and back into the woods as if afraid of what was coming.

"Do you think they'll be able to hurt us?" I asked Brandon as the ghosts pressed in closer, creeping slowly.

"I don't know. Well, not me, anyway, but if they decided to use up ghostly energy to make contact with the physical world, it could be possible." Brandon eyed one ghost wolf who seemed to be a bit closer than the others, perhaps the leader. "This is not a good time for your pet wolf to be so scared. What is he even scared of, anyway? Can he see the ghosts?"

I spared a glance to Gryphin who was now cowering into the grass, his eyes on the trees. "I think there's something else out there. Did you hear that deeper howl?"

"Excellent. Time for me to be the hero." Brandon took a few steps in front of me and toward the leader ghost-wolf. "Hey, you there. Can you understand me? I know there's a human inside of you somewhere."

A low growl rumbled in the ghost wolf's chest. It didn't sound like the usual growl but more echoey, as if coming from somewhere other.

"Brandon, I'm not sure you should do that. I don't think he likes it." I glanced back at Gryphin and realized he was also making a sound, but it was more like a whine and less like a scary growl.

And in this case, the whine scared me more.

The ghost wolf came to a pause, and the others stilled behind him. All of them stared at us, and my body reacted to their smoldering looks like it had when first seeing Gryphin's wolf. My muscles froze, and it was the most I could do to keep pulling in shallow breaths. I had been growing more comfortable dealing with ghosts, but undead, wild wolves were another matter.

Gryphin was so low in the grass that I couldn't even see him anymore, but his whines told me he was still there.

There was no sound to warn us as another wolf walked into the clearing, this one very much alive. He was easily the biggest werewolf I'd ever seen, and by then I could claim I'd seen several, even if they weren't all alive. While Gryphin was the size of a minivan, this one was easily the size of one of those church buses that drove around and picked up old ladies on Sunday. His fur was an amber brown, and his eyes were a calculating gold.

Despite this wolf having a physical form, he was still as silent as the ghost wolves as he walked closer to Gryphin. He held his large head high and looked down on my friend with superiority. If Gryphin hadn't been cowering before him like a scared puppy, I would have still assumed that this wolf was more dominant. Size wasn't everything, but a wolf such as this newcomer was bound to be powerful.

"Okay, so, that's a werewolf. Why is he hanging out with a bunch of ghost wolves? Are they following him? Does he even know they are there? Do you think he'll try to eat you after he mauls your new boyfriend to death?" Brandon asked, standing as still as I was.

I'd seen other ghosts touch each other, so it stood to reason that these ghost wolves could touch Brandon, but I had no idea if they could do any harm since, you know, he was already dead and all that.

As much as I wanted to correct Brandon's errant comment about Gryphin being my boyfriend, I was too scared to say anything. Heck, I was too scared to breathe in case the movement brought more feral attention in my direction.

I still couldn't see Gryphin's crouched form in the grass, but as the larger wolf approached, my friend whined again. If I hadn't been so paralyzed, I would have walked closer so I could at least see what was happening, but as it was, I wasn't brave enough.

The amber wolf bent its head down in Gryphin's direction, and my heart hammered inside my chest. *Please, please, please don't eat my friend,* I thought to myself. *I don't want that to be the last thing I see before I get viciously mauled to death.*

Whatever the bigger wolf was doing, he finished with a huff into the air and then turned its gaze onto me.

I didn't know my heart could beat any faster than it had been going, but, at that moment, I learned it could. Gulping in small sips of air, I forced my body to stay still instead of running away screaming like my instincts were yelling at me to do.

As the large wolf came nearer, I got a good look at his power-ful shoulder muscles, thankful that at least its mouth was shut so I couldn't see its teeth. Although the time for that seemed to be fast approaching.

"It's coming over here. It's getting closer. What do we do? What do we do?!" Brandon fidgeted, glancing between me and the big wolf and the ghost wolves who encircled us.

Gryphin rose from the grass behind the bigger wolf. His ears were pressed down and back while his head was still bowed low, shoulders slumped.

At least he hadn't been eaten.

When the giant wolf was a mere ten feet away, it stopped, regarded me for a moment, and then glanced back at Gryphin who nodded encouragingly. As if reaching a decision, ripples in his fur waved down his body, and he looked up to the sky with closed eyes as the change began.

Horrified, but still too scared to move, I watched it all. It made sense as to why I had heard so many bones cracking and snapping during Gryphin's change. Human bodies were not the same as wolf bodies, and they had to completely rearrange themselves to become the other. The transition looked as painful as it had sounded. While the fur receded, his jaw stretched and then shrank, muscles spasmed all over, and bones popped in and out of places as they worked to fit themselves back into a human form.

Brandon cursed and backed up a few steps. "Remind me never to get bitten by a werewolf."

"Don't get bitten by a werewolf," I said, finding my voice hoarse and small.

The ghost wolves had begun to relax slightly even though they hadn't moved from their places. A few had even sat down, watching us curiously.

I couldn't have been sure, but it seemed like this wolf had been able to change faster than Gryphin had and was also able to recover quicker. In a matter of minutes, a human man was standing before us, still large but not near as big as the wolf had been. It begged the question of where all that mass went after the change, but perhaps that was a question for another time.

His hair was the deep amber that the wolf's fur had been, and I could see a resemblance to Gryphin's jaw structure. The man's eyes were also the same gold as the wolf's, and they found their way back to me. "It's been a long time since a Seer visited us."

I gulped, trying to get my organs to work again. "There might be some shorts in here that might fit."

I crouched slowly as I tossed the bag Gryphin had given me at the man's feet.

Frowning, he looked down at the bag, then at his nakedness, and back at me.

"I get the feeling he's not used to worrying about clothes," Brandon said, keeping his hand over his face to block out the sight of the man's muscled and lean body.

As for me, fear had kept my eyes pinned to his face. One of the last things I wanted to see in my life was Gryphin's dad's...manhood bits.

Gryphin was still several paces behind the naked man, but his ears had perked back up, and he'd taken a seat in the grass. I could have sworn his wolf mouth curled up into some kind of amused and terrifying smile.

"I suppose it would make you more comfortable. You reek of fear," the man said and leaned down to pick up the bag.

As he dressed into a pair of Gryphin's basketball shorts, I worked hard to avert my eyes and study the trees. I didn't know much about trees and could only guess as to what type they were, but as their leaves were turning and falling, I could deduce they weren't pines, at least.

"I'm sorry if I offended you. I'm not used to talking with outsiders. It's been many years. Usually, I let the others in the pack deal with things like that." Gryphin's dad said as he dropped the bag back into the grass and took a few more steps in my direction.

"It's okay. I er... I can see why it might be weird to find me here. I'm sorry if I'm trespassing." The words came out thickly which made sense since I felt like I'd been scared spitless.

"Gryphin has explained it. I'm not happy, but I'm not going to attack you. My name is Bertram Swift, and I'm alpha of the Blue Ridge Pack which I assume you know about since you're on our land and going for joy rides with my son."

"Right. Uhm, nice to meet you, Mr. Swift. I don't want to correct you or anything to make you mad, sir, but we weren't going for a joy ride." I glanced at Gryphin who nodded at me in encouragement. "We're...er, that is, I'm trying to help find a ghost, because like you said, Mr. Swift, sir, that I'm a Seer. That's the kind of stuff I do, you see."

"Smooth." Brandon had relaxed his arm now that Bertram was dressed, but he still kept glancing at the ghost wolves who were seemingly content to watch us.

A small shadow of a smile pulled at Mr. Swift's lips. "Please, just call me Bertram. I understand you're a student of Billy's?"

"Oh, yes. I call him Mr. Tyler." I tried to smile but it felt like my cheek muscles were still too frozen.

"Ah, yes, you would."

"Ask him about the ghosts." Brandon needlessly nodded his head in the direction of the closest ghost wolf to us. "See if he knows they're there."

"So, uhm, did Gryphin say who we were looking for?" I glanced at the silver-grey wolf, hoping I wasn't divulging the secret.

Bertram sighed and swiveled his head in Gryphin's direction for a moment. "Not outright, but I'm not a fool."

At Bertram's gaze, Gryphin's ears and head lowered. They perked back up when his father turned his attention back to me.

"No one thinks you a fool, I'm sure." I nodded earnestly, sensing that being in trouble with this guy was nothing nobody wanted.

Bertram sighed and cracked his neck. "They might not try to think it or say it out loud, but sometimes I wonder. They've seen fit to keep me in the dark about this scheme to find Sarah. The thing is, they shouldn't have bothered. I know where she is."

Chapter 13

"Oh, do you think he means she's one of these ghost wolves?" Brandon spun around again, this time slower and studying each wolf carefully.

"You do? Well, I have to admit that would help make all of this a lot easier. Is she...here, right now?"

Bertram laughed, but it wasn't one filled with happiness. Instead, it was an angry laugh. I didn't even know those were a thing. "Whatever they've told you about me, I'm not insane. I know she's dead."

"Right. I didn't mean—"

"Of course, you didn't. No one means to let me know these things, but neither do they give me much credit. I'm not that old. I'm not crazy."

"I know that. I'm not saying—"

"No, of course you're not. You're just here in my territory, roaming around, looking for my dead wife so you can talk to her and figure out what happened so you can come to me and give me peace of mind. Well, let me tell you something." He took a few more steps toward me. I would have taken a few back, but the pond was right behind, and I really didn't feel like falling in. "I know exactly what happened. I don't need answers to help me find peace, because none of those answers are going to bring her back. She's far too gone. Her body's missing, and not even a necromancer could bring her back now. Not even with *your* help."

I took a breath and glanced at Gryphin, really wishing he could step in and help me figure out the right things to say, but all he did was lower his ears again. If he'd been talked to like this his whole life, I could understand why his father would scare him so. I understood why he was the alpha, and I wondered if there were any other alphas who weren't also bullies.

"Wait, I get the feeling he's not talking about raising her as a zombie." Brandon's attention, as usual, was not on the important things. "What else can necromancers do?"

"You're right that we're trying to get answers, sir." I pulled my shoulders back and attempted to stand straighter. He might have been able to turn into a giant werewolf and probably didn't even need that form to pummel me into a pile of Jell-O, but I wasn't about to let him bully me with words as well. "But have you ever thought about the effects your distress is having on your pack?"

Bertram turned a burning glare on Gryphin who visibly wilted under his father's gaze.

"No, not just Gryphin, although I do hope you can see how much he's afraid of you, not a good thing, I might add. I mean the whole pack. They all can feel your anger and confusion, and all they want is relief and answers. No, it won't bring Sarah back, and I'm really sorry that I can't do that, but what I can try to do is get answers. This might not give you peace or help, but it might bring some to the pack. Isn't that your job, at the end of the day? Helping your pack? Protecting them? Or do you just want to give up, crawl into a deep hole to never come out, and let another wolf take control? Because from where I'm standing, that's exactly where you're headed."

Silence descended on the meadow, and all I could hear was the rapid pulse in my chest and the wind stirring the dying leaves high in the treetops. The alpha's steely glare bore into me, but I kept my footing solid, mostly so I didn't fall into the pond. Also, I'd had enough of his bullying and Gryphin was a sweet guy. He might have been my friend's dad and the alpha of a large werewolf pack, but he wasn't *my* father or alpha. It was time someone else stood their ground.

Okay, so maybe I was betting on the fact that he wouldn't dare hurt a Seer a little too much, but I had already said the words and had to deal with the fallout.

"Wow, that was some brave talk for someone who has just seen werewolf teeth up close." Brandon's eyebrows were high on his head, but the small smile on his lips told me he approved.

After what felt like at least thirty heartbeats later, Bertram finally moved, and, thankfully, it wasn't to come over and punch me in the face. Instead, he turned to look at his son. Gryphin again pressed his ears to his head. It was almost comical to see such a big wolf show deference to a man.

"Some fear is important for an alpha. How can we control feral wolves without fear?" Bertram turned back to me, again with the intense golden eyes. "You don't understand how wolves work. Part of us is all animal instinct. The alpha must keep all parts, including the animal part, in line. If they weren't afraid of me, there would be attempts on my life all the time as others fought to control the pack, thinking they could do a better job. Or worse, the wolves wouldn't listen to me and cause havoc and chaos wherever they went, including killing innocent humans they may run into. Humans like you, I might add."

I considered his words and glanced back at Gryphin. "It's true that I don't know much about werewolves, and what you say does seem to make sense, but that doesn't go with what I see. Does your own son need to be so scared of you?"

"This guy is a sure piece of work. My dad wasn't great, but I'm glad this fool isn't my dad," Brandon said.

Bertram again took a minute to think but then waved away my question with his hand. "None of that matters right now. What matters is that you need to get off my territory before you get hurt. I can only do so much to protect you, and if a wolf decided it wanted you dead, there isn't much I could do, even for a Seer."

I huffed and glanced at the ghost wolves, feeling quite sure that one of them was Sarah and that if the alpha would help us, we'd be able to get the answers we needed. "Sounds like your rule of fear isn't that strong, then."

"Ouch. That was brutal, even for me." Brandon's wide eyes glanced between me and the alpha.

Gryphin crouched down and whined while Bertram let out a howl that was more wolf-like than human, despite his human vocal cords. "Get her out of here before I tear her throat open!"

I wasn't sure if it was the howl, the words, or the way his rage-fire eyes bore into my soul while the change rippled over his skin again, but I was finally scared enough to run. Slipping on the mud, I scrambled to get away from the pond and head back into the woods.

The ghost wolves also reacted to the alpha's anger, and they all stood at attention, their fur spiking up and eerie snarls warned of impending attacks.

"They better not take a run at me!" Brandon faced the ghost wolves with balled fists.

Gryphin, either to save my life or to follow his alpha's orders, probably both, launched into action and was next to me before I could take three steps. He leaned down slightly so I could scramble up his side, and we bounded out of the clearing and into the woods before Bertram could complete his reversal into thick fur and sharp teeth as big as my forearm.

The woods rushed by us in a flurry as Gryphin ran. Before, I had thought he'd been going fast, but apparently he'd been holding back. Trees zoomed by us so quickly, it all became a blur. It was all I could do to close my eyes and cling to his back, praying I didn't fall, barf all over him, or get snatched off by an alpha wolf's powerful jaws.

Somehow, none of that happened as we made it back to the commune in record time. Gryphin's pace slowed as we approached the van. Once we made it, he gestured with his head for me to get inside, and I scrambled to obey him. I wasn't sure the van could stop an alpha werewolf, but it was better than waiting out in the open for Gryphin to change back.

Brandon had been left in the woods but had probably popped back to his haunt once he'd seen I was safely leaving on Gryphin's back. At least that's what I hoped had happened and not that the ghost wolves had figured out how to tear his ghostly body apart.

Thankfully, being in the van muffled most of the terrible sounds as my friend turned back into a human. As I waited, I watched the woods out of the front window, expecting to see a large amber werewolf emerge at any second.

Gryphin was still putting his shirt on as he opened the driver's side door and climbed into the seat. I got another glimpse of his toned abs before he pulled his shirt all the way down. "Oh man, I'm so sorry. That was not a good situation. Are you okay?"

Warmth spread through me as I looked into his earnest eyes. I was still breathing heavily, but the serenity in his gaze helped calm me down somehow. "Yes, I'm okay. Are you okay?"

He nodded, glanced at the woods again, and then put the key into the ignition. "Yes. I'm fine. We should get out of here."

I nodded, trying to take deeper breaths.

As we pulled out of the gravel parking lot of sorts, Kage jogged up to the van. Gryphin rolled down the window to talk to the second in command. The van was so old, he had to use a manual crank. His arm muscles bulged as he rapidly spun the crank around.

"What happened? Did he find you guys?" Kage asked and looked back and forth between us as if trying to search for any injuries.

"Yes." Gryphin looked back at me for a second. "He wasn't happy to see us, just like you suspected. He's convinced he doesn't want answers about Sarah."

"Actually," I said holding up a finger, "his exact words were that he already knew what had happened and that we were just getting into stuff we shouldn't be."

Kage frowned and glanced back into the forest. "He's coming back. I'm sure if he really wanted to hurt you, he would have already, but y'all still shouldn't be here when he gets back. Fill me in later, okay?"

Gryphin nodded and rolled the window back up. He drove us out of the commune and onto the gravel road.

"I didn't have time to tell you, but there were ghosts with him." I clasped my hands together to keep them from trembling so much. Adrenaline and fear still flowed through my veins, and I couldn't help but keep looking in the rearview mirror for a wolf bounding down the road behind us.

"There were?" Gryphin took a second to glance at me before putting his eyes back on the road. He must have seen my shaking fists because he switched hands on the steering wheel so his right one was free to cover mine.

His skin was almost hot to the touch, and the heat helped relax my muscles. I didn't dare move my hands though in case any movement made him think I didn't want his touch or that I did. Either way, it helped calm my nerves.

"Yes, they were all wolves, though. It was weird. I've never seen an animal ghost before. I guess because they're werewolves they can be ghosts, but also because they're werewolves, they are wolves. Does that make sense?"

He shrugged. "As much as anything right now."

"I'm wondering if Sarah is among the pack of ghosts. What did her wolf form look like?"

"Remember that family picture of us? Her fur was the same color as her bright red hair. Did you see one with red fur?"

I shook my head. "It's hard to say. Ghosts are always this blue transparent color so trying to determine the colors before they died is really hard. Mostly, I saw varying shades of blue. Anything else stand out about her that I might be able to recognize?"

"I'm sorry. Not that I can think of. She was about average size for a werewolf."

"Which is like huge, by the way. Why didn't you warn me about how big you guys are?"

A small smile returned to his face, and I was relieved to see it instead of the cowering shoulders and the flattened ears. "Would you have believed me if I'd told you?"

"Probably not. I'm sorry I messed all this up. I should have been nicer to him… I just couldn't stand to see him being so mean to you. Is he always like that?"

The smile disappeared. "He's right, though. Wolves, at least were-wolves, have to operate like that. We might be part human, but we're also part animal. Our instincts can overrule the human side of us, especially when we're in wolf form."

"That seems like a hard way to grow up. I'm sorry."

He lifted one shoulder in another shrug and left it at that.

Brandon must have decided it was time to check in, and he popped up next to me, crouching between the two front seats. "Woah! That was intense! Let me see you. Are you missing any limbs? Why didn't you summon me when you were out of danger?"

He stretched his neck out and visibly looked all over my body as if checking for injuries. When he saw our hands touching, he frowned with a pouty lip. "Alright, guess you're fine. I'll leave you two alone, then."

"Wait!"

He disappeared again and I let out a frustrated huff, pulling my hands out from Gryphin's warm fingers.

"What was that?" Gryphin put his hand back on the wheel and gave me an amused glance. "Did the ghost come back?"

"He did." I shook my head. "He's so exasperating sometimes. I could call him right back and make him listen to me but that seems like a bit much."

"Yes. It sounds like something an alpha would do." Gryphin's lips twitched in a grin, so I knew he wasn't trying to be too bitter.

After we'd made it back into town and in front of my house, I popped my door open and hopped out before he could come around and open it for me. He was polite enough not to comment as he stood next to me on the side of the road.

"So, what do we do next? How do we get access to talk to Sarah if she's in that ghost pack? And then, even if we have access, how do I get her to turn into a human so we can talk and get answers? Can werewolf ghosts even turn into humans?" I frowned as I shut the van door behind me.

"Those are all really good questions." Gryphin sighed and leaned on the door, his arms over his chest, and his eyes on his worn shoes.

"I wish Gran were still around. She might be able to help." I leaned on the car next to him, careful not to get close enough to touch his big arms, although I could still feel the heat radiating out of his skin.

"Is there anyone else we can ask?"

"I guess we can start with Mr. Tyler, or Billy, or whatever you call him. He seems like the kind who knows things. He knew about Seers before I did, anyway. Maybe he knows about wolf ghosts too."

Gryphin nodded. "I can do that tonight. See if he's got any ideas."

"Something we need to investigate might not be the most pleasant thing." I gave Gryphin a sympathetic look before going back to staring at the gravel around my shoes. "Your father mentioned something about knowing already what happened. I'm not sure he does from what you've said, but we need to figure out at least what he thinks he knows."

A muscle in Gryphin's jaw tightened. "That's not going to be easy."

"I know. I'm sorry."

"I'll do my best to get what I can out of him."

"Alright. I'll ask Caleb too, just in case. It's possible he has run into something during his several hundred years terrorizing the earth."

"Wow, is he really that old?" Gryphin's slim grey eyebrows rose.

"Around three hundred he said. I can't imagine how bored of living he's gotten."

"Well, it sure seems you've been giving him a run for his money lately."

We shared a grin.

"Okay, I'd best get back home. Hopefully, Dad will run off his anger before coming home again."

"Hey, Gryphin," I said while putting my hand on his shoulder to stop him from walking away for a second. "I'm sorry, again. I shouldn't have made him angrier. I'm also sorry that you have to live in such a world of fear."

He smiled and nodded before turning away. "It's fine. I'm used to it."

I watched him drive away from the comfort of my front porch and vowed to myself not to anger his father again, if on the unfortunate circumstances that I had to actually see him any time soon.

Chapter 14

Since the next day was Sunday, I had plenty of time to catch up on my homework. I wish I could say that I had gotten it all done, but it was really hard to focus with werewolf ghosts and a brooding 90s skater ghost constantly whirling around in my thoughts. Later in the evening, after struggling through some math, I put my pen down in frustration and texted Caleb.

Feel like going for a drive? I was hoping we could talk a bit.

He didn't bother to text me back, and, instead, I heard the now-familiar tapping on my window.

I winced slightly as I got up from my chair. My leg muscles weren't used to much running, and they felt a bit weak and sore after the eventful day I'd had yesterday. As I threw up the blinds and opened the window, Caleb popped off the screen.

"We have a front door, you know. I'm sure my mom would let you in now," I said, backing up to let him crawl in through the window.

"And take all the fun out of it?" Caleb's megawatt smile lit up my room almost as much as the pinkish sunset did.

"I suppose someone as old as you would enjoy trying to find anything to make life more interesting." I plopped down on my bed and gave him a cheeky smile.

He shook his head and turned my desk chair around so he could sit on it backward, his arms crossed on the top of the backrest. "Young people these days. No respect for the elderly."

I shrugged. "Hard to think of you as elderly when you were just about to go on a date with my sister. You guys planning trying again any time soon?" I raised my eyebrows scandalously.

Caleb surprised me by taking a second to consider the question. "We really shouldn't, probably."

"Okay..."

"I mean, it's no good to date a vampire. I can't tell you how many girls I've...dated and then seen die. In fact, I'm not even sure I'm up for more heartache. Even if Trina lives to a good old age, it'll still only feel like a drop in the bucket of life for me."

I frowned. "Wow. That's deep and dark. I had no idea you were capable of such depth."

He shrugged. "Yeah, well. So what did you want to talk about?"

"I was hoping you could drive me over to see Stephanie for a minute, and while we go, if I could pick your brain a bit about a problem Gryphin and I have encountered. I know it doesn't sound like the most enjoyable evening for you, but Mom would let me go somewhere with you, even after dark. You're pretty much the only person she trusts right now...you know, after the whole...incident."

"Right. And I'm not protesting, but why don't you just summon your friend here to talk to her? You can do that, right?"

"I could, but then we wouldn't get to spend some quality time in the car bonding as the in-laws we are bound to be." I grinned and started putting on my tennis shoes.

"I can think of some other things we can do in the car." He winked.

"Ew."

He chuckled a deep laugh that rumbled through his chest. "Sorry. Old habit."

"Do you mind terribly if we go through the front door?" I stood and put on my jacket.

"Oh, fine. I'll meet you out there. I have to go grab my car, anyway. It's parked at my house." He hopped silently out of the window and fitted the screen back in while I shut it.

Mom and Trina were watching TV as I walked into the front room.

"Are you going out? It's getting late." Mom glanced at the clock on the wall.

"Yes, just going to visit Stephanie's ghost and see if we can work on getting her closer to crossing over. Don't worry, Caleb is taking me. He's meeting me out front with his car."

Trina made a face I couldn't read but didn't say anything.

Mom sighed and nodded. "Okay but be back before ten. You know how I worry."

"I certainly do. Love you guys!" I waved before stepping out of the front door.

Caleb's sleek black car pulled up just as I walked off the porch. He leaned over and popped the door open for me while he stayed in his driver's seat. Normally, I wouldn't have had a second thought about that and considered it a nice gesture, but, after hanging out with Gryphin, I kind of missed trying to dodge the wolf's gentlemanly ways.

"It's so much slower to drive around," Caleb said as I got into the car.

"Yes, I'm sure. It must be terrible to have to follow driving laws and all that when you could just use your vampire speed and zip around so fast no one can see you."

He nodded and pulled onto the road. "Exactly. Is your ghost friend joining us this evening?"

I couldn't help but sigh. "No. I seem to have run him off...again. I've never known someone so emotional before."

"Didn't you say he was a teen in the 90s? Those were hard times and teenagers were weird." Caleb shook his head at the memories. "I blame Kurt Cobain."

"Okay... I guess that might have something to do with it, but I worry he's becoming a little more unstable in his ghostliness."

"I suppose that could be it too. What did you say to him?"

I shifted my legs and butt and wondered how a car that looked so expensive didn't have super comfortable seats. "It wasn't so much of what I said. This time, anyway, but more of what he saw."

"Oh," Caleb took his eyes off the road to give me a waggled eyebrow, "were you and wolfy making out?"

I smacked his arm that was resting on the gear shift near my leg. "No!"

He laughed, unfazed by my girly attack. "Whatever you say. You could do worse, honestly."

"You approve of me dating the wolf? Wow. Have I fallen through a looking glass?"

"Maybe. I don't know. If there's something I've learned from being around for so long, it's that loneliness is a real and powerful thing."

"I promise you I am far from being lonely. In fact, there are so many people, dead and alive, around me all the time that a little space would be a welcome moment." I looked out the window as the town's shops and businesses whizzed by us.

"Hmm, maybe that's the vibe your ghost buddy is picking up on. You never did say what he saw to make him upset."

"Oh, right. We'd just gone through a scary situation involving his angry father, and Gryphin was trying to steady and calm my hands by holding them. It was innocent enough, but Brandon saw it and thought the worst. He didn't even give me time to explain before disappearing. That was hours ago, and I haven't seen him since."

Caleb hummed in his throat but didn't say anything else. It gave me a few seconds to think about what he'd said about loneliness and Brandon. Honestly, we'd started hanging out because he'd looked so lonely. The image of him sitting alone in the grass popped into my head, and I felt a curl of sadness unfurl inside my chest.

After a few minutes of silence, Caleb spoke. "It must be very hard for him to see you holding hands with someone you can actually touch. I'm sure he's grown some strong feelings for you whether he's wanted to or not. After all, you're the only person he can talk to, so it's basically like you're the only person left on earth. That's bound to make him feel something for you, even if he otherwise wouldn't have."

I blinked a few times and gave him a side-eye. "Er, thank you?"

Again chuckling, he turned onto the road leading toward the bridge. I was surprised we'd made it so quickly, but I shouldn't have been with Caleb at the wheel.

"I only meant he cares about you, and it has to be difficult for him to see you interacting with others whether because he feels some kind of ownership over you or because he's unable to make those kinds of connections himself."

"I guess that makes sense. Maybe you have learned some things in your old age."

"A few."

We pulled onto the side of the road near the bridge. I could already see Stephanie sitting in the middle of the bridge, watching traffic whizz by with a bored expression.

"Oh, I'm supposed to be asking you about wolf ghosts, but you distracted me."

"Wolf ghosts?" His dark eyebrows rose in surprise as he shut off the car.

"Yes, we've found a roaming pack of wolf ghosts that the alpha knows about. He's able to sense them in some way, and it looked like he'd been joining them on a run, all by himself. Well, that is to say without anyone else alive."

Caleb frowned and tapped the steering wheel with his fingers a few times. Traffic rushed by on the busy road and once in a while the car rocked from the windy vibrations of another vehicle passing too quickly.

"And why are you asking me about this? Just because I've been around doesn't mean I know much about wolves. We tend to keep apart from each other to avoid wars and all that fun stuff. The separation has worked for years and has allowed the humans to live and thrive... Although many feel like humans have gotten too powerful, and we need to rise again to show them who is really in charge."

"Er... Well, that's terrifying."

His broad shoulders lifted in a shrug. "It's only a minority. There's still plenty of others who don't look at it that way."

"Great. Add that to my plate of things to worry about. So you've never heard of a ghost wolf before?"

"Maybe. I need time to think about it. Three hundred years make a lot of memories to sort through," he said with his predator grin and got out of the car.

I waited to make sure there was no one passing by before opening my own door and quickly getting to the sidewalk. "You know, with as old as you are, you'd think you would have kept some of those gentlemanly, old-timey habits."

Caleb walked ahead of me toward the bridge. "Like what?"

"I don't know. Maybe like opening the door for a girl? Or even walking on the outside near the traffic and keeping her on the inside?"

"You didn't seem like the type that would appreciate those kinds of things. I thought perhaps using every bit of spare time I had keeping an eye on you and following you around while you do your lame teenager things would be enough. Do you want more from me?" He stopped and turned abruptly, and I nearly ran into his solid chest.

Forcing myself to look up into his dark eyes with dignity, I shook my head. "Never mind. That will be quite enough."

His deep chuckle rumbled behind me as I forged past him and made my way to Stephanie who had seen us and was waving.

"Hey, Steph!" I said brightly and leaned against the cement railing next to her. "Lovely evening for watching cars."

It was one of the warmer nights of November and while a jacket was still required, the wind didn't slice through it quite so sharply.

"I see you brought me some eye candy to look at," Stephanie said, dragging her gaze up and down Caleb's body as he stood slightly behind me.

"I figured you could use something new, although now that you're dead and you've come to terms with me having a weird power to talk to dead people, I suppose it's safe enough to warn you that Caleb is actually a vampire." I shot him a cheeky smile and nodded my head to the right, indicating he could stand over there without disturbing anyone.

He gave me a flat look and moved to lean over the edge next to me, peering down twenty feet or so at the swiftly moving water. "Just because she's dead doesn't mean you should be giving away my secrets. That seems rude, Miss Complain-about-manners."

At the same time, Stephanie was talking. "What? A vampire? Are those even real? He looks normal to me... Well, now that you mention it, he is a bit *too* handsome."

I shrugged. "Hey, I have to tell someone," I turned back to Stephanie, "and yes, vampires are real. Believe me, I've been thrust into a world full of crazy stuff ever since..."

Brandon. That's what I wanted to say, but I stopped, saddened by the thought of my friend. I was getting closer to summoning him again just to see his face, even if he didn't want me to.

Stephanie didn't notice my thoughts had gone somewhere else, and I couldn't blame her after dropping the vampire bomb. "Does he drink blood? Oh, ask him why he didn't turn me into a vampire that night to save my life! Wouldn't I look so hot as a vampire? I could go around seducing men into dark alleys where I drain them of blood and walk out without smudging my bright red lipstick."

I blinked a few times. "Wow. I didn't know you were so dark."

She had the decency to blush and smile out of embarrassment. "Yeah, I don't know if I'd be like that. It was mostly a joke, really."

"I'm sure we'd all be different after being turned into a vampire. Hey, Caleb, did you used to open doors for girls before you were turned?" I nudged him with my elbow and gave a teasing grin.

He rolled his eyes. "Are we here to make fun of me?"

I shrugged. "I have to make fun of someone when Brandon isn't here."

He shook his head and went back to watching the water. "Guess you'd better kiss and make out... I mean, up."

"Ugh, vampires. Anyway, Steph, did you figure out anything that might be your unfinished business yet?" I asked, figuring I might as well get down to business, even though it was tempting to keep stalling and avoiding going home to more homework.

She shrugged and fiddled with the ends of her hair which had been curled down the length of her back, giving more sass to her police officer Halloween look. "I mean, I've tried to think of things, but it's hard to say. I am so young... Okay, I was so young. Is it possible my unfinished business is the life I didn't get to live? Like all those fun college parties I missed out on and those stolen kisses where I make sure I'm actually into boys? What about getting married ten years later to a rich lawyer and giving him three perfectly adorable children?"

"Er, well, I don't know. It could entirely be possible, but that's not something I can help you with, so I hope that's not the case. Unfinished business is something we're supposed to be able to take care of so you can pass on, not living the life that you had lost, right? I think?" I glanced between the two of them.

Steph looked off into the distance, still playing with her hair, while Caleb gave me a vague shrug.

"As far as I know, Linda—er, your gran—was able to help most of the ghosts she tried to help. Some took far longer than others, but yes, most of the unfinished business was something possible to do for a Seer. I would assume this would be the same," Caleb said, able to add to the conversation even though he could only hear my side of it.

"Right. So let's assume that it's not living the life you lost. Do you have any regrets, Steph? Anything you feel like you need to do right before you leave? Anyone you need to apologize to or something?"

She frowned with a pouty lower lip. "I mean, I felt bad for how we treated you sometimes, but I already said sorry for that."

"Yes, if that were it, you'd have gone over by now."

Caleb stopped leaning and turned toward me. "I feel like I should tell you guys something before you get too far into this crossing-over business."

"And what's that? Does it have anything to do with where you've taken her body?" I crossed my arms over my chest and gave him an expectant look.

"What? *He* took my body?" Stephanie pulled her eyebrows together in disgust and leaned in closer to whisper into my ear, which was quite unnecessary. "Is that like...a vampire thing? What did he do to me, and would I have enjoyed it?"

I wanted to smack her arm. "Ew! Gross! Steph, you really have a dirty mind."

Looking more amused than chagrined, she backed up a few inches. "Sorry. Guess it comes from hanging out with all the football players all the time."

"I guess." Shuddering, I turned back to Caleb. "Well?"

He sighed and rolled his neck to the side until it popped. "I didn't tell you this before because I didn't want to get your hopes up, either of you, and it's not something I should be sharing, especially with such a blabber-mouth like you, Hanna."

I stared blankly at him until he continued.

"Anyway, with the help of a Seer, necromancers can sometimes... Well, the really powerful ones, anyway. They can sometimes bring people back to life."

Steph and I looked at each other with wide eyes and then back at him.

"Are you serious?" she said.

"Did you just make this up?" I narrowed my eyes suspiciously.

"Why would I do that? I took her body to the necromancer order—a place I do *not* enjoy going to, I'll have you know—and they put it into stasis until the master can come back, and they can work on putting her back together again. That's why I was trying to push you to stall working on her unfinished business. If she crosses over, it won't work."

"You should have just told me all of this from the beginning!" I tossed my arms up into the air, trying to release some frustration. "Do you know how important this is for me to know? If they needed my help, I'd have to know anyway! And what do you mean the master to come back? Did he go somewhere?"

Caleb watched me with amused eyes as I went off on my tirade. "It's alright, darling. Slow down. You might scare the ghost."

Stephanie huffed. "Yeah, right."

"Can we focus here? I'm guessing that the master is the only necromancer strong enough to bring her back?"

Caleb nodded.

"And he's gone somewhere?"

"Yes, apparently out of the country for a few weeks."

"And that's not too long to be able to...fix her?"

He shook his head and shrugged. "According to them, as long as they can keep the body in good shape, it shouldn't be a problem?"

Steph took in a sharp breath and put her hand on her chest in dismay. "Wait, are we talking about turning me into a zombie? I refuse to be a zombie!"

I nodded. "That's a fair point. Are we turning her into a zombie? I've seen those things in person, and that is *not* a look she'll go for."

Caleb laughed. "No, not a zombie. They'll really bring her back to life. That's one reason necromancers love Seers so much. With their help, a dead person can be reunited with their spirit, as long as they turned into a ghost and their body was preserved, and that person can be normal again, mostly."

"Will she remember being a ghost? How come I didn't know this yet?"

"There are lots of things you still don't know, doll. And there are lots of things I still don't know." Caleb's smile turned a little kinder. "It's still a long shot. I don't know all the details, but I do know it doesn't always work. There is some risk, of course. You'll have to ask the master or your necromancer friend or someone who might know what effects it could have on a person or what she'll remember."

"This seems like a big thing I should know about," I grumbled. "You bet I'll be asking Noah about all of this. So, what do you think, Steph? Is this something you want to try? I won't do it unless you want it."

Her eyes darted around from Caleb, to me, to the traffic, and finally the bridge, before coming back to me. "I'm not sure. Did you say Noah was involved in this? Andrea's boyfriend-type-guy Noah? I always thought there was something weird about him... What's a necromancer, anyway?"

I grinned. "Guess we have a few more things to explain."

Chapter 15

Sunday night found me alone in my bed, staring up at the swirls in the ceiling spackle. I was mostly okay during the daylight hours, despite the whirlwind of ghosts, vampires, and necromancers in my life. It was when the world was quiet, and I was alone, that the anxiety and fear crept in.

It wasn't the memories of glazed zombie eyes staring up at me or even the empty eye sockets of older zombies that bothered me the most. It wasn't the crowded room of the vampire seethe as I was brought in before the queen.

It was the terror of not being in control of my own body.

While I had been entranced by the vampires, preventing me from contacting the ghosts for help, they could have easily given my body the command to stop breathing, and I would have suffocated right there on the plush carpet.

I hadn't even been able to talk or go to the bathroom without their consent. I might not have even been able to blink.

I'd read online about panic attacks and tried to employ some of the tactics in dealing with them. First, I acknowledged that I might be having an attack or feelings of intense anxiety, that these feelings were situational inside my head, and there was nothing threatening going on at the moment.

I was safe in my bed with Caleb watching over me, or, at the least, with a protection spell around my house that was supposed to protect us from creepy things in the dark.

Repeating these reassurances in my head did not help much.

I tried distracting myself, focusing on my breathing. Forcing my brain to only think about the air that went in and out of my chest. I brought it in slowly and exhaled slowly. This only worked as long as I kept focused. Too bad being focused wasn't one of my strengths.

Conversations from the day floated into my mind. Along with it, came the anxiety of probably having said or done something to offend or upset someone without even meaning to.

I realized then there was definitely someone I could and should apologize to as soon as I was able. While he might not enjoy being summoned right at that moment, he was just going to have to deal with it.

"Yes, my master?" Brandon said with a flat voice as he appeared inside my room, standing next to my bed.

My breathing had gotten out of control, and it was all I could do to keep gasping without dissolving into screams that would surely awake Mom and Trina. The last thing I wanted was for them to have more worry.

It only took a few milliseconds of strained breathing before Brandon's heart thawed, and he dropped to his knees. His face was inches from mine, and his glowing blue eyes were earnestly focused on my face. "Oh, Hanna. It's okay. I'm here. Just breathe. All you have to do is breathe right now. Don't worry about anything else. School doesn't matter. Homework doesn't matter. Those stupid boys don't matter. It doesn't even matter that you're a Seer and everyone in the whole world seems to want to use you for something."

"Not. Helping," I gasped.

"Oh, sorry. Here." He placed a cool hand over my own that had been clutching at my chest.

"Brandon, don't..."

He shook his head to silence me and squeezed harder, pulling energy from me so he could manifest a physical form for a few minutes. Like before, I couldn't feel the drain, but we still didn't know what the side-effects might be.

"It's fine. Don't worry about it. Wait...unless worrying about it will help distract you? Or would that cause you more anxiety? Yeah, probably best not to worry about it. Listen, Hanna. I'm here. I'm not going anywhere for as long as you need me. You're safe, and no one is coming after you. It's okay."

My mouth was dry as I swallowed thickly. The rapid breathing had slowed somewhat, but I could feel the pounding of my heart all throughout my body, which at that point could have easily been from the close contact of my favorite person and not just anxiety.

"I'm so sorry, Brandon." My voice quivered and hitched in my throat.

He sighed and rested his now solid chin on the corner of my mattress. His expression was soft and kind as he studied me.

I focused on the green of his eyes that I loved...no, yearned to see, despite the fears that what we were doing wasn't right. The focus helped calm my breathing even more.

"Hanna, no." He sighed again and rubbed a thumb over my fingers. The ridges of his fingers were soft against my alert skin. "I'm the one who should be sorry. I've been jealous and petty and acting more childlike than I should at thirty-three years old."

His lips pulled up at one corner as amusement crinkled in his eyes.

I couldn't help my own smile from peeking out. "You're such an old man."

"If only I would act mature, though, right?"

"Maturity is overrated. You were jealous?" I had suspected it but had been too afraid to admit the suspicion to myself. Voicing the thought out loud brought warmth into my chest that I didn't know what to do with.

"You were holding hands with another dude, and then it all made sense as to why you hadn't summoned me back. You hadn't wanted me back." The pain in his eyes pulled at my heart.

"What? No!" I flipped my hand over and grabbed at his so we were holding onto each other. I tried to ignore how I was pressing him to my chest, but a part of me liked it. "I only didn't summon you back because I don't want to be manipulating you like that. It doesn't seem right to summon you all the time whether you get a say or not. Especially when you're mad."

"Oh." He tilted his head to the side, and his usual charismatic grin spread across his mouth. "Guess I shouldn't have joked about you being my master when I first popped in."

"Yes. That wasn't helpful."

The teasing smile faded. "I'm sorry. Like I said, I was just feeling angry from being jealous. You didn't deserve it."

"And you don't deserve to be my slave, beholden to whatever a whim I have. It just doesn't seem right."

The grin came back. "Listen, I'll be your slave any time you want me. Just say the word, and I'll do whatever you want, and I'll like it, too."

I narrowed my eyes. "Why do I have a feeling we're suddenly talking about something other than just popping in to help me solve ghost mysteries?"

He was still grinning as he leaned in and kissed the back of my hand.

Monday started a new week, and I had to slog through the last five days of school before my birthday. Mostly, I kept quiet about the upcoming event, but I did have to invite some people to the party, or they wouldn't show up. That's how parties and invitations worked.

Addy was excited while Emma was more thoughtful when I told them during our Monday morning jog around the gym. Their company helped ease the pain of having to plod around in a circle with sore muscles and concerns about smelling sweaty and looking bedraggled for the rest of the day. This was certainly the last time I allowed my schedule to have P.E. for first period if I could help it.

"Sounds like a great time!" Addy added an extra jump in her running to emphasize her point.

"Of course, we'll come," Emma said with a smile. "It's nice to be invited."

Addy looked around to make sure no one was close enough to listen to our conversation. "Are there going to be any...other kinds of people there?"

I shook my head and smiled. "I don't know. A few others might show up. Remind me to tell you about other things in our world besides ghosts. Although, I probably shouldn't...but it's just too amazing and terrifying to keep it all to myself."

"Ghosts are easy to believe, but there are other things?" Addy's eyes widened.

"Right. I probably shouldn't have said anything. It's fine." I waved my hand to push away the subject. "Do you guys have any plans for Thanksgiving break?"

We chatted more about "normal" things, and I managed to keep my foot out of my mouth for most of the rest of class.

After history, Mr. Tyler asked to meet me in his classroom again after school. I agreed, even though I still had no idea what to do with the renegade alpha and his ghost pack of wolves.

As was my usual new thing, I spent lunch in the library. Unfortunately, it appeared to be Noah's new thing too. He sauntered in not long after I had arrived, forcing me to put down the book I was enjoying and look at his handsome, annoying face.

"Hey, what's up?" He plopped down into the chair next to mine even though there were several others at the table I'd chosen to sit at.

"Aren't you going to be missed in the cafeteria? I'm sure your girlfriend's butt will be cold from not sitting on your lap." I tried to make my tone snarky, but it probably came out more bitter than anything.

He laughed. "Wow, was that supposed to be an insult?"

I frowned. "I'm not so good at those, apparently."

"There are worse things to be bad at. I told them I had to take a makeup test for Chemistry."

"Couldn't even tell them the truth about hanging out with me." I sighed at my book. "Not saying I don't blame you. I am an outcast and all that."

He rolled his eyes. "We all know you're way more interesting than them. That's probably most of the problem, really."

A small flutter of warmth bloomed in my chest, but I ignored it, hoping it would go away. "To be honest, I have been wanting to talk to you about something."

He leaned in closer, much too eager. "What about?"

"Well, first, I am curious as to how the group is handling Stephanie's absence. Are they sad or have they stopped thinking about themselves for two seconds to even realize she's gone?"

Noah raised his eyebrows and sat back in his chair. "That's a bit harsh, isn't it?"

"Is it? Andrea can't take her eyes off a mirror to save her life."

He sighed and put his hand through his hair. It was a motion I used to love to watch, but, this time, it had me thinking of another head of hair with a silver curl.

Poor Brandon. Maybe he had a right to be jealous and angry. I did lead him on but then later I was off thinking about other dudes. I tried to tell myself it was a better and healthy thing since there really was no future with Brandon. It was good to distract myself from his stupidly charming smile and dumb jokes.

"I know she's been tough on you. I'm not blind, but she also does have some good qualities."

"Is that why you love her so much?" This time it came out successfully with snark and sass.

"I told you, there's a bigger reason I've got to stick around her. You can think of as…she needs some extra help."

I narrowed my eyes and thought for a second. "Does this have anything to do with your other hobby that's not football?"

He glanced around to see if anyone was paying us attention. Apparently satisfied, he turned back and leaned in to speak quietly. "Yes, it might. I promise things would be different, very different, if she didn't need my help, but I just can't abandon her."

I shook my head. "Yeah, I'm sure that's what all the guys say."

"Well, you're one to talk. I hear you've been hanging out with a wolf. Was having a vampire on your payroll not enough for you?"

"Ugh, I'm just helping him with a ghost thing. That is my job, isn't it? I mean, if I didn't know better, I'd say you were jealous. Is there something going around these days?"

Noah gave me a flat look. "So, what if I'm jealous? It's not like I'm trying to be. In fact, if I had it my way, I'd never think about you again unless it was important."

"How rude," I found myself echoing words that Brandon said all the time.

"Ugh." He put both elbows on the table and his hands clutched into his hair. "This is not how I wanted our conversation to go."

"Me neither." I crossed my arms over my chest and frowned. "Why did you come here anyway?"

He flopped his hands onto the table, causing a few people to look in our direction for a second. "Is it so hard to hear that I missed you? I guess when you have choices between a vampire and a wolf, the necromancer seems like a stupid, weak human."

"What? Who said anything about any of that? I'm not interested in either of them. Besides, aren't you forgetting about Andrea?"

"I could never forget about her," he sighed, "but probably not for the reason you're thinking."

Silence settled in between us for a few minutes. Light chatter and laughter from the group of kids a few tables over floated around. They always looked like they were having so much fun playing whatever card game they were so obsessed with they spent every lunch playing it.

"What else was it you wanted to talk about?" Noah asked eventually.

"Oh," I straightened up in my chair, "I was actually hoping to get some information or more like confirmation, on something Caleb told me yesterday."

"Oh great. I'm sure this will be good."

"Actually, it's a good thing. Well, kinda. For Stephanie, anyway. Is it true that with a Seer's help you can bring someone back from the dead?"

"Shh!" Noah glanced around panicked and then leaned in again. Whiffs of his mall-brand cologne stirred in the air. "He told you *that*? It's supposed to be one of our top guarded secrets."

I shrugged. "Sorry. Yes, but he thinks you guys can help Stephanie. Isn't that worth it?"

"I wonder how he found out in the first place."

"He is pretty old. I'm sure he's seen things."

Noah shook his head. "Anyway, I've heard that it's possible, yes, but it's also rare for the spell to be successful. Lots of things have to add up just right for it to work. First off, the body needs to be in near-life shape. Do you know where her body is?"

"Yes. Well, I mean, Caleb does. My wolf friend dragged her body out of the river, but before we could get it to the authorities, Caleb came by and took it, saying he had an idea we could try. At the time, I was probably in too much shock to wonder much about it. The action was so weird, he had to eventually tell me what his plan was, even if he was trying to avoid getting my hopes up."

"Okay, so where is it?"

"Oh, right. He said it's with your order. That y'all know how to store a body and keep it ready to be fixed or resurrected."

Noah's eyebrows rose. "Wow, I hadn't heard about that at all."

I shrugged. "Maybe you didn't need to know. Caleb said they were waiting for the master to come back into town before they could try anything. Apparently, he's out of the country?"

Noah nodded, his eyes staring at some bookshelves across from us as he thought. "So, my order has already agreed to help with this?"

"Maybe? Sounds like it."

His focus came back to my face. "I'm telling you. Don't get your hopes up. Even if we get everything ready for the ritual, that doesn't mean it will be successful."

"Okay. I'll try not to, but it would be awesome if it worked."

"The other thing we need, obviously, is your help and her ghost. Do you know where her ghost is?"

"I do," I suppressed a smile, "and you'd think it was hilarious if you could see what she died in."

"Or not."

"I mean, yes, it's totally sad, but both her and I, and Brandon of course, shared a laugh over her Halloween costume."

He stared at me flatly for a few seconds. "Your sense of humor is growing darker from hanging out with us occult people all the time."

"Oh, come on! You raise zombies for Pete's sake!" I made sure to lean in closer and hissed those words at him in a hushed tone.

He scoffed and sat back in his chair again, crossing his arms over his chest. "Life is still sacred. You, of all people, should know this."

The bell rang to signal the end of lunch. As I shoved my book back into my bag, I gave him a side-eye. "Of course, I know this, but I also know you've got to find laughter during the dark times, or else the will to live shrivels up and dies."

He pushed his lips into an appreciative frown. "Alright. Hanna coming out with the deep thoughts."

We stood up together, and then I remembered this weekend. "Oh, there's a birthday party this weekend. If you want to go."

While standing, we'd gotten closer. I could feel the warmth from his body and smell his cologne all around me. If he decided to bend down just a few inches, our lips could have easily been touching.

"Whose birthday party?" His voice was kind of floaty, perhaps also distracted by how close we were standing.

"Mine." I shrugged and took a step back before Noah tried anything we would both regret.

A wide smile stretched across the lips I had been contemplating. "I'd love to come."

Chapter 16

Gryphin was waiting with Mr. Tyler as I walked into the classroom after school. I'd told Trina and Caleb what I was doing and that Gryphin could escort me home afterward so neither of them worried. Again, Caleb probably only agreed to it because he was nearby on the football field and could put out an ear for me in case I got in trouble.

Honestly, it was nice having people keep tabs on me in case something went wrong, but it was also super annoying at times. I was starting to miss my freedom.

"There she is," Mr. Tyler said as I walked in. He was standing at his desk organizing a stack of papers while Gryphin sat in an undersized student chair at the back of the row, closest to his uncle's desk.

"Seen any ghosts lately?" Gryphin said with a teasing smile by way of greeting.

"Funny." I shook my head and took a seat a few rows away from Gryphin, not wanting to get any closer to him than I needed to and not because I didn't like him.

His chair squeaked in protest as Mr. Tyler sat down. "Gryph tells me you may have found Sarah, but that she's in her wolf form."

I nodded. "Yes, this is way above me, I'm afraid. I don't have my gran to ask advice from this time."

Mr. Tyler stroked his grey beard. It was a lighter color than Gryphin's hair and had been earned through old age. "It is quite a conundrum, indeed. And he says you found Bertram running with them?"

"Yes. That was not the ideal situation for meeting the alpha." I shuddered at the memory of his angry golden eyes.

Gryphin frowned. "I'm really sorry about that."

"Not your fault. How were you to know that he'd be running around the forest with a bunch of dead werewolves?"

"Actually...we all have a connection, and I could feel that he was out there. I just... I don't know. I didn't expect him to come hunt us out." Gryphin picked at a spot on the desk where some bored student had dug a hole into the wood.

Mr. Tyler sat forward toward Gryphin, and his chair squeaked again. "You didn't think he'd come hunting when he sensed a strange presence in his territory?"

The younger wolf seemed to sink into his leather jacket. "I was hoping we'd be done before he'd notice."

Shaking his head, Mr. Tyler sat back. "No wonder he was upset at finding you. You know how he feels about outsiders when he's not grieving, let alone after just having lost his mate."

Gryphin rubbed at his forehead and eyes. "I know. I messed up. Can we just focus on fixing the situation now?"

I tried a wobbly smile. "It's okay, Gryphin. You got me out of there quickly. No harm is done."

He gave me a small, lopsided smile of appreciation.

"Mr. Tyler, have you ever heard of ghost wolves before? I mean, you knew what a Seer was before I did so that means you're familiar with then. At least a little? Maybe you've heard of a Seer working with an animal ghost?"

He was shaking his head before I finished my list of hopeful questions. "No. I'm sorry. I knew about Seers, of course, because everyone does. They're powerful and useful."

"And apparently someone to kidnap if you're feeling froggy," I grumbled.

Mr. Tyler chuckled and Gryphin found an amused smile from somewhere.

"It's interesting that as useful or helpful or sought-after Seers are, or however you want to say it, the local werewolf alpha wants nothing to do with me," I said, quietly looking at my shoes. "I mean, it feels nice not to have to worry about a werewolf sneaking up behind me to carry me away into the woods, but at the same time, I'm just trying to help."

"I know, dear." Mr. Tyler nodded sympathetically. "We appreciate it more than you can know."

I sighed, and we fell quiet for a second.

"The basics are this: we know there is a pack of ghost wolves, and, hopefully, Sarah is among them. They run with the alpha, but they're probably stuck in the forest while he isn't." Mr. Tyler looked at the ceiling as he thought out loud. "There's got to be a time when we can get them together without the alpha around."

Gryphin nodded. "Yes, we can do that. Surely that's the best first step, anyway."

"He probably sleeps sometimes, right?" I said, trying to hop on their train of thought.

"Yes. He's been coming home at night around two or three a.m.," Gryphin said.

Mr. Tyler adjusted the glasses on his nose. "So, we can sneak out there while he's exhausted and try to find them."

"I'm afraid I have a lot of issues with this plan." I frowned. "I promise I'm not trying to be difficult here, but my mom will not let me run around werewolf territory at night without Caleb to watch my back in hopes that we can somehow track down a creepy pack of dead wolves. Not to mention that when we do find them, how do we get them to change back into humans so I can talk to Sarah? We don't even know if they can change into a human while being a ghost."

The silence was back as we all frowned down at the terrible brown carpet.

"We need a witch," Mr. Tyler said after a few moments of heavy thought.

"Uhm, I'm sorry?" I said, scrunching my eyebrows. "Why do we need a witch? I thought the ghost thing was my department."

"How do we find one?" Gryphin asked, careful to wait until I was finished talking so he wouldn't interrupt.

Mr. Tyler put his elbows on the armrests and steepled his fingers together in front of his chin. "It's true that the witches don't typically have the in-depth relationship with ghosts that a Seer can form, but they can offer some help. I've heard of them doing some pretty unique things. In fact, that's why Sarah went looking for a witch. She'd heard of one raising a person from the dead."

"Wait. Isn't that a necromancer thing? How did a witch pull it off?" I asked, pulling my eyebrows in.

Mr. Tyler shrugged. "No idea. But for some reason, she felt if the witch was powerful enough to do that, then they could help her."

"Do you think the witch needed help from a Seer to do that? Like a necromancer would?" I'll admit I felt kind of proud knowing these details, even if I had only learned them that very day. Maybe I could get a handle on all this insane occult stuff.

Mr. Tyler shrugged his narrow shoulders. "Maybe if we find a this witch, we can ask them?"

I sighed and leaned back onto the sidebar keeping the student desk and chair together. "Yes, because we've been so successful at finding witches lately."

Gryphin's left eyebrow rose. "Have you been trying to find a witch?"

"For over a month, actually." I frowned and looked back down at the carpet. There were more than a few dark spots where gum had been squished into it. "I made a mistake when first dealing with the ghosts and helped a nasty witch enslave several spirits."

"Don't be so hard on yourself. I helped too." Mr. Tyler wore a kind smile that was probably in an effort to make me feel better. It didn't work.

"Well...anyway, we've been trying to find her ever since and none of us have been successful. However, we did find a lead from a vampire queen."

This time both of Gryphin's eyebrows rose in surprise.

"It's a long story, but basically, we learned about Rose the witch, her background, and her real name, which is actually Ann, apparently. I had hoped that would help us find her better, but so far, we haven't found anything. Not even with the help of an expert researcher history teacher." I nodded my head subtly in Mr. Tyler's direction in case Gryphin didn't get who I was talking about.

"That sounds frustrating," Gryphin said.

"You have no idea. So how are we supposed to find a witch who can help us with the ghost wolf thing?" I asked with a frown.

Mr. Tyler smiled. It was kind, but also a little bit mischievous. "Just because we can't find a witch who clearly doesn't want to be found, doesn't mean we can't find *all* witches. Some of them like money and will do quite a lot for a couple of Gs."

"A couple grand?! I don't have that kind of money."

"Relax, Hanna," Mr. Tyler said soothingly. "This isn't all on you. You're doing the pack a favor. Why would we make you pay for it?"

"Oh. Right. That's good. Sorry."

Gryphin smiled and shook his head. "It must be hard being a lonely Seer where all the ghost problems are on your shoulders. You're probably used to solving your problems on your own, and it might be hard for you to accept help from others."

A rush of relief and gratitude went to my eyes, and I was horrified to feel tears threatening to spill. I blinked the emotion away and tried to laugh it off. "Oh, well you know, that's the Seer's life, I suppose. Thankfully, I've been able to get lots of help from my family and friends."

I realized that, as I spoke, I did feel alone being a Seer sometimes. While the pressure was easily overwhelming if I let it be, I honestly did have several people who had helped me and or were willing to help. Even though I might have felt alone sometimes, I didn't need to.

Most of the emotional reaction was probably because I'd felt seen by him. It was like Gryphin knew me nearly as well as anyone else in my life, despite only knowing me a few days.

"Yes, we've got your back, as the kids say." Mr. Tyler smiled again. "I'll find the witch. Hopefully they'll be able to help us within the week, and we can solve this whole situation before our alpha goes completely insane."

"Oh! I just had a thought. Caleb knows a witch. We can ask him about her? Maybe she'd help us," I said.

Mr. Tyler thought for a second. "We'll have to see if this is her area of expertise, but we can start with her. I can also check with the witch who helped ward my classroom. If neither of them knows how to help us, maybe they know of someone who can."

"Okay. That sounds good to me. It's not like we have any other ideas," I said, standing up to stretch and get the kink out of my back. "Let me know when I can help and what the next step is. In the meantime, I'll try to figure out how to get my mom to let me out of the house so late at night."

Gryphin stood with me. "I'll walk you home."

Mr. Tyler gave us a knowing smirk and wheeled his chair back toward his desk. "I still have some work to do back here. I'll see you two kids later."

As we left the classroom and walked down the empty halls, I said, "I'm sorry you have to escort me all over the place. It's so dumb to need a babysitter."

Gryphin chuckled. "I think of myself more as a bodyguard and less as a gum-popping, phone-talking, blonde-ponytail kind of babysitter."

"You would look good with a blonde ponytail, though."

"Too bad I've left my wig at home."

We shared a laugh before Gryphin jogged ahead of me a few steps so he could open the door before I got there.

"My lady," he said with a teasing smile and gestured for me to go through.

I rolled my eyes but didn't comment again about how he didn't need to do that. He already knew how I felt, and I might have, maybe, kind of, sort of missed it.

"I know we're working on an important thing with your dad and all, but maybe you have time for some fun later?" I asked as we walked through the parking lot toward my neighborhood.

"What kind of fun do you have in mind?" Gryphin's smile spread slowly and heat inside my chest grew with it.

"Oh, nothing crazy. It's my birthday on Saturday. I know we just met, and it's kind of been under weird circumstances and all that, but I figured I should at least invite you anyway. Don't feel any pressure to go or anything. I get it if you don't want to—"

Gryphin's rumbling laughter stopped me from continuing on my rant. "I'd love to come. Saturday, you said?"

I nodded, trying to hold in the bright smile that wanted to beam over my face. "Yup. It's just a chill thing. No big deal."

"Honestly, it's my first birthday party outside the commune. It's kind of a big deal to me. Plus, it's your birthday, surely a day that needs to be celebrated."

Blushing, I turned my focus on our walk, so, hopefully, he wouldn't notice the redness in my cheeks.

Chapter 17

Tuesday through Friday actually went by relatively quickly and without too many absurd things happening. Wednesday evening Trina and I went shopping for cute birthday outfits. We didn't feel guilty at all for using vampire money that Caleb had paid me after the whole debacle with his previous seethe.

It had been a pleasant enough trip, and we got some cute things, but the conversation stayed relatively light. We still weren't talking about ghosts or her necklace. I figured she'd bring up that stuff when she was ready. We'd all experienced our own kind of trauma from that night.

Each night that week, Brandon laid next to me until I fell asleep. Either I was growing used to the feelings of anxiety, or they were lessening with time, because I hadn't had any breakdowns where he'd been encouraged to pull energy to calm me down. Mostly, we quietly shared giggling conversations in the dark as he told me about some of the pop culture things of his day, or we made fun of the others in my life.

I did go to visit Stephanie a few more times, but there wasn't much progress to make on that front while we waited for the necromancer master to come back to town. Caleb came with me and assured us they were doing all they could and that some things just took time.

Stephanie and I shared a mutual look about Caleb's sense of time being way more skewed in his old age than it was in reality.

On Friday evening, Dad took us out for dinner to celebrate my birthday with just him.

"I'm sorry I won't be at your party tomorrow," Dad said around a mouthful of lo mein noodles. "I've got to get some assignments prepared and submitted before Thanksgiving break."

I shrugged and ate a small bite of rice. "It's okay."

"She's going to be so busy with all of her boyfriends there that she won't have time to breathe, let alone entertain her dad." Trina grinned over her glass of soda.

I shook my head but couldn't fight the small smile that appeared. "I don't have a boyfriend. They're just friends."

Dad's salt and pepper eyebrows popped up in concern, and he put down his fork. "How many boyfriends are we talking here, T?"

I rolled my eyes.

Trina grinned. "At least three. You've met most of them. There's Caleb," she used her fingers to count, "and Noah, and this new guy, Gryphin. And of course, Brandon."

I gave her a sharp look. "Ugh, none of them are my boyfriends. If anything, Caleb is *your* boyfriend. Weren't you guys supposed to go to Homecoming together?"

As any good sibling knows, the best way to deflect an attack from a parent is redirection.

"Oh, really?" Dad turned his gaze to Trina.

"Well, we all know how that turned out, don't we?" Trina frowned and poked at some chicken on her plate.

"Actually, no. *We* don't all know. I want to know," Dad said looking back and forth between us.

Trina sighed. "It's just that things went a bit chaotic and his…"

"Family," I supplied helpfully.

"Right. His family. They kept him home and wouldn't let him come, but then…some other stuff happened and…"

"It's just a bunch of high school drama stuff." I waved it off with my hand in the air. "It's not a big deal. Their date got ruined is all, but that doesn't mean they can't try again. Why don't you guys try again?"

She looked up from her plate long enough to glare at me in annoyance. "I suppose one could say he's a bit too old for me."

"What? How old are we talking here?" Dad narrowed his eyes.

I chuckled, unable to help it. "Not much. Technically, he's a senior just the same as you, right Trina?"

She grunted and shoveled noodles and vegetables into her mouth.

Dad's shoulders relaxed, and he sat back in his chair and picked up his fork. "If he's in the same grade as you, he can't be that much older, right?"

"Exactly." I nodded.

What neither of us wanted to point out to him is that he had indeed met Caleb before. We'd been sitting down for a similar dinner. When he'd shown up, blood had been on his shirt, and he'd looked distraught, both things that were quite out of his character. It wouldn't be good to remind Dad of *that* first impression.

Conversation beyond that was mundane and the usual things. We fed him information about school and classes and different stuff that had happened that made us sound like a completely normal and ordinary family.

All of us avoided the topic of Mom except only to say that her photography business was going well, and she was getting lots of clients.

I ate just enough not to raise concerns from either of them, and since I hadn't eaten much the entire day before, I hoped the calories wouldn't add any fat to my slimming thighs. It had taken weeks, but I was finally getting closer to the weight that I wanted to be.

Saturday morning dawned cloudy and dark, a sign I should have cancelled the whole day and hid under my bed. Unfortunately, my powers didn't extend to seeing into the future.

Which, after thinking about it, probably wouldn't have been super fun anyway.

Mom, Trina, and I went to the pancake house after a decent amount of sleeping in. I used to love going to get pancakes on summer or Saturday mornings when I was younger. But, in the last year or so, I'd grown to dread it. However, my family knew that I used to love the trip so much that if something drastic happened, like me not eating my food, they'd surely get suspicious.

So when the warm syrupy smell of the restaurant hit me and my stomach grumbled angrily, I decided to give in a bit. As the waitress placed the full plate of fluffy strawberry pancakes in front of me, I lost all the rest of my self-restraint.

Trina even gave me a look after a few minutes of stuffing my face. Mom only seemed pleased with my appreciation of our pancake breakfast.

"Did you invite lots of friends to come over later?" Mom asked as she took a bite of her bacon.

I shrugged one shoulder. "I invited the ones I wanted to come over, but I didn't feel like having the entire high school squished into our house. A vase or two would be bound to be broken."

One side of Mom's mouth tipped down in sympathy. "I'm sorry we have to have it at the house."

"At least we'll be able to tell if someone is secretly a vampire if they try to enter our house and can't," Trina said.

"Hah, wouldn't that be funny to find out someone at school we had no suspicion of was actually a vampire?" I grinned thinking about how funny it would be for that witch's spell to stop Andrea in her tracks.

Of course, if she were a vampire, Noah probably wouldn't have been defending her so much. Plus, he'd insinuated something else was happening, and I was willing to guess that something was probably more secret necromancer knowledge I didn't yet understand.

"A year ago, I would have laughed to find out Caleb was a vampire," Trina muttered to her sausage.

"At least he's one of the good ones?" I gave her a sympathetic smile. She shrugged.

Mom studied her oldest daughter for a second and then turned back to me. "There might be good things about him, dear, but a vampire is still a vampire. It's like having a pet tiger around. They might not have attacked you yet, but they're still a dangerous animal. It's smart for Trina to be wary of him."

"And even if he does manage to never attack you, he'll outlive you easily. You'll be an old lady before he's even gained a wrinkle, which is what apparently happened to Gran. What I wouldn't give to hear their full story," I said thoughtfully.

"I think I'm good with not hearing it." Trina frowned.

"At least until you get over your crush, right?" I grinned while Mom gave me a chiding look.

"Speaking of crushes, is that ghost here with you today?" Trina said with a taunting bob to her head.

"He's not, I'll have you know."

Mom took a sip of her coffee. "Why not? It seems like he's been going everywhere with you lately."

Guilt welled up inside me as I thought of his nightly visits she didn't know about combined with the feeling that I was kind of using him only when I needed his help.

"We've decided to back things up a bit." I poked at the last strawberry on my plate. "Things were getting a bit...intense."

Trina scrunched her eyebrows together. "What does that mean?"

"How do things get intense with a ghost?" Mom's look was less confusion and more concern.

I really wished I hadn't said that last part.

"Right... Well, it can't, obviously. I just mean we were getting too dependent on each other, is all. I've got to focus on homework and getting good grades and my real-life friends, and he's got to...focus on crossing over and all that ghostly stuff."

Trina narrowed her eyes with a frown while Mom stared at me with her knowing-everything-because-she's-a-mom look.

My cheeks flushed under their scrutiny.

"It kind of sounds like you dumped him," Trina finally said.

"Maybe she was right to." Mom went back to eating her pancake.

Trina looked back and forth between us. "How can you say that after all he did for us?"

She was referring, of course, to his help in their rescue and escape from Caleb's former vampire queen. Without Brandon's help, they wouldn't have known where to go or even if I was alive. Trina had been brave enough to take off her necklace, thanks to the previous suspicion that I was in contact with ghosts due to my super-odd behavior of talking to myself, and she'd spent a few harrowed hours running from vampires with Brandon's quirky comments following her around.

I suppose she knew him best, second only to me, of course.

Sadness pulled at me, and I dropped my head. "We've agreed to keep working on ghost projects. We still spend plenty of time together, it's just that we both realize we need some distance before things get...well, you know."

"Poor kid. It must be hard being a ghost," Mom said.

"Does he even want to cross over? Have you tried to help him work on that? Do you even *want* to help him work on that?" Trina asked, probably getting as close to the ghost topic as she was going to.

"I've tried! He won't tell me hardly anything about his life. All I know is that he lost his three siblings before he died, and it really crushed him, which I totally understand."

Mom and Trina shared a look before turning their gazes back to me across the table.

"Even if he did tell you what he needs to cross over, would you help him do it and risk losing his friendship?" Mom asked, getting to the angry truth at the center.

I poked my strawberry some more. "I'd like to think I'd help him do whatever it is that he wanted. He deserves a choice to do whatever he wants with his...not...life."

The topic put a downer on the rest of the meal, but we were able to work past it and talk about happier things, mostly thanks to a few funny stories Mom shared from her photography adventures with toddlers.

After breakfast, we headed to the mall where we shopped around, got fancy coffee drinks, and eventually ended up at a salon for mani-pedis.

At first, it had been surreal talking to my mom and sister about ghost, vampire, and werewolf problems, but as time went on, we all got used to it. I updated them on the wolf situation and how we saw the ghost wolves, omitting of course the terror of being so close to an angry werewolf or even details about how giant a werewolf actually was. I explained about Mr. Tyler thinking a witch might help us and about how he'd find one that he knew. I was careful not to give them a reason to think I'd started developing my own little crush on some certain gentlemanly werewolf, but I did casually drop that he'd agreed to come to my party.

Mom seemed to accept it all with only a few strained winces, but Trina remained quiet through most of it. I had expected her to give me the third degree about Gryphin's good looks or how Caleb reacted to having to take me to the bridge to talk to Stephanie. Instead, after I thought about it for a bit on the car ride home, she was probably thinking about her own life and how she would be going through such chaotic, weird stuff if she embraced her powers and started trying to help the dead things around us.

I didn't blame her for wanting to keep her life as normal as possible, even if she still had to listen to my craziness.

Chapter 18

Around four o'clock, I came down the hallway and into the front room wearing my new birthday outfit. We'd decided to go for a more casual look since a big fluffy dress celebrating a day all about me was not really my style. Instead, we'd gone with an autumn-colored floral skirt that came to almost my knees, a white lace top, and a jean jacket.

While I'd been getting dressed, Mom had transformed the front room. The couch and chairs were all pushed to the wall. The dining table had been covered with a plastic purple tablecloth and displayed several bowls of junk food, trays of vegetables, finger sandwiches, and fruit. A cooler full of ice and drinks sat on the island counter in the middle of the kitchen. She'd strung purple streamers all over the walls and tied several balloons on chairs around the room.

It wasn't a fun bowling alley with black lights, loud music, and fresh pizza, but it was pretty good, all things considered.

"Hey, sweetie. What do you think?" Mom grinned from the kitchen and gestured with a hand towel.

"It looks really good, actually." I walked over and hugged her. As I breathed in her comforting vanilla scent, I closed my eyes for a second. "I'm sorry I gave you a hard time about not wanting to do it at home. I know things are harder now, but this place looks really great. Even the vampires won't have anything to complain about."

We shared a laugh at my dumb joke.

"Listen, before everyone gets here, I want to give you my present first." Mom tugged on my hand and pulled me to the couch.

Sitting on an end table also pushed to the side was an ornate box I hadn't noticed before. It was small, about the size of two fists put together, and carved beautifully. Mom grabbed it off the table, and we studied it together. Small designs were etched into the wood. Some were abstract, and I had no idea what the meaning or purpose was, but a prominent carving set right under the metal clasp.

I was startled by the carving and leaned in closer in case my eyes weren't seeing it right.

"Yes, I believe that's exactly what you think it is," Mom said with a smile.

It was a wavy form with two eyes shaped in such a way that they looked haunted and tormented. Two arms stretched out from the carving that ended in wicked, sharp fingers, and it didn't have any legs. Definitely a ghost.

"Where did you get this? What is it?"

"It's a funny story, actually. A few years after we sold your grandma's house, I got a strange phone call from the new owners. They said they were redoing the backyard and had found something that looked like an important family heirloom. I stopped by, and this is what they gave me." She paused and ran a soft finger over the top of the box. "The funny thing is that it's mentioned in the will, but no one could understand it. When I saw the box for the first time, I didn't even know what it was until I thought about it on the drive home."

Thank goodness we hadn't decided to go dig up that backyard yet. We obviously wouldn't have found what we were looking for, and we'd probably have been caught and fined. I didn't need all that on my record.

"Okay, so what is it?"

"I don't know. So far all I can tell is it's a pretty cool box. The will had strict instructions that were super vague at the same time. It only said something about a family heirloom inside a box that was to be given to the next seeing person in our family. At the time, I had no idea what that meant. I mean, I knew Mom had special powers to see things, but I didn't know she was called a Seer or anything like that. It was worded in such a way that we couldn't understand until a Seer was made known. I think that would be you, dear. I wanted to save it for you until a special day. Today seemed like one of those."

"Should I open it now?" My fingers trembled as I took the box from her and brought it closer to study more of the small carvings. "What if there's like a curse on it or something? I've recently learned about a whole list of things that could potentially be cursed."

"Do you really think your grandma would give you something cursed?"

"Yeah, okay, hopefully not."

Trina bounced down the hallway wearing her new clothes and smelling like hairspray and perfume. "You guys ready to party?"

Feeling weird that I got a secret creepy gift having to do with ghosts and Trina didn't, I quickly stashed the box behind me. "Absolutely. People should be coming any minute now."

Mom stood, perhaps sensing what I was feeling. "Come help me break up the ice some more before they get here."

I flashed her a grateful look before running back to my bedroom and stashing the box underneath my pillow.

The doorbell rang with our first guest before I'd finished coming back to the hallway. "I'll get it!"

Behind the door were Addy and Emma. They were both baring brightly wrapped presents and cheerful smiles.

"Happy birthday!" they both said at the same time.

"Oh, thank you! I'm so glad you guys could come!" I found the words were true as I ushered them inside.

And thus started the parade of guests, some later than fashionably late, but even Caleb showed up in the end.

Brandon popped up shortly after Addy and Emma, and I wasn't sure if I'd summoned him, or he'd decided he did want to come. All it took was a fleeting thought that I kind of missed having his dumb snarky comments, and there he was. It had either gotten super easy to summon him or he'd popped in coincidentally at the same time.

Perhaps it didn't matter whichever way it happened.

"Hey, birthday girl. Did you get your birthday spankings yet?" Brandon said as he appeared next to me while Addy and Emma were busy talking to my sister for a second.

"No, and even if I approved of that weird tradition, I wouldn't let you do it." I gave him what I hoped was a subtle side-eye while talking quietly.

"Maybe I'll just have to sneak some in when you're not expecting it."

I didn't even need to look at him to know what kind of grin was on his face. The flirty comments might have been annoying, and sometimes downright weird, but I couldn't deny the little flutters I felt in my chest or the smile that wanted to peek out on my face.

Noah arrived next, only two minutes late. His face was flushed, and his hair was wet as it hung into his eyes. He wore a slightly wrinkled polo shirt and a pair of jeans.

"I had to rush here after practice. Sorry I'm late! Happy birthday!" he said and handed me a gift bag.

"It's fine. You're not late." I smiled and noticed a lack of fluttery nerves in my stomach at the sight of him. Perhaps my crush was fading slightly, even though I still found his facial features quite pleasant.

He leaned in for a hug, which kind of surprised me. Hopefully, I covered up my surprise by hugging him back, trying not to inhale much of his cologne and freshly showered scent.

"Oh yeah, now we can get this party really started. Do you think he'll let us play pin the arm on the zombie?" Brandon grinned as he leaned against the wall.

Trina and Mom came up to greet Noah politely, leaving me to look outside and spot Gryphin's van pulling up.

When the werewolf came in, his large presence filled up the front room, and suddenly my house felt smaller than it had a few minutes before. He was wearing a red plaid button-up shirt and nice jeans, ones without any holes in them even. His silver hair was styled neatly, but that curl had sneaked out as if determined to be free.

Gryphin's smile added to the excitement I already feeling. "Happy birthday, Hanna. Thanks for inviting me, and you must be Ms. Sanchez. Your home is lovely."

My mom may have blushed as they shook hands. "Thank you. And you are Gryphin, I assume? We've heard so much about you."

"Well, you mustn't believe everything you hear," he said with an amused smile.

Mom giggled in a way that made her sound several years younger.

I introduced him to everyone around the room which included Addy, Emma, Trina, and Noah. Brandon was there but I wasn't about to introduce a ghost while everyone was together, even though they all knew about him.

Which was totally surreal.

What was the social protocol for hosting a fairly large group of people who all happened to know a weird secret about me being able to see ghosts? I had no idea and was only making everything up as I went along.

"You really did invite all your boyfriends," Brandon said with an eye roll.

Noah gave Gryphin a visual appraisal, and his mouth tightened into not quite a frown. The tension was eased by a cheerful laugh from Addy in response to some joke Trina had made, but Noah's intense gaze didn't fade.

If I had thought the tension between them was uncomfortable, it was doubly so when Caleb finally showed up.

Not even bothering to knock, he opened the door and strode right in. "I hear this is the place to be today."

Leave it to the vampire to show up in leather pants and a dark V-neck shirt that opened enough to reveal a few curls of chest hair and defined muscle.

Trina was the first to recover, and she stepped up to greet him. "Arriving fashionably late so we all have to stare at you? Seems like your style."

Caleb's dark eyes softened as he looked down at my much shorter sister. "My date ditched me at the last second, so I had to debate with myself in the mirror for several minutes before I could convince myself to come."

"Oh, feeling a bit shy, are we?" Trina's flirty grin amused me, but I figured the whole room didn't feel like sitting there and watching them make eyes at each other.

"I'm so glad you could make it, Caleb," I said, coming up to them. "I hope you're empty-handed because my gift is too big to fit in through the door."

"Or just in my pocket," he said with a vampire canine look before pulling a small box out of his pocket.

"Thank you," I said, taking it to put with the others. Hopefully it wasn't an engagement ring or something equally as stilly.

Caleb's eyes moved over the rest of the room. When they rested on Gryphin, they narrowed slightly, but he didn't even pause to look at Noah before heading to the kitchen and greeting my mom. Guess he was over the whole necromancer thing.

"Why do all the boys insist on flirting with you in front of me?" Brandon said with a huff. "It's like they don't even know I'm here. How rude."

I shook my head slightly and gave Trina a reassuring smile as she watched Caleb's long stride towards the kitchen.

After we did some, perhaps unneeded, introductions, Mom started with a couple of fun games. Thankfully Addy and Emma were great at participating and getting the others to play as well.

At some point, Caleb pulled me to the side. Music was playing loudly from Trina's phone that was hooked to a speaker. I had let her pick the music to avoid our usual fight about how her taste was better than mine.

Everyone was chatting and eating cake after that group singing where everyone makes the birthday person feel totally awkward and unsure of what facial expression to wear while they get sung at. Personally, I always felt that was the worst thing about birthdays, spankings aside. Thankfully the presents kind of make up for it.

"I've been thinking about your question," Caleb said quietly as we stood near the drink cooler.

"What question? I ask so many of them even I can't keep track."

Brandon meandered over to us, the snoopy ghost that he was. "Oh, is this a secret clandestine meeting in the middle of a birthday party with people all over who could easily overhear?"

"About the ghost wolves. I was sorting through some memories and came across something that your gran talked about with me."

"You make it sound like your brain is just a room full of filing cabinets."

He shrugged a muscled shoulder. "In a way, it kind of is. Do you know how hard it is to keep track of three hundred years of memories?"

"No," I said flatly.

"Right. Anyway, Linda mentioned them one time."

"What did she say? How much of them is the wolf and how much is human? Is there a way I can communicate with them somehow?"

"Good job providing a solid example of how many questions you ask." Brandon gave me an appreciative nod and a thumbs-up.

"Apparently there is a way to turn them back into a person, still in ghost form, of course."

"Let me guess." I took a sip of my diet soda. "We need a witch."

Caleb's eyebrows rose. "Okay, maybe you already know this already."

I sighed. "No, just that Mr. Tyler is already looking for one. He must know something of what you're about to say. Tell me," I frowned into the soda can, "why I need a witch."

"Linda had said she'd needed to talk with a ghost wolf, similarly to what you're facing now, and she had a witch friend who was able to make a potion."

"Gran was friends with a witch?" I asked, unable to keep from thinking about Rose.

"How does a ghost drink a real-life potion?" Brandon asked, getting to the more important bit of the information.

"Not all witches are evil," Caleb said with a twitch of his mouth. "She was actually a very good friend. They helped each other many times over the years."

"I guess it would come in handy to have a friend like that." I frowned and then glanced at Brandon who had his arms crossed over his chest, tapping his foot expectantly. "How does a ghost drink a real-life potion?"

Caleb glanced around, and I followed his gaze. Addy and Noah were in some kind of deep conversation on the couch while Trina, Gryphin, Emma, and my mom were all sitting at the table chatting, their plates mostly smears of melted ice cream with a few crumbles of cake mixed in.

Satisfied no one was giving us too much attention, he turned back to me. "Someone has to die with it in their pocket, and preferably this someone has to be certain not to cross over immediately but to become a ghost and stick around. Plus, their haunt needs to be obviously nearby...or it would be if you didn't have your Seer powers of summoning a ghost."

The information was shocking enough that both Brandon and I stared at Caleb, mouths open slightly ajar, and eyes wide with disbelief.

Caleb nodded. "Yup. It's that crazy."

"What—What are we even supposed to do with this?" I finally said, remembering we were in a room full of people who might look at me any second and decide to come find out what was wrong.

"That's beyond crazy. Are we supposed to kill someone? Who would agree to do that?" Brandon shook his head. "There's got to be another way."

Caleb shrugged. "Hey, I'm as lost as you. As far as I can remember, that's the last she talked about it to me. I have no idea if they tried it or not, and if they did try it, I have no idea if it worked."

"That's all very helpful." Brandon shook his head.

"And do you think Mr. Tyler knows all of this and is ready to sacrifice someone to be a part of it? That doesn't sound like him." I chewed on my lip and looked over at Gryphin who paused in his conversation and shot me a friendly, albeit curious, smile.

"You're right. It doesn't sound like him. Maybe he's got another plan?" Caleb asked, following my gaze.

"He better. I'm not going to ask anyone to die so I can get a potion to a werewolf ghost. I doubt any kind of information is worth all of that."

Trina came over then and I was grateful to her for stopping our morbid conversation.

For the rest of the party, my mind was reeling with thoughts about how I could do what I needed to do without killing anyone to do it. Nothing came to mind except that Gryphin's pack was just going to have to handle their alpha's anger and grief on their own. If they couldn't, well, then I guess someone would challenge his dad for the pack and he might die. I had done as much as I could for them.

There had to be a line somewhere, and I was pretty sure we'd found it.

Toward the end of the party, I found myself being tugged outside into the backyard by Noah. We'd been using the backyard for extra sitting space even though it was a bit chilly, but it was empty for the moment.

"I've been waiting all night to spend a few minutes with you," Noah said as he shut the door behind me.

"Oh, should I be worried? Am I in trouble?" I tried making jokes hoping that it would chase away some of the weirdness I was feeling—nervous and awkward combined with a worry as to why he'd want us to be alone together.

"Only if being beautiful is a crime." Noah's smile changed the comment from possibly coming out as a joking quip into more of an honest compliment.

I sighed. "Noah... Aren't you—"

He held up his index finger and barely touched it to my lips. The sensitivity of my skin brushed past the ridges on his fingertip, sending thrills through my body. "Let's just not worry about anything else right now, okay? It's just you and me."

I didn't mention that a ghost might follow me outside at any second and that, frankly, I was surprised he wasn't out there already. Maybe he'd gotten distracted by something shiny.

"Why?" I breathed the word past his finger.

"Because I've been thinking about doing this for months."

He moved his finger past my mouth and extended the others, putting his palm onto my cheek, leaving this thumb to caress my bottom lip.

"Doing what?" I croaked out past the lump in my throat.

"This." He moved his thumb and leaned in to kiss me.

The first thing I thought was how warm his lips were compared to the other kisses I'd had. The second was that he tasted faintly of soda.

One part of me wanted to kiss him back, bury my hand into his hair, and push him closer toward me.

But another part of me, a bigger more assertive part, grew annoyed.

"What are you doing?" I pushed him away.

"What are *you* doing?" He said as he took a few stumbling steps backward.

"I'm standing up for myself, finally. Look, you can't have it both ways—the hot cheerleader in public and then be sneaking kisses from the weirdo ghost girl in secret."

"Weirdo ghost girl? Is that how you think I see you?" His eyes were wide, full of panic.

"Isn't it? You just want everyone to think you and Andrea are together like you're some hot couple."

His shoulders slumped. "That's not it at all. I promise. Don't you believe me that I have to be with her to help her, and it has nothing to do with my feelings? If there was nothing else going on, I'd have left her a long time ago and have asked you to be my girlfriend."

"Yeah, right. And no, I still don't believe you. What could be so important that you have to be with her all the time? What is more important than your personal feelings?"

He ran his long fingers through his hair in frustration. "I'm really not supposed to talk about this."

I folded my arms over my chest. "If you can't trust me with the secrets, then what's even the point?"

"What? Wait—"

I didn't give him time to finish as I walked back into the house, fuming.

Chapter 19

Gryphin was the last person to leave the party, and I walked him out to his van. Caleb had left pretty early, but there was a good bet he was still hanging around, at least within hearing range, anyway.

Trina and Mom stayed inside cleaning up from what we'd all decided was a decently successful night, even without the bowling alley's black lights and the loudspeakers.

Brandon also stayed behind. As I stepped out of the door to follow Gryphin to the van, Brandon sighed from where he was sitting on the couch. I gave him a look that I hoped he could read as something like, "I'll be right back."

He just sighed again.

"Thanks for coming, Gryph. I hope you had fun."

He nodded, the curl on his forehead bobbing slightly. "Oh yes, I did. Thank you for inviting me. It's not often I get to hang out with others outside the commune."

"I bet. Before you go, I wanted to check with you if Mr. Tyler had found a witch yet or not."

Gryphin leaned back against the van and crossed one ankle over the other. "He was just telling me this morning that he's meeting with one tomorrow. We weren't sure if we should invite you or not since we're not sure how much we want the witch to know, or even if this witch will be able to help us."

I nodded. "I could just be there, and we don't have to tell her what I am. I could just be a friend."

"We definitely need to keep your powers a secret."

"Caleb would say there are too many people who know about me already."

"I'd agree with that. Do you want to come then?"

"I'd like to learn more about what witches do. Anything I can learn more about them, the better."

Rose's elegant face floated inside my mind, and I wondered if the witch we were dealing with the next day knew anything about her. However, even if she did, it would be weird to ask about Rose randomly, and I definitely didn't want word getting back to Rose that I was looking for her.

Or maybe I did as it could draw her out, and I could finally confront her.

Ew. Confrontation.

"Okay, you can come. We'll just say you're a friend and leave it at that."

"Great. I'll see you tomorrow."

He smiled and stood straight. "I'm looking forward to it."

A swirl of awkwardness floated in between us, and I tried to wipe it away with a smile. "Yeah, it should be fun, or at least it will be good to get closer to some answers, even if we might not like those answers."

"What do you mean?" He leaned in a little closer and narrowed his eyes.

The wind pushed his wild and free scent in my direction, and it made me think of wildflowers bobbing in the breeze.

I shrugged it off, trying to play it cool. "Oh, I don't know. I'm not super comfortable working with witches. I feel like there's always a catch somewhere."

"True enough." He backed up a bit and smiled warmly. "Alright, well, see you tomorrow."

Grateful—and also maybe disappointed—that I hadn't had to fend off a second kiss that night, I waved.

Later, after I'd helped finish cleaning up the house, I brought all my gifts to the bedroom and set them on my desk. I hadn't had the birthday party for the sole purpose of getting gifts, but it was a bonus of being able to hang out with everyone.

"You got a good haul there, even if I'm not quite sure what all of it is," Brandon said, following me into my room, the rule about him staying out long disregarded since he nearly spent every night in my bed.

"Life has evolved some since you were around." I grinned as I read the back of the box of the smartwatch Caleb had gotten for me. If it had come from any other friend, I would have refused such a nice gift, but as it was from him and his hoard of vampire money, I didn't feel too bad.

"I got to admit smartphones and the Google are pretty cool." Brandon spread his arms out and fell backward onto my bed.

"I just can't imagine life without being able to have a phone all the time. That must have been weird." I put down the box, shut the bedroom door in case Mom or Trina walked by, and sat on the bed next to Brandon's transparent arm.

He shrugged. "We didn't know any different. We managed."

"I suppose you would have to. So want to see something cool?"

He sat up partially, propping himself up on his elbows. His mischievous smile framed his question, and I didn't have to guess what he was implying. "How cool are we talking here?"

"Ugh, boys. No, nothing gross. Get your mind out of the gutter."

"I can't help it. I think it's stuck in there."

I gave him a flat look and then turned to retrieve the weird box Mom had given me only a few hours earlier. "Do you remember the mysterious item Gran had tried to tell me about before she left?"

Furrowing his eyebrows, he sat up all the way and leaned in closer to study the box in my hands. "This is what she had buried in her yard?"

"Yes. The new owners of the house found it and thought it important enough to get it back to my mom. She wanted to give it to me because she figured since Gran and I shared the same powers—"

"And Trina is still in denial about them," Brandon added.

"Right, that too. She thought I should have it."

"While I wish you were going to show me something else, I have to admit that this is pretty cool. What's inside?" Brandon tried to touch the intricate designs on the top of the box but couldn't make contact.

"I don't know. Honestly, I'm a little scared to open it."

"Want me to stick my head out the window and holler for your vampire bodyguard who is bound to be stalking around nearby?"

Laughing, I shook my head. "No, I don't think that will be necessary."

"There could simply be nothing in there."

"Then why would Gran spend her last words on trying to tell me about it?"

"Maybe it's like a box where you can stuff bad ghosts. I'll be naughty if you want, and you can put me in time out." He batted his eyelashes over doe-like innocent eyes.

I rolled my eyes. "You're almost as bad as Caleb can be."

He kept batting his eyes innocently.

"No, I'm sure it's not that. I'm just worried I'll let a curse out or something if I open it."

"Oh, Jumanji!"

"What?"

"Maybe it'll suck *us* in!"

"Now I really don't want to open it." I lowered the box onto my bed and snatched my fingers back.

Brandon laughed and shook his head. "I'm sure it's fine. Gran wouldn't have given us something dangerous."

"Us?"

He tilted his head to the side with a pleasant smile. "We're in this together, girl, whether you like it or not."

"Right..." I looked back down at the box. "Fine. Let's do it."

Without giving myself any more time to doubt, I pushed down the metal latch and raised the lid. No curses came out, no angry ghosts wailed as they clawed their way to freedom, and we did not get sucked in, thank goodness.

Instead, nestled inside some soft red fabric was a pair of steampunk-looking glasses. They had thin golden frames with delicate golden circles swirling around the glass lenses and down the earpieces.

"Glasses? Sure, they're super cool looking and everything, but all this," Brandon gestured to the box, "for a pair of glasses?"

"Obviously they're important."

"Put them on and see what happens."

I obliged and peered out through them. "Everything looks the same."

Brandon bobbed his head back and forth and gave me a wave. "You can still see me?"

"Of course."

He shrugged. "Just checking to make sure they weren't like the necklace your sister has."

"The golden metal does seem similar. Maybe they come from the same place?"

As I spoke, memories flitted across my mind. "Wait..." I pulled the glasses off and studied them with creased eyebrows. "This couldn't be what that woman was looking for, could it?"

"What woman?"

"The woman who killed Gran. I can remember she was looking for something. Maybe these are it!" The more I spoke, the more my heart picked up pace.

Brandon, however, frowned. "That's not good, if it's really them, I mean."

"Why not?"

His now blue eyes that I knew to be pure green kept bouncing between my face and the glasses. "Because they got her killed."

Frowning, I closed the earpieces and placed them carefully back into the box. "Oh, right."

"Maybe this isn't that and it's just something else? Without Gran here to tell us, we can't know for sure."

I nodded and kept staring at them. The beat of my heart combined with that super annoying logical voice inside my head insisted that this had to have been what the woman was looking for, though. There was nothing else it could have been. Now all I had to do was figure out why.

Chapter 20

Mid-morning on Sunday, I updated Trina and Mom about Gryphin and Mr. Tyler's progress with the witch, leaving out, of course, any concerns about what we were doing or if it could be dangerous.

Mom seemed to be more assured that I would be okay when I mentioned that Mr. Tyler would also be there. Trina appeared to be less concerned about my safety, more so that time had probably made her feel more comfortable with it rather than how much she cared about me. At least, that's what I told myself as she kept focus on her phone instead of our conversation.

Shortly after that, I went outside to the front porch and summoned Brandon. "Ready to go see if a witch can help us go wolf hunting?"

"No." He frowned and put his hands into the large pockets of his jeans.

I stifled a teasing grin. "I'm sure the other ghosts can't hurt you, even wolf ghosts. What are they going to do? You're already dead."

His eyebrows pulled into a glare. "I know. Maybe it's just not my cup of tea to hang out with wolves all day, especially ones who look at you like you're their next snack."

"Ugh, gross."

Brandon shrugged, unapologetic. "Well, he does."

"You could stay home, you know."

"And lose out on time with you? No thanks."

My eyes softened, and I smiled. "I'd like to have you around too."

Gryphin pulled up in his van, and even though he knew I was expecting him, the routine had become familiar so it would have been totally fine for him to sit in his van and honk the horn or send me a text to say he was there. Instead, Gryphin being Gryphin, he got out of the car and walked toward me.

"Well, howdy!" A big smile beamed on his face.

"Cheery this morning?" I teased but didn't resist returning his smile.

"Ugh, this is just as terrible as I thought it would be," Brandon grumbled.

Gryphin shrugged while we walked toward his van, oblivious to the ghost following behind. "Seems like a good day for smiling. I get to hang out with a beautiful girl, perhaps get some more answers for my dad, and there aren't any school classes today. Seems like a good day, indeed."

A swirl of trepidation whirled inside my stomach. I hadn't told him everything Caleb had told me about the possible witch's spell, and I worried about what we were walking into. I couldn't decide if it was better to warn him to stave off any hope he might have or to keep my mouth shut in case the witch came up with a different way to help the pack that might be a lot more attainable.

Gryphin opened the door for me again, somehow moving faster than I could track with my eyes, and grinned at me as I got inside.

Shaking my head as he climbed into his chair on the driver's side, I said, "Thank you for calling me beautiful."

Brandon groaned in the back seat behind me. "Can we at least not do the whole flirting thing?"

"Who says I was talking about you?" His grin told me he was teasing as he turned on the van, and we hit the road.

"Hopefully he was talking about some other girl that's going to be there. Maybe the witch will be super hot," Brandon said while he frowned and stared out the window.

It was a pleasant ride out to the commune, despite Brandon's grumpy huffs. As the town flashed by, my thoughts dipped slightly into sadness. If we got the answers we needed and were able to help the pack, this could possibly be our last trip out there together.

Stealing a glance at the wolf while his focus was on the road and singing along to some old song on the radio I didn't recognize, a pang of sorrow threaded through my chest. His forest brown eyes bounced around as he watched the road for dangers, the silver curl of hair bobbed as he swayed his head to the music, and his big hands gripped the steering wheel and gearshift confidently.

Being with Gryphin felt unlike being with anyone else. Caleb was so intense, and it just felt dark whenever he talked, perhaps due to being a vampire, perhaps due merely to his brooding personality. With Brandon, I felt a lot lighter, playful, and free to be myself, but there were moments of darkness when he let his guard down or grew super grumpy for some reason. Something deep stirred inside my ghostly friend, and I was afraid to both find out what it was or never know.

Gryphin, however, was free and relaxed. He seemed to take life as it came, had a healthy respect for others, and was able to live in the moment. It was obvious that out of the two of us, I was the one who worried the most.

I was going to miss being around him.

When we got to the commune, the ride had felt much shorter than the other times he'd driven me out. I glanced one more time at him while he maneuvered the van into a parking spot, and he flashed me a happy smile. I decided then to take a page from his book and just live in the moment.

It wouldn't do to dwell on future sadness. What was coming would come.

As I stepped out of the van, Gryphin almost making it in time to open the door for me, I noticed a few different cars were sitting in the parking area. Mr. Tyler's truck was there with some others, but there was one in particular that stood out from the rest—a bright red Ferrari with shiny rims and the top up.

Gryphin saw my line of sight and chuckled. "It appears our witch likes to travel in style."

"She's already here?"

Brandon whistled and walked over to the car for a quick inspection. "I would love to have one of these."

"She must be. No one else in the commune drives that car." Gryphin gestured for me to walk ahead, toward the path leading to the heart of the werewolf village.

"Honestly, I'm surprised the pack let an outsider know where the commune is and let them drive up to it like that."

"It is unusual," Gryphin said with one more glance at the bright car. "Perhaps this one is a friend of the pack or knows about us already."

"I guess werewolf packs aren't as secret in the occult world as they are in the human world. After all, witches already know you exist." I shrugged.

He nodded and scratched at this stubble, which, if he had shaved that morning, had already grown into a prickly fuzz. I imagined it was quite difficult for a wolf to say clean-shaven.

"That they do, and for the most part, I'd put my bets on a werewolf pack versus a single witch, if it came down to it."

I raised my eyebrows. "Is that something that could happen?"

Brandon jogged to catch up with us. "As awesome as that sounds, it better not happen while you're here."

Gryphin's large shoulder muscles rippled under his t-shirt as he shrugged. "It's happened before. Might happen again."

"Terrifying."

"Don't worry." His grin exposed white, sharp teeth. "We'll keep you safe."

"Thank you?"

He chuckled and the sound alone made me smile.

"They better keep you safe. It's the least they can do for all of this chaos," Brandon said, shaking his head.

As we got closer to the village, I looked up to the sound of crunching gravel and saw Kage walking toward us. "Hey, you two. Billy is showing the arcanist around on a cursory tour so we could wait for you guys to get here. We're supposed to meet in the lodge afterward."

"What's an arcanist? I've never heard that before." I crinkled up my eyebrows, still finding it funny that Mr. Tyler was called "Billy" by some.

Kage turned to walk back with us to the lodge, standing on my other side.

I tried not to feel too much like I was being escorted somewhere.

"I just learned the term for myself today as a gender-neutral word for a person who uses magic," Kage explained with a kind smile. "I suppose I should have known it before now, but I'm not usually hanging out with the magic-user crowd. I tend to run with the furrier types."

I grinned at his description.

"That's cool," Gryphin said with an appreciative nod.

"What's gender-neutral? I'm not sure we had such a term when I was alive." Brandon pulled his face into a thoughtful expression.

I agreed with Gryphin by using a mirroring nod, making a mental note to explain the concept later to Brandon when it wouldn't make me look like a crazy person. "Does the arcanist seem...not evil?"

Kage laughed. "I'm not sure what that means, but they seem like they're eager to help and will want to do it in the best way possible."

I frowned. "I guess that's the best we can hope for, for now."

"Why are you so worried about it? Not all magic users are evil." Kage glanced down at me with well-manicured eyebrows.

"I've just had some not-so-good experiences so far. I thought I was helping a witch do some good, but it turned out I was doing the opposite."

Gryphin gave me a good-natured pat on the back. "It'll be okay."

"It better be."

As we walked toward the lodge, we saw several people out and about going through their routines and daily business. A few ladies were standing in a circle, holding coffee cups, and chatting loudly.

Several men and women walked past us going somewhere else. All of them greeted our group with polite nods, but I couldn't help noticing none of them would look Kage directly in the eye. It must have been a pack thing, and I started to wonder if I was breaking some kind of werewolf rule by freely giving out my eye contact with everyone.

Hopefully, they were more lenient on outsiders.

Kage led us up the stone steps toward the lodge, and I took a second to again appreciate how grand the wooden structure in the middle of the woods was. Memories of being in Gryphin's arms as he'd shown me around that first day threatened to heat my cheeks, but I fought to keep calm and focused on the task at hand.

"I have to say there are a lot less holes in the walls and a lot more order to this little village than I would expect from werewolves. The ones in the movies are always getting violent and smashing things," Brandon said as he looked up and around, not too dissimilar to what I was doing.

As Kage was walking in front, and Gryphin was off to the side a few steps behind me, I allowed myself to offer Brandon, who was walking right next to me, an amused look.

It took a few minutes for my eyes to adjust to the relative dimness after we walked into the building. Everything seemed nearly the same as the last time I'd been there, except there wasn't anyone at the various tables and the large sitting area appeared empty.

Then a familiar voice echoed out through the room as Mr. Tyler walked in from one of the side areas. "There you are, and just in time too. Poor Phoenix here was just getting so bored of listening to my rich, but sonorous, tones."

I rolled my eyes but couldn't help a small smile. Apparently, Mr. Tyler was as much of a jokester here as he was in class.

"Apologies, Billy." Kage gestured us to follow him as Mr. Tyler turned back and went the way he'd come.

Inside one of the many alcoves was a door leading to a small and more intimate room. It was still large enough to hold several people, but a round table took up most of the space, making it feel like a conference room of sorts.

Standing at the back of the room, looking out a large window that displayed more of the village, was a tall person, made even taller by high-heeled boots. They wore pantaloons and a bright floral shirt. Their hair was shaved on one side and was long and curly on the other side, dyed a bright red.

"Salutations!" they said, turning to greet us with a wide smile and bright teeth. "You have such a lovely place here. Do you have to be strictly a werewolf to live here?"

Kage smiled and walked confidently toward them, his hand outstretched. "Thank you for saying so, and thank you for coming to visit. Unfortunately, anyone not a werewolf probably wouldn't enjoy living here, especially on nights of the full moon."

"Sounds like a party to me." They grinned and joined in the handshake wholeheartedly.

"It can be if you can get past all the capricious violence. I'm Kage, second in command here at the Blue Ridge Pack."

Both let go of each other's hand, and the arcanist nodded. "Billy was telling me about you. Pleasure. I'm Phoenix."

Kage smiled and turned to introduce the rest of us. "Here is Gryphin, the son of the alpha, and his friend, Hanna. They're here to see if they can offer any more insight that you may need."

"Nice to meet you. Thank you for coming all this way to help us out." Gryphin also shook their hand with a charming smile.

"Pleasure to be here." The arcanist placed a manicured hand on Gryphin's bicep and squeezed. "Quite a pleasure to be here."

Blushing for the first time I'd ever seen, Gryphin grinned.

"Nice to meet you," I stepped up and offered a hand to shake.

"Oh, how lovely to meet a Seer!" They nearly squealed and vigorously shook my hand.

I glanced at Kage, unsure how to respond.

"Yes, I know what you are. Sorry if it was supposed to be a surprise, dear." They said, letting go of my hand and giving me a kind smile. "It's kind of a hazard of my occupation. Seers just have the brightest aura around."

"For once, I'm glad I'm invisible," Brandon said, still standing in the doorway. "I feel like this person would stare straight into my soul and know all my secrets immediately."

"Can you read everyone's auras?" I asked, my eyes wide with fascination.

"Oh sure! Like Gryphin here, he's got one of the purest auras I've ever seen." They pursed their lips together appraisingly. "His heart is pure as pure can be."

The wolf blushed again and looked down at his worn shoes.

"What about other magic users? Can you see their auras too? Are you able to look at a person and know exactly what they are? Like werewolf or vampire or witch? Or is that something you can only do with Seers since we have such a distinct aura?" The questions poured out of me so quickly, I was unable to stop them.

Mr. Tyler laughed and gestured to the table. "Woah, Hanna. Let's give them a minute to settle in before we ask the hard questions. Please, have a seat. Gryphin, will you come help me gather some stuff from the kitchen? We may be savage wolves, but we can still host an amiable teatime."

Gryphin nodded and followed Mr. Tyler out as the rest of us took a seat at the table. Brandon kept standing near the doorway, leaning against the frame with folded arms.

"I'm sorry to ask all these questions," I said, feeling a bit embarrassed. "I've just been wondering a lot about witches or arcanists or whatever for a while now."

"It's alright, dear." They placed their elbows on the table and rested their chin on their long fingers. "I'm used to getting lots of questions. Am I the first arcanist you've met?"

"Kind of. I did know a witch of sorts who had a store in town. Her name was Rose or...maybe Ann. She kind of helped me with some ghost issues but then disappeared. Do you know her?"

Phoenix tilted their head from side-to-side a few times in thought. "No, I'm not sure that I do. I'm sorry."

My shoulders slumped. "It's okay. I've been trying to find her for a while, but she seems to have disappeared completely. Maybe I imagined her all along."

"She's real, Hanna," Brandon said. "She's just really good at hiding. She's probably done it all her life, and that's a lot considering she's older than even Caleb."

"Oh, dear. I'm sure you'll find her again someday." The arcanist gently patted my shoulder. "Would it help you feel better if I asked around about her? Maybe I can get a lead from the magic community?"

A small smile perked on my lips. "That would be nice."

"We might not want her to know we're looking for her, though." Brandon frowned.

I couldn't reply directly to him right then, but he was voicing concerns I did have about looking for her in the early days. If she knew I knew what she had done was wrong, she might not want to confront me. However, by this point, I was too desperate to find her to right the wrongs that I was willing to risk it.

Mr. Tyler and Gryphin came back to the room bearing a tray of finger sandwiches and two pitchers, one lemonade, the other water.

"How delightful!" Phoenix said, clapping their hands lightly.

"Who would have thought such tough wolves even knew how to make delicate finger sandwiches?" I said, grinning at Gryphin who placed the food on the table like a hospitable server.

He smiled back at me. "We have many talents."

The arcanist laughed while Kage gave Gryphin a raised eyebrow.

After a few minutes of passing around food and pouring drinks, we settled in.

"I've told Phoenix some of why we're here today, but I think we should start from the top," Mr. Tyler said after taking a sip of his drink. "Gryphin, will you do the honors?"

He nodded, put his sandwich down, and told Phoenix about the alpha's grief and how the pack is suffering so much that they needed to try and find as many answers as they could. None of them wanted the alpha to get displaced or murdered, but they also didn't want to keep suffering like this.

"And so Hanna here has agreed to help us track down my stepmom's ghost to see if we can get more insight into what happened to her," Gryphin concluded.

I smiled self-consciously.

Mr. Tyler gave me a kind look and turned back to Phoenix. "She has helped us locate the ghost, possibly, we're not sure."

"Let me guess," Phoenix said with a curl of their lips, "you found a roaming pack of ghost wolves."

"Yes! How did you know?" I nearly bounced out of my seat.

Phoenix laughed. "Well, firstly, because Billy had mentioned y'all needed help with a ghost wolf, and second because that's what happens to dead werewolves. Didn't you know?"

"Right, because I'm the Seer." I pulled my lips back in an awkward grimace. "No, I didn't know. All werewolves turn into roaming wolf ghosts after they die?"

"Well, the ones that don't cross over, of course," Phoenix said.

"Of course. Did you guys know that?" I asked Mr. Tyler, wondering how in all the history of werewolves, they'd never once had a Seer mention something about wolf ghosts.

His bushy eyebrows scrunched together. "Can't say that I've ever heard that."

"I'd be willing to bet my dad knows. It does explain some of the eerie howls I can sometimes hear at night, though," Gryphin muttered, perhaps more to himself than the rest of us.

"Creepy," I said, sitting back in my chair with a frustrated frown.

"So here's the real question." Mr. Tyler leaned forward over the table. "Do you know how to get a ghost wolf to change into a human so Hanna can find out the truth of what happened?"

Phoenix pressed their lips in thought. "There might be a way, but it isn't pretty."

My heart sank as Caleb's words came back to me. Part of me had hoped that Phoenix knew of a different way to help the ghost wolves that didn't involve someone willing to die with a potion in their pocket. Judging from Phoenix's expression, I was sure I knew where this conversation was going.

Gryphin and Kage glanced at each other before Kage asked, "What is it? What's not pretty?"

The arcanist sighed and took a swallow of their lemonade. "I have a feeling Hanna already knows. Perhaps she can explain it to us."

My chest froze for a second before I reminded myself to breathe. "Ugh, yes. I mean, I might? Caleb told me of something he'd heard from my grandmother who was also a Seer. Are you sure you're not some kind of mind reader too?"

Phoenix smiled kindly. "No, dear. I'm just also good at reading people. By the way, you may not want to plan to get into poker playing."

I probably would have laughed if I wasn't so depressed about what I was going to tell them. Glancing at Gryphin first, I turned back to Phoenix. "There is a potion a witch can make that a ghost wolf can drink which will turn them into a ghost human. The bad part is that for the potion to get to the ghost, it's got to be on a person who dies. Then the newly made ghost can give the ghostly potion to the wolf ghost, and then I can talk to her and get all the information we need."

"Well put, m'dear." Phoenix nodded. "Yes, I'm afraid that's the heart of it."

Shocked silence entered the room as the wolves all took turns looking at each other and then me and the arcanist.

"Too bad we can't bring me back, kill me again, and let me handle this. I mean, woo, I'd just be a ghost again," Brandon said while sarcastically waving his hand around in the air.

"Wait a minute!" I stood up from the table and almost spilled my water. "I've got an idea!"

Brandon frowned. "Oops."

Everyone turned to look at me expectantly.

"Well?" Kage said.

"We're going to need a necromancer as well as a magic user. Luckily for us, I happen to know one, or a few, depending." I started pacing around the room, excitement from my idea stopping me from being able to rest.

Phoenix raised one perfect eyebrow. "That could work, I suppose. Honestly, I've never had a Seer's help before so I hadn't considered such a thing, but yes, with all the right players, we might be able to get it to work. Do you have access to a fresh corpse?"

"Someone please tell me what is going on," Kage said, putting deep authority in his voice.

"I do happen to have access to a fresh corpse, and we've already set things in motion to get her ghost put back into her body, thanks to my vampire friend who knew about this little trick necromancers like to keep quiet," I said, the gears in my mind whirling.

Mr. Tyler narrowed his eyes. "I think she's saying we're going to raise a zombie, give it the potion, and kill it again."

"Is it considered murder when the zombie has already recently been dead?" Brandon tapped his lip in thought as, like always, he was asking the important questions.

Kage frowned. "I'm not sure I like this. It feels like we're bringing in a lot of extra people to know pack secrets."

Phoenix shrugged their narrow shoulders. "I'm sorry, dear. I know pack secrets are well guarded, but I don't see another way through this."

Leaning back into his chair, Kage crossed his arms over his chest and frowned. "We cannot let the alpha know what we're up to. Seer or no Seer, he would murder us all."

Gryphin took a deep breath. "Then we'll just have to do this without him knowing. Hopefully, when all this is over, he'll forgive us."

"He'd better or else we'll all be dead," Mr. Tyler said, shaking his head.

Chapter 21

Caleb agreed to take me to see Stephanie again that night. After setting some tentative plans, we'd dismissed our small party at the commune and Gryphin had driven me back home. We'd each been given a homework assignment and my first step was to check in with the potential zombie in question.

"So, tell me the plan again?" Caleb crinkled his forehead as we drove away from my house.

"I'm pretty sure this will work. We'll put Steph back into her body, give her the potion and let her die again. Once the potion is tangible for ghosts, we'll feed it to the wolf we think is Sarah, and Steph can be put back into her body again. No one will get hurt or dead, and we already know Steph has unfinished business so we won't have the risk of killing someone who doesn't turn into a ghost. Plus, she was talking about wanting to help people more, and this gives her a chance to do that."

Caleb gave me an odd look. "And that's the best you came up with?"

I frowned. "I thought it sounded pretty good."

"Sounds complicated. How exactly will you get the wolf to drink the potion? How do you know which wolf is hers and not someone else you accidentally give it to?"

Silence fell onto us like a wet blanket as I fumbled inside my brain trying to answer his questions.

"Right." Caleb chuckled kindly. "It's all coming together."

I slumped my shoulders and rubbed my eyes. "Do you think wolf ghosts can hurt human ghosts? I've seen ghosts touch each other before. It seems possible that a wolf ghost could harm a human ghost."

Pursing his lips in thought, Caleb was quiet as we pulled up to the bridge and he parked alongside the road. "They might touch, but could it harm the human? Can the ghost body be changed? What's the worst that could happen? They are already dead."

I shook my head in frustration as we got out of the car and met each other on the sidewalk. "I have no idea. It's going to be a risk we'll have to take, I guess."

"And you're sure Stephanie is the best candidate for this?"

I shrugged as I headed toward her blue form sitting on the railing of the bridge, her knees tucked into her chest and her eyes staring thoughtfully over the water. "She's the only one, really, so yes. I guess she's the best."

"You could stuff Brandon into a random zombie's body for a moment. Would that work?"

I laughed at the mental image. "He'd probably like that, actually, but it doesn't seem super ethical. Does it?"

Caleb shrugged. "Guess you could use that as a backup plan."

"I don't know… Can the necromancers put a ghost into a body that doesn't belong to that spirit?"

Caleb shrugged. "I'm not sure. It's just that Steph might not want to die again after just getting her body back."

"That's true." I frowned and waved at her ghost as we got within a few feet. "Hey Steph, how's it going?"

Late evening traffic whizzed by us on the busy bridge, stirring my hair every time a car zipped by. The sun had already set as days were getting shorter for the coming winter months. The cold air pecked at my jacket.

"Hey guys," Steph said without her usual gusto.

"Are you feeling okay? You seem kind of down." I stopped to stand next to her while Caleb stood on my other side, leaning back onto the railing and watching the cars drive by.

Steph took a look at me. "I could say the same for you. Is something bothering you guys? Did something happen to my body?"

I smiled and glanced at Caleb awkwardly for a moment. He kept staring and chewing on his lip in thought. Sometimes I forgot he couldn't hear the ghosts because he was capable of doing so many other things.

"No, your body is safe with the order still, as far as I know." I glanced at Caleb again. "Maybe we should check on the status of your body."

Caleb's dark eyebrow rose and turned to look at me. "It's fine. The master will be back any day."

"It strikes me as odd that you have such a good relationship with the order when you and Noah seem to be angry rivals. I thought vampires and necromancers hated each other?"

Stephanie watched our exchange with mildly interested eyes.

Caleb shrugged, grunted, and turned back to stare at the traffic.

"Okay then." I looked back at Steph. "Sounds like your body is fine. Are you excited to go back to it? We'll need to come up with a story of where you've been the past few days, but thanks to Caleb's quick thinking, no one ever saw your body. So instead of dead, you'll just have been missing. Maybe you washed up down the river, and a kind old lady took pity on you and nursed you back to health, but you didn't have your memory for a few days so she didn't know where to find your family for a while."

Stephanie shrugged. "I guess. I've had a lot of time to sit here and think."

"Oh yeah?" I leaned against the railing, facing the water. "About what?"

She shrugged again.

"It's unlike you to be so quiet. Usually, you're bubbling with energy. Are you feeling tired today?"

"Not really. Just death puts life into a different perspective, doesn't it? I'm afraid if I go back... I'll forget what I've learned here and get sucked in again to the shallow and dumb stuff I was so obsessed with during life."

I watched a ripple in the dark water I could only see because it reflected light from the bridge. The circles grew bigger and moved down with the current. "I suppose that is a risk, but the only one who can have power over your choices is you."

"That's what I'm afraid of."

I gave her a small, empathetic smile. "I'll be there to help you. I'm not going anywhere. If you want, I can smack you any time you get distracted."

A small smile perked back at me. "That's very kind of you."

"Listen, I have something weird to ask you."

"What's that?"

I took a breath and hoped I didn't sound too insane. "I need your help. Once you get brought back, I need you to take a potion into the ghost realm and give it to a wolf. After that, I promise we'll bring you back to life again. Do you think you could do that?"

Slowly, she turned away from the water, brought her legs down so they dangled over the rail towards the traffic, and gave me a flat look. "I'm not sure which part I should be more confused about."

"I know it sounds ridiculous." I shook my head. "I wouldn't be asking if I had any other ideas. We need to get this wolf to change back into a human so we can talk to her about some important information. The potion is getting made by an arcanist in the living world, but the wolf is in the ghost world. There isn't another way for the potion to get into a ghostly form without someone dying. If you help us, at least I know you'll come back as a ghost, and we won't risk hurting someone for no reason."

Steph frowned and glanced at Caleb, probably trying to see if what I was saying was all part of an insane joke or something. "There's a lot wrong with this."

"I know. I'm sorry. After we bring you back the second time, I promise we'll leave you alone to live a totally normal life. Caleb can even help erase some memories if you'd like. Vampires apparently can do stuff like that." I glanced at him for confirmation.

He nodded, his gaze still on the cars passing by.

Stephanie looked down at the bridge, thinking things over. "It is weird knowing that werewolves and vampires exist and that you can chat with ghosts on the regular while still being expected to go back to cheerleading and math tests."

"I know that's right." I nodded, my eyes wide.

She glanced back up at me and laughed lightly. "I'm sure you do know all about that."

I smiled and shrugged. "It is what it is. Will you think about it? I won't do any of it without your permission."

"Didn't you say this is the only way to get the information you need?"

"Yes, but I won't force you to do it."

We shared a steady gaze for a moment before she nodded. "I'll think about it. It might be nice to help someone with something."

"Helping others can feel really good." I nodded.

Caleb dropped me off at my house a little while later. We hadn't spoken much in the car as we each thought about our own concerns. He'd brought up some good points, and I wasn't sure what the answers were going to be. I could hear Brandon's scoff in my mind that he would make once he'd heard my incomplete plan. He hated incomplete plans.

It was the best I could do for the moment.

Monday morning dawned dark and cloudy. I pushed myself to make it to school on time and work my way through the day's classes.

On the walk home from school, Brandon popped in on me.

"Hello, love!" he said with his awful British accent.

"Hi, Brandon."

"Where're all your boyfriends this fine afternoon?" He made a show of looking around thoroughly.

I sighed. "We've been over this so many times. I don't have a boyfriend."

"Are you sure?" He squinted his eyes while wearing a teasing grin, keeping pace with my hurried walk.

The clouds were still grey and ominous but hadn't spilled their rain yet. Even if it wasn't raining, the wind kept it chilly enough that I didn't feel like keeping my pace leisurely.

"Of course, I'm sure. One guy likes to drink blood on the regular—the warmer the better—was involved with my gran on some level and is now being crushed on by my sister. The other one is super confusing, insisting on hanging out with my former friend while continuing to say he likes me, and the other is a werewolf."

"The last one felt kind of anticlimactic there." Brandon pursed his lips in thought. "Are you sure there isn't anything else wrong with him? Maybe you're just keeping your options open because you have a secret hope that someone else might become available?"

I glanced at him through my wind-blown hair. His grin told me all I needed to know about who he was insinuating.

Pretending to think for a second, I looked up at the bare trees above our heads. "Hmm...nope. There's no one else I can think of. All the other guys I know are just ugly."

He huffed. "Sounds like you need to get your eyes checked."

I gave him a teasing smile so he could tell I was kidding, although he probably already knew that. We were spending so much time together these days, he had to know I thought he was anything but ugly. Even if I could see straight through his head.

"I'm sorry I'll probably be super boring tonight. The only plans I've got are to do homework. Are you sure you want to stick around?" I asked as we neared my house, eager to get out of the sharp wind.

He shrugged. "Even watching you scribble the wrong answers down on a math worksheet is better than sitting in the skatepark and watching grass grow."

"If you were really helpful, you'd make sure I got all my homework answers correct."

He shrugged again. "Too bad I believe in turning in your own work. I guess you could always copy off your friend Andrea's homework?"

I winced and scrunched my nose. "Ouch."

He smiled and bumped through me with his shoulder. "Just teasing."

Trina wasn't there when I got home, probably giving one of her friends a ride. Mom was there sitting in the kitchen and chewing on her lip as she looked at her computer.

"Hey, sweetie," she looked up for a second when I walked in.

"Hi, Mom."

I walked down the hallway to my bedroom and dumped my bag onto my bed. Turning, I saw the wooden box Gran had left me sitting on my dresser. A sudden thought occurred to me.

"Hey, mom?" I hollered from my room and grabbed the box. "Can you do me a favor?"

I must have startled Brandon with my abrupt turnaround because he looked surprised and kept standing in the doorway.

"What do you need?" Mom called back from the kitchen.

Quietly, I raised my eyebrows at Brandon. "Excuse me"

Blinking, he stepped aside. "Well, at least someone around here has manners, not walking through me all the time."

We shared a smile before I walked back into the kitchen.

"Can you put these on and tell me what you see?" I asked as I walked toward the kitchen table.

"Wow! These are...amazing! Where did you get them?" she said as she examined the golden glasses.

"Would you believe that's what was in Gran's box?"

Mom paused and looked up at me, blinking a few times. "*These* were in that box?"

I nodded. "I tried wearing them, but I couldn't see anything different. So far, they seem like regular, non-prescription glasses."

"Pfft. I think you mean an awesomely cool Halloween accessory," Brandon said as he stood next to me.

Mom's fingers were suddenly trembling as she raised the glasses to her face. As soon as the lens passed over her eyes, they widened in shock. "I never imagined these were still around. In fact, I'd kind of almost thought I'd imagined my mom even talking about these. I feel kind of dumb not even considering that these were what could have been in that box."

"Hanna..." Brandon edged closer to me. "I swear she's looking right at me."

Chills went down my spine as realization set in.

"That's because I *am* looking right at you," Mom said, slightly awed. "Hanna, is this what you see *all the time*?"

I glanced between Mom and Brandon. "I mean, if you see a blue transparent kid from the 90s with too-big pants and blond hair that doesn't know about gravity, then yes. Yes, I pretty much see it every day."

First, she smirked and then busted out into full laughter. "Oh my gosh! I can't believe we have these!"

"So...she can see me with those on? I'm not sure if I should be happy or scared." Brandon's eyes kept bouncing between me and my mom.

"I'm thinking scared. Be afraid. Very afraid," I said, watching my mom have some kind of happy breakdown. Was that a thing? It was like a nervous breakdown but with laughter instead.

Mom wiped at a tear from underneath her eye, lifting the glasses for just a second. "I'm sorry, sweetie. I'm just having a hard time coming to terms with this. Gran talked about them once when I was a teenager, but I'd almost forgotten the whole thing until now. Are you going to introduce your friend to me?"

"Oh, right. Yes, this is Brandon. He's...uh, my friend?" I gestured my arm up and down in front of him.

"Nice to meet you. Though, I have a feeling you've been around quite a bit lately." Mom smiled, seeming more in control of her emotions.

"Do you think she can also see me as well as hear me? Those things don't really come with headphones," Brandon said out of the side of his mouth while still giving my mom a polite smile.

"Yes, dear. I can hear you as well as see you. They're made from the same Seer that made Trina's necklace and pretty much do the opposite of what the necklace does." Mom fiddled with the earpiece as she talked.

"Okay. In that case, it's nice to meet you too. Yes, I'm around a lot but don't worry, we have strict rules and stuff to keep everything...you know, like proper and stuff."

I shot Brandon a scandalized look while my mom raised her eyebrows.

"I suppose that's good to hear," she said, glancing between the both of us. "We do have a no boys in the bedrooms rule, and I'm happy to hear you guys are following it, even if there's less risk with him being all...well, dead."

Brandon and I shared awkward glances.

"Right," I jumped in. "It's just that we like to keep things above board is all. Following the rules, that's us."

"Glad to hear it." She smiled. "Now that we know what these are, we need to make sure to keep them safe. Do you understand how valuable they are, Hanna?"

I nodded, thinking about all the uses one could have with them. It would certainly make a Seer obsolete, and it had been shown several times in the last month or so how valuable people thought I was. These glasses couldn't even talk back like a mouthy Seer could nor could they lie like a Seer might if they had their reasons. Not to mention, you wouldn't need to kidnap and then feed them like a certain alive Seer would require.

A thought occurred to me that made me frown. "The night that Gran died, the lady was looking for something, demanding Gran give it to her. The lady, if we can even call her that, said something about needing an item so she could talk to someone. Do you think these are what she was after? Are these why Gran died?"

Mom frowned as silence settled onto us, burdened with heavy thoughts.

After several seconds, Brandon was the first to speak, unsurprisingly. "If that's true, these are more dangerous than valuable. Maybe we should destroy them?"

I looked at Mom with questioning eyes.

She was already shaking her head. "They're too precious even for that. What if we need them in the future for something? We might need them even to save a life. If we'd had them when you were taken by the vampire queen..."

She trailed off and our own thoughts finished the sentence for her.

"Actually, I could use them right now with the wolf ghosts," I said, chewing lightly on my lip. "If I could get a werewolf to be able to talk to the wolf once we get her in human form directly, then maybe they'd help her calm down faster and get better answers than I ever could. They even might be able to get better closure."

Brandon nodded slowly. "That might help, but that risks letting several people know you have them, including the witch who is supposed to be meeting us there and giving zombie Stephanie the potion. Do we know them well enough to trust them already?"

Mom's eyes widened in alarm. "Just what exactly are you getting into? A witch is involved now? A zombie? I thought you were just going to the commune to track down one of their ghosts, not involve a whole circus of supernatural creatures."

I sighed, went to the fridge, and grabbed two bottles of diet soda. Placing one soda in front of my mom, I pulled out a kitchen chair and sat down. "There's a lot more to it than that now, I'm afraid."

Brandon helped me fill her in on more details, and, while I didn't like adding to her list of worries, I felt it was the responsible thing to keep her informed. After all, not knowing all this could have made her worry more. Not to mention, she had a hand in helping me with the vampire seethe and keeping her updated may provide her more opportunities to help me when I desperately needed it. Even if I couldn't see those situations at the present.

After we were finished, Mom was shaking her head. "I don't like this very much."

"I don't either, now that we hash it out like this. Hanna, there are just too many things that could go wrong," Brandon said, pursing his lips.

I sighed. "I figured you'd say that, and I can't say I disagree, but I also don't know what else to do. I can't not help the wolves. Their pack is falling apart. Gryphin's dad is on the verge of losing his hold on them every day. If we fail, he'll most likely die."

Mom grabbed my hand from across the table after pushing her laptop to the side. "Listen, honey. I know you feel it's your job to save all the ghosts in the world, but there will just be some situations you can't help with. Life is hard like that. There are times when things don't go as you'd like, no matter what and how hard you try."

Brandon nodded. "She's right, Hanna."

I frowned and looked down at the wooden grooves in the table. "But what if I can do something to help, but I give up too soon? I've got to at least try or else all this struggle I've had with my powers is useless. If I can't use them to do something good, what good am I?"

Mom smiled and squeezed my hand again. "I wish more people thought of their assets like you do."

"Helping one ghost cross over is one thing. Trying to wrangle a pack full of not-talking werewolf ghosts is a whole other thing." Brandon frowned and crossed his arms over his chest.

I gave him a half-smile. "You know, part of this is totally your fault. I was good with avoiding ghosts as much as I could until you came along."

He narrowed his eyes and snorted.

"I'm sorry, Mom. I've got to try, but I promise I'll be careful. Gryphin and Mr. Tyler will be there to help protect me should anything go wrong. They might not be a supermen vampires, but werewolves are quite powerful themselves."

Mom pressed her lips together in thought. "I know Caleb can't go with you to the werewolf commune, but do you think they'd have anything against necromancers?"

I shrugged. "I could ask, but I'm not sure Noah would be much help if it came down to any kind of fight. He can take a vampire, sure, but we're not dealing with those right now. No, wolves would be better for this situation."

"I wish I had some superpower or something," Mom frowned and pulled her hands away. "Then I could help. It's so hard to see you work through this stuff on your own."

Frowning at the pooling water in her eyes, I said, "I know. I'm sorry too. The last thing I want to do is add more worry to your plate, but I figured you'd rather have me keep you informed than not."

She nodded, a small grateful smile on her lips even though her eyes were still pained. "I do appreciate that, yes."

"I'll be there if that helps?" Brandon said and smiled awkwardly as we both turned to look at him.

I tried not to grin but probably wasn't too successful. "Yes, that's very kind of you, Brandon."

Mom was better at giving him a kind smile. "Yes, Brandon. It does help."

Chapter 22

Tuesday morning started with the usual routine. Emma and Addy asked me about ghosts sometimes during P.E., but I didn't want to involve them any more than I needed to. Mostly, I just kept them updated on Stephanie's progress, which was to say, we hadn't done much except give her some possible false hope that she'd get reunited with her body. However, I was definitely not going to share that last part with my new friends.

Mr. Tyler stopped me after history class, and I waited behind as all the students filed out. Noah seemed to hesitate for a second but looked at Mr. Tyler's face, gave me a small smile, and left.

"Are you any closer to getting your friend back into her body so we can take her back out again?" Mr. Tyler asked once all the students had finally left.

Only a little worried about making it to my next class on time, I winced. "Still waiting on word from the necro master. They're going to contact us as soon as he's back and ready to go. It's supposed to be any day now."

He frowned and rubbed at the grey scruff around his chin. "I'm worried we're running out of time. The pack is getting restless. Kage is trying his best to keep everyone in line, but the next guy, the third in line, is going to make a move soon."

I shifted the books in my arms. "I'm sorry. If it helps, Steph seems willing to do what we need. She wants to help us since we're working so hard to help her, I think. I didn't realize she was such a brave person."

Mr. Tyler's mouth perked in a sympathetic smile and nodded. "Alright. We'll just hope things come together soon. I understand there are others here making sacrifices. Please let me know as soon as you can when you're getting her body back."

I nodded. "Of course."

The rest of the school day was pretty mundane, comparatively. Andrea and Randi were standing by their lockers at the end of the day, and, as I walked by on my way out of the school, I heard Andrea mutter something to Randi and then they both burst into scandalized giggles.

My old self would have been upset by the exchange, but this new one had much more to worry about than dumb girls at school talking bad about me.

I spent that evening doing homework again while Brandon played with his pocketknife and made random comments as he sat on my bed. Every once in a while, I'd glance at the box sitting on my desk where we kept the glasses nice and snug inside. We needed to find a safer place to keep the box, but it was okay sitting there for the time being only because no one knew that we had them...so far.

Wednesday at school was much of the same, and as I walked home that afternoon, I finally got the text message we'd been waiting for.

Noah: The master is back and ready to go. I'll pick you up in 5.

I blinked a few times at my phone, standing still on the sidewalk and letting the message sink into my brain.

"What's up?" Brandon peeked over my shoulder and looked down at the screen. "Oh, it's go time!"

I looked up and blinked. "Yes. I've been eager for this to happen, but why am I suddenly nervous?"

"I'd be nervous too. It's new. We don't know what to expect. Maybe you should take Caleb with you." Brandon smiled thoughtfully and something about the expression made me wonder if he was feeling bad about not being able to help me more.

"I probably should, and as much as I'm really sorry to say this, perhaps you shouldn't come."

"What? No, I—"

I stopped his protest with an upraised hand. "Listen. What we're about to do might not be so exact that the spell doesn't get confused with more than one ghost in the room. Do you really want to wake up in Steph's body by accident?"

He furrowed his brows. "It probably wouldn't be so bad... I've always wondered what being a girl was like."

I smirked and shook my head. "I promise to contact you as soon as we've made progress, okay?"

Sighing, he frowned down at his shoes where only the tops could barely be seen peeking out from underneath his large pants. "Okay, I guess."

I blew him a kiss and turned to run the rest of the way to my house so I could be there when Noah showed up.

After ditching my bag in my bedroom, grateful that the house appeared empty, I paused for a second and stared at the ornate box sitting on my desk. I didn't know quite what to expect from the evening, but there was a chance that the glasses would come in handy. I made a decision, and I pulled out a jacket from my closet with big pockets. Carefully, I took the glasses out of the box and fit them into an old sunglasses case I'd gotten for my birthday last year. I stuffed the case into my jacket and made sure it was lodged securely in the pocket.

Then I ran back outside and got out my phone. I texted Mom and Trina so they'd know where I was, and, just as I was about to text Caleb, he appeared in my yard.

"Ready to go raise some dead?"

"Holy Moses!" I clutched at my chest. "You're worse than the ghosts!"

Laughing in a low rumble, he said, "Sorry."

"No, you're not. You do that on purpose. I need to get you a bell. How did you know where I was going?"

"Noah texted me. He wants me to be there just in case. I know. It's weird, but I'm glad he included me."

"Well, if he hadn't, I would have," I said with a pointed eyebrow and put my phone away.

He grinned and turned his head toward the street. "Here comes your boyfriend."

I rolled my eyes as Noah's car came around the corner and approached my house. "Why does everyone say that?"

"Because we all know you want it to be true."

I huffed. "Not anymore."

Noah rolled down his window and peered out through the passenger side. "You guys ready to go?"

I nodded, and like the considerate person I was, climbed into the back seat and let Caleb take the front where there was more room for his long legs.

"Did you guys have to skip football practice?" I peered up from between the two front seats.

Noah pulled onto the road and glanced back at me. "Are you wearing your seat belt?"

Caleb laughed, earning a sharp look from Noah.

"Woah, it's fine." I scooted back and put on the belt. "I guess he's right that I shouldn't rely on vampire reflexes to save me every time."

Caleb's dark eyes shined in amusement as he glanced toward me. "As you wish, dear."

I shook my head in frustration.

"Yes, we had to ditch practice," Noah said, locking eyes with mine in the rearview mirror for a moment long enough that it had me wondering at his intensity.

"Can't Caleb just use a mind trick on your coach and make him think y'all were there the whole time?" I asked, tearing my eyes away from Noah's before we got into an accident.

The faux-leather seat creaked as Caleb shrugged his shoulders. "I could."

"But that would be helping out a necromancer," Noah said dryly.

"Seems to me that we'll owe you guys if all this goes well," I said, fiddling with my phone in my lap.

"Maybe *you* will." Caleb shot me a grin. "But they're not doing *me* any favors. If anything, they owe me for grabbing the body and bringing it to them so quickly."

Noah scoffed.

I decided to ignore the last part of his comment. "Will the order expect any payment or something for this service?"

It was Noah's turn to shrug. "They might. This type of spell requires a lot of costs."

"But it probably won't be money they're after," Caleb said with another glance in my direction.

"Oh. Right." I had enough time on our drive over to stew about what I was doing. Were a grieving werewolf alpha and the happiness of a pack really worth all of this? They were going to owe me big time, and Stephanie too, for that matter.

After about twenty minutes or so, Noah pulled up in front of a large house with manicured lawns and a four-car garage. It was situated in a sizable neighborhood with many of the homes as large as it was, most of them boasting wide swatches of grassy yards.

"This is not what I would expect from a necromancer order," I said as I climbed out of the car, thinking about what kinds of funny comments Brandon would have made were he with me.

As I felt a pang of sadness from missing him, I chided myself. I had been spending way too much time with him.

"This is *exactly* the kind of place I would expect," Caleb said, standing next to me.

"What's that supposed to mean?" Noah growled as he walked past us and headed up the walkway.

"You're too smart to need an explanation," Caleb grumbled and followed behind Noah.

"You know, no one is forcing you to be here, Caleb," I said, trying to come across helpful instead of rude.

Not sure I succeeded.

He stopped abruptly and whirled around so that I smacked right into his solid chest. Whiffs of minty frost floated in the air between us, and I got the sudden urge to hug him again if only to feel the rock-like strength of his embrace.

Thankfully, I resisted.

"And leave you alone with these maniacs? Your gran would kill me."

I smirked, unable to help it. "Too bad you're already dead."

He rolled his eyes and turned around again.

"It's just that you seem to really hate these guys. I mean, I guess I would too if they had the power to possess me at any second. That would be pretty terrifying. Of course… I do hang out with you though, and you kind of have that same power over me, but I don't hate you."

I could see his head shaking as I rambled on, and we followed Noah into the house.

Noah opened the door and stood back so we could come in. His eyes lingered on mine again, and I got the feeling he really wanted to say something but couldn't quite do it.

Instead, he said, "The only reason he hates us is because he knows we won't hesitate to make sure he doesn't do anything questionable. He realizes his free will here is near obsolete."

Caleb bristled. "You don't even—"

I pushed my way in between them and gave the vampire a pointed look. "Tut tut. Relax. We're all friends here working to help other friends. We're with allies and nothing bad is going to happen."

It took a few seconds for them to back off slightly, but their angry glances at each other would probably never go away completely.

"Now," I turned to Noah, "let's get this started."

He nodded and led us through the house and down into a basement. I was a bit sick of basements at that point, but it didn't seem right to do such a dark ritual anywhere else. The inside of the house was decorated more like a model home than a place actual people lived. The wall hangings were tasteful—vases with fresh flowers sat on end tables and recent magazines sat on the coffee table. There wasn't even a dish in the sink.

The basement was another story. We passed several rooms and while most of the doors were shut, a few were cracked open, and I spotted beds, personal belongings, and piles of laundry. At the end of the hallway, there was an open door that led to a larger room, more industrial-looking than the rest of the house. It was like they'd finished the basement except for this last room, leaving the cement flooring, the insulation-exposed walls, and the visible pipes and electrical wires exposed.

As we walked into that room, Noah stepped aside and greeted the several figures standing inside. I recognized a few of them from when they'd come to save me from the vampire seethe. In the middle of the room was a large table with one of those corpse bags you see at crime scenes. I figured it was Stephanie's body, ready to be reanimated.

"Was it necessary to bring the sucker?" Grady, I think his name was, asked from where he stood on the left, wearing khaki work pants and a dirty plaid shirt.

I was kind of disappointed that they weren't all in dark purple ceremonial robes or something, but alas, it appeared they wore regular garb for their clandestine rituals. At least this time no one was in their pajamas.

Caleb growled but didn't waste words on answering the question.

Alberto was there, as well as the doctor, Marcus, and the older fellow who had seemed to be the leader the last time I'd seen the bunch. However, he must have only been second in command because an older man was sitting in a motorized scooter closer to the body. This guy looked so old, I wouldn't have been surprised if he was a second corpse. With hunched shoulders, a nearly bald head, sagging pale skin, and a wrinkled face, it was surprising to see that his hands were steady and his eyes sharp.

"Now, now, that's no way to treat our guests. Welcome to our inner sanctum, of sorts," the old man in the scooter said. "I'm David Fellows, master of this order, and I owe you an apology for the time you've had to wait for this day to happen."

I nodded politely and resisted the urge to bow or curtsy or something else as ridiculous. "Thank you. We understand sometimes important things take time."

David nodded. "Indeed. I was traveling on another mission, and then we needed to gather the ingredients for such a spell. We haven't had a Seer to help us resurrect someone in some time."

"Are the ingredients hard to find?" I asked, trying to subtly look around the room and spot anything odd they might have brought in for such a spell.

The only woman in the room scoffed, drawing my attention to her. She stood with most of her weight on one leg, her hip cocked, and arms folded across her chest. "Why are all Seers so frustrating?"

Alarmed, I glanced at Noah, afraid that I had said something wrong, but he only gave me an encouraging smile.

David gave the woman a flat look and then turned back to me. "Forgive Mariah. She's worked very hard the past few days."

"I'm sorry. I feel like this has been a lot to ask of y'all. I wouldn't have asked this if there was any other way. Poor Stephanie was so young and full of life..." I didn't need to fake the emotion that welled up inside my chest.

"Honestly, my dear, while this is a risky thing, I'm humbled that the opportunity has come to me. I've seen this done a few times, and it's not every day a necromancer order gets to do something so helpful," David said with a kind smile and bright white teeth that looked much younger than his frail body.

Mariah scoffed again.

I glanced at her before going back to David. "Noah has explained some about the costs on a necromancer when doing big spells like this. I feel horrible that this could possibly...hurt you in any way. He also told me only the master can perform the ritual."

David spared a look to Noah who winced slightly under the gaze. Perhaps I shouldn't have divulged that information, but I wanted them to know I understood they were making a sacrifice. "Yes, that's true. This spell can cost much, but one reason we have the rule of only a master being able to do this is because of the ability a master has to siphon energy from his order members. This way, the group can come together to pay the cost, making it less severe on any one person."

"Wow. That's..." I shook my head. "Now I feel even more terrible for asking for this. Maybe we should go home."

I was kind of kidding but also kind of not. How could I ask them to make such a sacrifice? It didn't seem right. It was made even worse by the knowledge that we were going to kill Stephanie again in just a few more hours, depending on how long it took to bring her back. There had to be another way to get the potion back to the ghost wolf without murdering someone.

However, I had still promised Stephanie we'd bring her back. One task at a time.

David steered his scooter around the center table and got closer to me. He gazed steadily into my eyes with solid purpose. "This is an honor. Please don't feel bad."

I nodded, trying to accept his words. "Okay... The least I can do is offer my services to help your order in the future, should you need it."

Caleb grunted and shook his head with a warning look in my direction, but I ignored it. Perhaps I was making a deal with a group of devils, but they were willing to help me. It didn't seem right not to offer help in return. Not to mention, it couldn't have been worse than helping the vampires, as great as that turned out.

Mariah rolled her eyes at my offered help, but David seemed pleased. "That's kind of you, my dear. Now, are we ready to get started?"

"I am if y'all are," I said, glancing around the group of necromancers.

"First thing is first." David smiled at me. "Is the spirit here? In the past, we've had to go to the haunt to unite the spirit with its body, but I understand that is unneeded in this case?"

"Right. Yes, I've somehow picked up the ability to summon ghosts to my location."

"A useful skill, indeed," David said while locking eyes with Alberto for a second.

I wasn't sure if I felt proud or creeped out.

"If you will please call the spirit in question, we will prepare for the ritual." David moved his chair back to the top of the circle.

Closing my eyes, I pictured Stephanie's long blonde hair, flirtatious smile, and the unfortunate policewoman costume. I hoped someone had been kind in the preparation of her body and removed the horrendous outfit.

It didn't take but a few seconds before the prickles on my neck announced her arrival. She'd been waiting for the call and that seemed to make all the difference in the time it took for the ghost to arrive.

"Seriously? This place is gross," Stephanie said, looking around the room.

I smiled at her. "We're just glad we don't have to do this on a bridge in the middle of traffic. For some reason, most Seers can't pull ghosts out of their haunts, except me, so we've got that going for us."

Stephanie gave me an appreciative nod while the alivers around the room gave me curious glances. I wasn't sure what they were curious about. Sure, I was talking to someone they couldn't see, but that was my entire purpose for being there.

"I suppose that helps put some perspective on it," my dead friend said.

"Are you ready?" I looked at the body bag on the table, and she followed my gaze.

"Not sure what to expect, but I guess?"

"It's okay. We'll get through this together." I looked back at David and nodded. "We're ready."

"You're up, Grady," David said and bobbed his head toward the door.

Noah, Caleb, and I shuffled out of the way for Grady to pass as he left the room, only to come back a few minutes later with a rather large goat in tow. He pulled at it from a rope around its neck, but the goat didn't seem too overly concerned. The clip-clop of its hooves clacked as it got onto the cement, and it let out an unenthused bleat.

My heart sank as it was pretty clear what was about to happen. We were going to bring life into a corpse. It made sense that we'd need to take life from something else. I felt bad for the little guy, but it was better him than a human, I supposed.

"Oh, does he have to die so I can live?" Stephanie asked with a sad pout.

I gave her a sympathetic shrug.

Grady led the goat towards David and hooked the rope onto a sturdy nail stuck into a solid 4x4 within reaching distance of the necromancer leader.

Next, Marcus went to the corner shelf, retrieved a fancy-looking vase or urn, and approached the body. He set the urn down carefully, and deftly unzipped the bag.

"I hope I don't stink," Stephanie said, eyeing her corpse with distaste.

"We've kept her frozen all this time," David said as if to answer her question. "This preserves the body and makes it more viable."

"So Stephanie died of drowning, right? How will her body revive from that without...other, unwanted consequences?" I asked, wanting to know as many details as I could get.

"What other consequences could there be? It works or it doesn't, right?" Stephanie looked between David and me with alarm.

David steepled his fingers and rested his chin on his thumbs. "That's actually one of the risks that makes this ritual such an uncertain thing. If done right, the spell does this kind of one-time healing cleanse where the body is restored to its healthy state."

"And if it goes wrong?" I asked before Stephanie could.

David glanced at Noah for a millisecond before looking back at me. "Then we'll deal with it as it comes. There's no reason to doubt that everything will go well."

Stephanie and I exchanged looks. She didn't seem super confident at his words, and I had to agree with her, but we also didn't have much of a choice.

"What do you need me to do to make sure her spirit gets into the body? You need a Seer for this, right?"

"I'm glad you asked that question," David said with a smile. "Besides contacting and readying the spirit, we need you to help guide it towards the body at the right time. They need to be touching for the spell to work."

"How will I know when it's the right time?"

"We'll help you. Don't worry," Marcus said kindly and then looked back to David to see if he should continue.

The master nodded and Marcus pulled back the plastic from off Stephanie's body.

"Ew, I look terrible." Stephanie frowned as she peered into her own face. "Please tell me that's not what I look like all the time."

"Of course not! You're dead," I said with a small chuckle. "And you've been frozen for a while. If you did look good after all that, I'd be worried."

The alivers in the room politely ignored my one-sided conversation, and Marcus carefully pulled her body out of the bag, rolling it over to get the plastic out from underneath.

She furrowed her eyebrows. "What am I wearing? Ew! It's so ugly! Plus, that means someone here had to take me out of my other clothes and see me naked." She looked around with a distasteful frown.

Thankfully, someone had changed her out of the Halloween outfit and put her into a simple cotton nightgown.

"Would you rather be in that costume still?" I pointedly looked at her ghost body that couldn't change out of its clothes like her physical body could.

She snorted and folded her arms across her chest.

"Don't worry. We'll find you something nice to wear after this is all over, alright?" I gave her a kind smile.

Marcus took the lid off the urn, dipped his fingers in, and started using whatever had been inside to write grey, dusty runes on Stephanie's skin. He started with her forehead, then went to her arms, and finally to her legs. Thankfully, he didn't have to do it somewhere that the nightgown covered.

"What is *that*?" Stephanie's eyes widened.

"That's not someone's dead ashes or something, is it?" I asked for the benefit of both of us.

"Would that be so bad? She's also already dead," Caleb said with a smirk.

Stephanie huffed. "Yes, it would be! I don't want a different dead person's insides on me."

Marcus answered my question while still maintaining focus on his task. "It's not ashes from a dead person, but rather ashes from an elder tree and a cedar tree. One for healing and the other for new life."

Stephanie pressed her lips into a line. "I suppose that's okay. Better than human bits at least."

After tracing several symbols onto her skin, Marcus stepped away and put the urn back onto the shelf. "She is prepared."

David nodded toward the group, and the goat let out another bleat.

Everyone shuffled into movement, and soon a circle formed around the table with David at the top. As I watched the necromancers carefully find their places, I finally noticed a pentagram was painted onto the floor with the table at its center. All ten of them stood evenly spaced along the ring and turned their gaze onto the leader.

Noah stayed outside of the circle, still near the door. I backed up closer to him in case there was an important place for bystanders to stand. Caleb kept his place between me and the circle but off to the side so I could still see what was going on.

David took several deep breaths as silence descended upon the room, save for the occasional goat snorts. He started chanting strange words, his voice undulating in pitch and tone. The atmosphere tingled and vibrated around us, and the small hairs on my arms reacted to the change by springing up in waves.

Stephanie turned to look at me with wide eyes, and I sent her a reassuring smile. This was new to all of us, but I trusted the necroes to do their best. They'd proven their support and loyalty when rescuing me from the vampires, so I had no reason to doubt them now.

Purple streaks darted across the lines of the pentagram, thickening as they grew stronger until finally uniting together around the entire circle. A wind stirred from some unknown source, but it only affected those around the circle. Hair waved, pants flapped, and shirts rippled, while Noah, Caleb, and I all remained untouched.

The chanting continued for several minutes, and I kept myself ready to look for an indication that it was time for Stephanie to make contact with her body. As for Steph, she kept to the outside of the circle, watching with a keen eye as her corpse's hair thrashed in the wind.

Finally, David's eyes focused on me, and he nodded firmly twice.

"Steph, are you ready? It's time. Can you get into the circle and touch your body?"

She took a breath to steel herself and glanced one last time at me. "See you on the other side," she said and stepped into the purple pentagram. The light fizzled where she crossed over and then reconnected stronger than ever.

With trembling fingers, she reached out to touch her body.

I gave David an eager nod, so he knew she was making contact. He nodded again and started chanting louder. This time, the others joined in with perfect harmony, as far as I could tell.

Shivers ran down my back from the sheer power I could feel in the room as the chanting got stronger.

At its height, David pulled out a shiny silver dagger with rubies inlaid on its handle. I cringed, having a feeling about what was coming next, and sure enough, he grabbed the goat, pulled it into the circle, and with a loud exclamation of some kind of word, sliced the goat's neck in a practiced and comfortable way.

The poor thing gurgled as its life juices drained down its body and onto the floor where it traveled into the lines of the pentagram and mixed with the purple lightning.

I gave Noah a sad, pouting look at the goat's demise, and he shuffled over two inches so he could put a comforting arm around my shoulders. He didn't speak, probably as to not interrupt their spell casting, but he gave me an extra squeeze of assurance.

Caleb shook his head, amused, but didn't bother to try and stop Noah. As for me, I wasn't sure what to do. The warmth from his arm was comforting, but it didn't bring the exciting tingles that it once had. Plus, I was still angry from our last encounter. If I hadn't been so flustered by the ritual, I might have shrugged his arm right off.

The spell fizzled and crackled in the air as the chanting started going faster. Stephanie was pulled in as she leaned down, looking quite dazed, and climbed onto the table until her spirit lined up with the body.

Noah winced as we watched the necromancers' faces bead with sweat and grimaces as the chanting grew faster and louder. The spell was taking its cost, and the hunched shoulders of the casters told me it was painful.

David looked to be in the worst shape as he scrunched his forehead in pain, and, while still chanting precisely, his body pulled tautly as if his nerves and tendons were being sucked up somewhere.

Just when I thought they wouldn't be able to chant any faster, they exclaimed in one final word, with all of them looking upwards and using their vocal cords to throw the spell into the world.

I couldn't help shuddering as the spell ended and the magic dissipated. None of the necromancers fell, but a few looked like their knees were about to buckle.

Mariah was the only one to shoot me a nasty glare as if the whole thing had been my fault. And, I have to say, perhaps it kind of was.

Quiet descended amongst the labored breathing. The purple lightning was gone, along with the blood, even though the goat's corpse was still laying on the cold cement. Stephanie's ghost wasn't anywhere to be seen, and I took that as a good sign.

Dying to ask if the spell had worked, I had to force myself to keep quiet in case the whole thing wasn't finished or something.

Caleb didn't share my concerns. "Did it work?"

Still breathing heavily, leaning against the back of his scooter seat, David said, "We'll know in a few minutes. Sometimes it takes a moment for the heart to get beating again."

His voice was raspy and slight, and I wondered if he was going to wither away right in front of our eyes.

Noah gave me another quick squeeze before removing his arm from my shoulders and making his way to the master's chair. Marcus also kneeled next to the man and started checking his vital signs.

Several of the necromancers finally allowed themselves to fold onto the floor and rest. Mariah pushed her way out of the room, bumping her shoulder into mine as she left so she must not have been *that* exhausted.

"What a rush!" Grady said, his eyes closed as he savored the feeling the magic spell must have given him. His legs were sprawled out in front of him as he sat on the ground.

I never thought about magic giving a rush to someone, and, after watching their faces, I wasn't sure I wanted to try it.

"Can I touch her?" I asked, walking into the circle that was once again mere paint on cement.

No one stopped me, so I decided that was as good an answer as I needed. Stephanie's body looked about the same. The dusty runes were all gone, having been absorbed during the spell at some point. Her skin was still a slightly grey hue, and my heart hammered inside my chest in fear that all of this had been for nothing.

Then her eyes popped open. She turned stiffly to the side and vomited enough water to fill several buckets. I was sure if we'd been turned into a cartoon at that moment there would have been several flopping river fish in the water that soaked the floor.

Chapter 23

About an hour after the ritual, we were sitting outside in the backyard of the necromancers' home. We'd been assured that food and evening sunshine would be helpful in Stephanie's recovery.

David had been limp enough that Marcus and Noah had carried him upstairs and out of our sight. I hoped he was going to recover, and there must have been enough worry on my face for Alberto to keep reassuring me that it was normal to need so much rest after such a spell and that the master was sure to recover.

"How do you feel?" I asked as I sat next to Stephanie's now reanimated corpse, while Caleb, who also happened to be a different kind of reanimated corpse, stood in the shade a few paces away.

"You mean compared to the last time you asked two seconds ago?" She shrugged and took a sip of her sweet tea. "The same, I guess."

The orange hues of the sunset spread across the sky and over the fluffy clouds, making the whole sight a beautiful welcome into the world. We sat on a wooden bench that was probably surrounded by a beautiful garden in the summertime, but, as it was, there were a few pansies hardily withstanding the cool wind of autumn.

Mariah, as unfriendly as she was, had found some clothes that Stephanie could change into, so instead of pajamas, she wore sweatpants, a gym t-shirt, a light jacket, and a pair of flip-flops. I was a bit envious that Steph could pull off that kind of outfit, but she was just one of those girls who could look cute in anything.

"Right. I guess that's better than worse?" I smiled, trying to ease some of the tension.

She shrugged.

"Are you wishing you hadn't done this? I kind of thought you'd be happy to come back, even though you're wearing those unfortunate pajamas."

Keeping her eyes on the sunset, she took another sip of the drink. "I thought I would feel excited and ready to tackle life with renewed energy, that maybe I'd even be more committed to living a better life. You know, like getting better grades and volunteering at senior homes and all that jazz, but I don't. I just feel...tired."

I frowned and put a comforting hand on her shoulder. "Perhaps you'll feel restored after some rest. What do you want to do from here? Perhaps we ought to help the werewolves before we bring you back home and give your parents the shock of their lives?"

I left it unsaid that we didn't want to get her parents' hopes up in case something went wrong with the next phase of our haphazard plan. Not to mention, they probably wouldn't allow Steph to leave the house for weeks after just getting her back.

Stephanie thought for a few moments and then nodded. "Yes, I think we'll go help the wolves first. I can't believe those are real, and that they need *my* help. It's crazy. After that, we'll go from there."

"Sounds smart. If you're up for it, we can go there tonight. My mom won't like it, but if we can get Gryphin to pick us up from here, there's no reason she has to know about it."

"Impressive. The Hanna I knew wouldn't have dared do any such a thing."

I winced. "I know. I don't feel good about it, but maybe more than one of us has changed in the last few weeks."

Gryphin was thrilled to get my text for him to pick us up, judging from the number of exclamation marks he'd used.

Caleb was not so thrilled, but he must have already been expecting it because he didn't put up too big of a fight. I had to promise to text him as soon as we were off werewolf land and update him on whatever went down. I also had to put him on the phone with Gryphin who assured the vampire over and over that at least three werewolf members would be personally protecting me and Stephanie from any harm, but the odds of that were low since we were in their own territory and nothing bad was going to happen.

Caleb's pinched face didn't look too convinced as I waved at him and Noah from the front seat of Gryphin's van.

Noah hadn't been thrilled about us going, either, but he understood that others needed my help. Plus, he seemed a bit distracted with concern for the order members who had worked hard to pull off that insane spell.

I really did owe them a big favor, but I tried not to think about it because there was no telling what a necromancer order might need help with. That was a problem for future Hanna.

"What kind of tunes do y'all like?" Gryphin asked as he pulled out onto the main roads and headed toward the commune.

I turned around in the front seat and looked at Stephanie who was usually the one to take control of the music. At least, she had the few times I'd hung out with her and Andrea outside of school.

Instead, Stephanie's gaze was far away, looking out the window and watching our world wash by.

"Steph? You still in there?" I asked with a kind smile.

"Huh?" She shook her head as if to clear away some inner fog. "Oh. Sorry. Did you say something?"

Gryphin wore an empathetic smile as he kept his eyes on the road. "Just wanted to know what kind of music you like to listen to."

"Oh, whatever you guys want." She shrugged and went back to staring out the window.

"Are you okay? I know you've been through a lot recently, like way more than a normal person will ever experience, but you okay in there?" I asked, trying to convey my sympathy.

"Yes, I'm fine. Perhaps finer than I've ever been in my life," she said in a groggy kind of way, still looking out the window.

I turned around to face front, locked eyes with Gryphin for a second, and gave him a shrug in response to his questioning expression.

I spent the rest of the thirty-minute drive worrying about what we were going to do. I'd been certain we could ask the necromancers for help again, but after what they all just went through to help Steph the first time, I knew I wouldn't be able to ask them to do it a second time. I probably should have called the whole thing off right after I made the choice not to ask them for help again, but I didn't have the guts quite yet.

Perhaps I was also waiting for a miracle of some kind or a stroke of genius to illuminate my mind.

We got to the commune about eight o'clock. It was dark by then, and the forest looked much more ominous in the dark than it had during the day. As we climbed out of the van, I swear gleaming eyes glittered at me from the nearby forest. And considering where we were, that wasn't too farfetched.

I hoped they were friendly eyes.

Lights were on in the commune, and I was kind of surprised to see that they had any outside lights at all considering they were wolves and probably had great eyesight at night. In front of the lodge, there was a large fire roaring, and several people were sitting around on benches, chatting, and drinking beverages.

"This is how werewolves live?" Stephanie asked, her eyes darting around in surprise. "This is not at all what I would have pictured."

Gryphin chuckled. "Yes, we get that a lot."

I shared a smile with him. "It's surprising until you think about it, and then it makes a lot of sense. Wolves need space, and being on their own out here is much safer for them...and humans."

She nodded slowly. "I suppose that makes sense."

"I'm sorry if this is a weird question, but how does your body feel after everything? Are you sore or anything?" I asked as our feet crunched gravel beneath us.

She paused for a second as her focus went inward. Then she shook her head. "No. It's weird. I should feel terrible, but I don't."

"That's good. They said something about healing properties, which makes sense as you'll need your body to be healed, but I was just curious if you were feeling any issues."

Stephanie shrugged. "Physically, I feel pretty good."

I nodded and smiled, feeling a little relieved, but still worried.

Before we could get too far into the village, Kage intercepted and directed us toward the outskirts, away from the fire and other wolves.

"Phoenix is on their way with the potion. They said it was a hassle to get completed, and they had to ask the coven members to get rare supplies they needed, but they were eventually able to get it together," Kage informed us in quiet tones as we stood behind one of the outer cabins.

My eyes were still adjusting to the darkness, and I'd almost tripped a few times as we'd walked through the grass, but Kage and Gryphin seemed to have no trouble with it at all.

"Oh, great. I hope they're not charging you too much for all of this," I said with a frown.

"Witches are notorious for being expensive." Kage shrugged. "If it works. It'll be worth it. If not, we'll just eat them."

His white teeth reflected what little light there was as he grinned a feral grin.

Stephanie looked to Gryphin for reassurance. "Please tell me he's joking."

Gryphin nodded with a laugh. "Oh yes. We don't eat witches or arcanists or magic users, whatever you want to call them. Their insides have a unique burnt taste that's not good for the pallet. Now, regular humans, that's something else entirely."

Kage brought his fingers together in a chef's kiss. "Mmm, delicious."

Stephanie looked at me in horror.

"They're kidding," I said. "Probably."

Gryphin laughed while Kage grinned.

"We are," Gryphin said. "Don't worry. We won't eat you."

"At least not until we get this ghost business over with," Kage said, still grinning.

They could have easily been telling the truth and disguising it as a joke, but my instincts didn't scream at me to run away. I'd spent some time with them and other various creatures of the night, and so far, the wolves seemed like folksy fun guys that liked to make jokes. As long as Gryphin's terrifying dad wasn't around anywhere.

As we waited for Phoenix, I thought about summoning Brandon to hang out with us, if only to get to see him for a few minutes, but I resisted. It was better that he stay out of the way in case something went wrong, like maybe some ghost werewolves decided he looked like a tasty treat. They probably couldn't really hurt him, but I didn't want to take any risks.

"I have to confess something to you guys," I said, after a few minutes of quiet, our eyes continuously darting to the incoming road, watching for Phoenix's car.

Gryphin turned a curious look in my direction, and the curl on his forehead waved lightly in the night wind. "Have you finally decided you want me to turn you into a wolf? The bite doesn't hurt...much."

His suggestion was so absurd that I burst out into a scoffing laugh. "No! That's definitely not it. Plus, if I did decide to become a werewolf, I'd let Kage do it. He looks like he knows what he's doing more than you would."

Kage grinned and nodded. "She's got the right of it there."

Gryphin huffed but still wore a side-smile so I knew he knew I was just teasing him a bit.

"No, my confession is that I have no idea if this is going to work. Aside from all the crazy other stuff, I've never summoned a ghost that I don't know before. Any time I've needed to summon one, I've at least interacted with them once, but with Sarah, the alpha's mate, I've never even met her."

Kage pressed his lips into a thoughtful pout while Gryphin studied me for a second.

"Wait, maybe you have met her, just not her human self?" Gryphin said.

I frowned. "She might have been in that pack of ghost wolves, and she might not have. We don't know for sure. Even if she was in that pack, they were wolves, and the only way I interacted with them was to stand there terrified, hoping they couldn't touch me as an aliver. I'm not sure that counts as meeting someone."

Kage shrugged. "Guess there's only one way to find out."

"Did you manage to get information from your dad about where she is? He did say something about knowing," I asked, giving him hopeful eyes.

Gryphin sighed, rubbed at the back of his neck, and shook his head. "No. I'm sorry. He's just been so...unapproachable lately."

It didn't take much to remember his giant, angry eyes, and I nodded. "I get that. I'm sorry. I'm not sure—"

Kage began talking, interrupting me. I let him continue because I didn't really want to say what I was afraid I needed to say. "The alpha has been under a lot of stress recently. Hopefully, we'll be able to alleviate the worst of it tonight."

As he spoke, Gryphin turned his head to the side as if listening to something.

"Do you hear a car?" I asked, straining my eyes to look through the darkness.

"No, I just feel—"

And suddenly Phoenix was standing in front of us, as if having appeared out of nowhere. "Hey y'all!"

Kage and Gryphin immediately shifted into defensive stances, and I swear one of them growled. Stephanie and I grabbed onto each other and shrieked.

Phoenix just laughed as we all calmed down and realized there wasn't a threat. "Oh man, I love doing that to new people. It's the best part of my job."

"Your job is to show up without warning and scare the pee out of people?" I asked, my voice a bit more high-pitched than I'd like.

They laughed again. "Y'all should have seen your faces. Didn't y'all know that witches can teleport? It's only to places we've been before, but still useful." As they talked, they held their arms out as if to put themselves on display and did a little twirl.

It was hard to see what they were wearing in the dark, but it could have been a skirt because fabric swirled around their legs. A few gems from their bag reflected light as they moved, and their hair bounced merrily.

"I did not know that," I said, exchanging alarmed looks with Stephanie.

"We're not as sneaky as vampires, but we can come close," Phoenix said with a sassy waggle of their shoulders. "Are we ready to get this show on the road?"

"Do you have the potion?" Kage asked.

Phoenix pulled a small vial from their bag and handed it to Kage with a smile. "Yes, this little guy took a lot of doing. I hope you're ready to pay me handsomely."

"I understand," Kage said, swirling the potion around. "It's smaller than I thought it would be."

Phoenix shrugged. "It'll do the job."

I took a breath, glanced at Steph who was still staring at Phoenix, and decided to be brave. "Listen. I know we've all worked hard to get to this point, but I'm not sure we're going to be able to continue."

Kage and Gryphin both quirked their heads to the side, and, under other circumstances, I probably would have giggled at their puppy-like actions. Phoenix merely looked at me as they listened.

"After having just gotten Steph into her body with the help of the necromancers, it's become quite clear we can't rely on that route again to put her back. It costs them too much, and I already owe them a big favor. I have a feeling that asking them to do it again on the exact same person they performed the ritual on will have some bad results. I'm not sure we can do this plan, after all."

Stephanie frowned as I talked, and she looked down at her borrowed flip-flops when I was finished. "Well...maybe..."

Phoenix interrupted whatever she was about to say with an upraised hand. "Hold on a minute here. While I was doing research for the potion, I stumbled upon something else that might help us. I grabbed the herb just in case I was right, and I have to say, I'm glad I did. We can use it to hold your friend's body in a type of waiting stasis while she does her business as a ghost. As long as we get her reunited in under the time limit, we should be good."

We were quiet for a second as we processed the new information.

"Wait, what?" I was the first to ask, my brain reeling with all kinds of different possibilities. "We don't have to kill her?"

"Well, yes, in a way, but she'll be mostly dead, not completely dead. It'll be fine, and you won't owe anything more to the necromancers, even if it might cost you a bit more to pay to the arcanist. Luckily for you, I'm the type that only deals in cash, not favors."

With crinkled eyebrows, I turned to Kage who was already nodding. "Good. I like this better, actually. Don't worry about the money, Hanna. We'll do what we need to do."

Phoenix beamed with happiness, either from the fact that they'd been able to solve one of our big issues, or that they were going to get some more money out of it, or both. It was probably both things.

I turned to Stephanie. "You know, you can still back out of this if you want to. I made a promise not to make you do anything you don't want to do. This might be your last chance."

Stephanie took time to look at both Kage and Gryphin and then toward the village behind us. Coming back to face me, she shook her head. "No. I've come this far. I've spent my whole life doing stuff just for me, now I want to do something for others."

"That's admirable of you," Kage said with a kind smile in her direction.

"We appreciate this more than you'll ever know," Gryphin said. "It's my dad you're saving, you know?"

Stephanie nodded. "Yes. Well, at least I'll try my best."

Kage handed the potion back to Phoenix, who tucked it securely in their bag, and pulled out his phone. "Okay, sounds like we're ready to go. I'm going to text Billy to meet us out there. He's been working hard to keep the alpha busy with extra work tonight. Gryphin and I will change, and then we'll run everyone out to the meadow."

Gryphin gave me a quick side-hug before he left to go around the building to wolf-up. "Don't worry. Everything will be fine."

"Is my expression that obvious?"

He laughed and the sound brought some warmth into my frayed nerves. "Maybe just a bit."

Chapter 24

Phoenix and Stephanie stood next to me as we waited for the wolves to change. They'd gone around the building we were standing next to, but it was still close enough to hear the snarling and bone breaking.

"This...is terrifying," Stephanie said, grabbing onto my arm.

Phoenix gave her a wicked smile. "At least they're out of sight. Watching them change is even worse than hearing them change. So glad I'm not a wolf. Though, I have to say it would be lovely to be as fit as most wolves are."

I patted Stephanie's hand. "It's okay. I'm still not used to it, but Gryphin assures me the pain is only temporary and quickly forgotten when the rush of being a free wolf takes over."

"I can't believe I'm about to ride a werewolf." Stephanie swallowed, and I didn't need any lighting to know her face was pale.

"Well, that part is actually pretty fun," I said. "Terrifying, but fun."

"It's one of my favorite rides to go on," Phoenix said with an eyebrow waggle.

Stephanie and I burst into giggles, partly because the joke was funny, but also to expel some nerves.

Not too long after, but long enough for me to wish I had brought a thicker jacket, Kage and Gryphin loped around the corner of the building with long legs and paws at least the size of my face.

I'd seen Gryphin's wolf before, and I knew how big he was, but it still took my breath away. There was one thing to see nature far away, like at a zoo or something, but it was quite another to be so close to a wolf that I could see the glint of saliva off his teeth.

And Kage was even bigger than Gryphin.

I supposed it made sense that Kage was bigger as he was the second in command and needed to have a sizable prowess, or else the other wolves would take his spot in the hierarchy. Frankly, I was just grateful he wasn't as big as the alpha had been.

If Gryphin was the size of a van, and Bertram was nearly the size of a church bus, Kage was somewhere in between. His fur was the color of midnight, so dark I could barely see his form even from only a few feet away.

Phoenix and Stephanie climbed onto Kage's back as he laid down low enough for them to reach it. Stephanie apologized several times as she pulled fur to get leverage. I tried not to laugh at her concern because I'd been the same way my first time riding a wolf, but it was hard not to. Phoenix sat behind her as confidently as a professional who had ridden werewolves since childhood. I was sure that wasn't actually the case, but what did I know?

Gryphin lowered down next to me, and I climbed on his back as quickly as I could. I only apologized once when I finally was in position, straddling his warm fur. Again, I was struck by how soft he was, and I couldn't help but run my fingers through the grey strands. I swear he almost purred for a second.

The last thing I did was to check and make sure the glasses case was still tucked securely into my pocket so it wouldn't fly out. Then as an extra added security, I pulled the pocket underneath my stomach and pressed it against my body so there was even less chance of being dislodged.

Then we were off.

We'd decided to do this again in the meadow because it was a known place that Sarah had enjoyed in life. We'd seen the ghost wolves there before, and we wanted to keep away from the village and other wolves of the pack who might get curious. There was the small chance that the alpha would come thundering back into the place while we were there, but Kage and Mr. Tyler had put some work into motion so that he was hopefully back in the village dealing with the wolf drama he'd been basically neglecting since Sarah had died.

I hoped he stayed there.

Being on Gryphin's back was even more overwhelming in the darkness. The trees whizzed by me so fast, I was under a constant fear that we'd run right into one of them. Logically, I knew Gryphin was perfectly capable of dodging trees while running at a pace he probably often ran at, but my poor human instincts were screaming that we were going too fast, too haphazardly. I had been determined to keep my head up during the ride so I could at least put on a brave face, but it wasn't long before I buried myself deep into Gryphin's rolling muscles and soft fur.

I hoped Stephanie was faring better than I was, but occasionally, I heard a shriek escape her lips, usually followed by a giddy laugh from Phoenix.

It wasn't long before we got there, but it felt like forever while adrenaline was rushing through me. Gryphin slowed to a trot as we entered the meadow. There were amazingly beautiful bright stars above us, unlike any I was able to see in the city, but there still wasn't much light to see by. The only reason I knew we had arrived was because the trees opened up and weren't threatening to jump into our path anymore.

Kage had gotten there before us and was leaning down so Steph and Phoenix could disembark. The arcanist had to steady my friend and basically support her the entire climb down. Her legs were shaking even more than mine were.

Hoping I was a little more graceful than I had been when getting on, I kind of half-slid off Gryphin's side and landed wobblily. I checked my pocket for the glasses, making sure they were indeed still there. I knew they hadn't flown out since they had been lodged against me, but I still wanted to double and triple-check just in case.

They were much too valuable to even be taking them out like this, but what was the point in having them if I couldn't use them when I needed to?

Once Stephanie was on solid ground again, she promptly sat down in the grass, groaned, and put her head between her knees. "I think I'm going to be sick."

I went to her side and kneeled so I could rub her back. "Just breathe through it. Focus on breathing."

Kage shook after the riders got off and busied himself with sniffing around the clearing, probably checking for anything out of the ordinary.

Gryphin was content to sit down next to us and use his wide eyes to keep watch.

Phoenix put their hands on their hips and looked up at the night sky while we waited for Stephanie to recover. "This is a beautiful place. I can see why the alpha's mate liked it here so much."

I spared a glance away from Stephanie to look at the sky again. "It's amazing both in the day and night. It would be one of my favorite places too, probably, if I were a wolf and all."

Stephanie just groaned.

Another wolf entered the clearing from a different direction. With golden fur, this one was a bit easier to see than Kage who had almost disappeared after taking a few steps away from us. Since neither Gryphin nor Kage seemed surprised by his entrance, I figured it must have been Mr. Tyler there to offer his services.

Indeed, when the light wolf entered our circle, he nodded in such a familiar way that it made me smile a little bit.

Phoenix turned to us and started rummaging in their bag. "Right. We're all here now. There's no reason to put this off any further, and since the wolves can't talk, guess it's up to me to get things started."

Steph was still trembling as I helped her stand but at least she didn't seem in danger of passing out or losing her sweet tea anymore.

"Last chance, Steph. Are you sure you're okay with this?" I asked, keeping my hand on her back in case she decided to topple over.

Her legs might have been shaky, but her nod was resolute. "Yes. I promise I'm good to go. I really want to help."

"Okay, and just in case I don't get to say it later, thank you so much for your help. I honestly don't know how we would be able to do this without you." I squeezed her shoulder in a quick side hug.

"That's if I can actually do what you need," she said with a nervous laugh.

"We've got this. No worries."

Phoenix handed her the potion vial and their long, manicured fingernails glittered in the dim starlight. "Alright, make sure this is securely in your clothes, preferably a pocket so that when your spiritual-self awakens, you will have it on your person."

Stephanie nodded, took the vial, and shoved it deep into the pocket of the sweatpants.

Phoenix turned back to their bag and pulled out a small plastic container that looked more like a spice shaker than a magical arcanist tool. "This is the herb we talked about. It will only take a few shakes on your tongue to mostly kill you. Anything else and we'll completely kill you, and you'd have to go see those grouchy necromancers again."

"Definitely don't want to do that." Steph glanced at me and laughed nervously.

I joined in her nervous laughter, once again wondering what the order was going to demand from me in return.

"Might be best if you lie down before I give you the herb so you don't have to endure a nasty fall," Phoenix said, indicating a nice place on the grass.

Steph settled herself in the tall grass, and Gryphin moved to stand next to her, probably to keep watch and make sure no one stepped on her or anything else during our mission.

I kneeled and grabbed her hand. "We'll be right here. When you appear as a ghost, you'll probably pop into your haunt again. I'll give you some time to orient yourself and then summon you back here, okay?"

"Okay." Her voice sounded small and worried, but mine probably sounded like that too.

Phoenix kneeled on the other side. "Are you ready, dear?"

Steph nodded and obediently opened her mouth.

With a concentrated look, Phoenix opened the spice shaker and knocked it twice onto Steph's tongue. She made a disgruntled face as she absorbed the herb.

It didn't take long for her eyes to droop, and her chest to stop moving. I carefully laid her hand down next to the body and stood up.

"And you're sure her body won't get any physical damage from being like that for a few minutes?" I frowned, staring down at my friend.

"As long as it's not more than fifteen minutes. This herb has been blessed with a spell as well, so it's got a little extra protection with it. She'll be fine. It's sweet how much you're worried about her, though. You two must be really good friends," Phoenix said with a smile as they set a timer on their watch.

I shrugged. "I wish we were closer, actually, but yes. I don't want anything bad to happen to her. I'd feel terrible."

"It won't, sweetie," Phoenix said. "But only if we get the other part of this. Are you ready to summon a ghost wolf yet?"

"I guess." I looked around the clearing with wide eyes, unable to see Kage, but Mr. Tyler and Gryphin's wolves were waiting nearby ready to jump in to help in any way they could.

I turned to Gryphin's grey form. "Actually, I know this is out of our plan, but I'm thinking it might be better if you can talk to your stepmom face-to-face. I hate to ask this of you since it sounds super painful, and, maybe I should have asked this before Steph went under, but could you change back into a human?"

Gryphin tilted his head to the side in a questioning puppy-like look again.

"Yes, I have an item that will help you talk to her. I think it'll be our best shot."

Gryphin nodded and turned back toward the trees for some more privacy. We hadn't brought any extra clothes with us since I'd failed to plan for this part, but I hadn't wanted to reveal the glasses unless I had to. At first, I wasn't sure if I would use them but being in the clearing had me remembering how scary those ghost wolves had been. If Gryphin was able to help calm them then the whole thing could go faster, and we could get Steph back in her body quicker.

Brandon had been right about my planning methods, but, luckily, he wasn't there to scold me about it. If it worked, he could scold me later as much as he wanted.

Phoenix narrowed their eyes at me as I spoke to Gryphin, but I tried not to get too concerned.

I took a deep breath and closed my eyes, remembering the lady I had only seen once from the picture in Gryphin's room. She had red hair, a fun smile, and was petite compared to Gryphin's towering dad. It took a few moments, but I could feel her inside the forest as a faint presence. She was running with the pack feeling free and happy, but, as I yanked her toward us, her happiness grew into confusion. She fought me a little, and it took me several more seconds to pull her spirit into the clearing with us.

I must have been getting better at the summoning thing to be able to feel and understand the ghost like that—even if it still had taken me much longer to summon her than usual, no thanks to the fight she'd put up.

It didn't help that while I was trying to focus on the wolf, Gryphin was snapping his bones and growling faintly only a few paces away. I was getting more used to the horrifying sound but was still feeling nervous and concerned. Part of it may have been some weird excitement at possibly seeing the guy shirtless again, but that would have been a dumb thing to be thinking about at a time like this.

The hairs on my neck prickled, and Mr. Tyler let out a warning growl as I opened my eyes to see a brilliantly blue, ghostly wolf standing nearly nose-to-nose with me. Kage whined nearby, and I figured that the wolf forms might have been more sensitive to the ghost spirits than the humans.

As for Phoenix, they appeared almost bored, one hand resting on their bag strap while they examined their fingernails on the other hand. What they could see in the dark was lost on me.

Sarah's wolf eyes were quite intimidating. They stared at me with a challenge, not but a foot away from my face. I wasn't sure what wolf protocol was here. Was it better or worse for me to back down and look away? I figured in this situation it would be best if I appeared to have some kind of control.

She was a smaller wolf than Gryphin, probably only the size of a car, so still really big. I couldn't tell her coloring while in ghost form, but I imagined her fur was a deep red, and her eyes had probably been some kind of golden brown, maybe.

A low growl rumbled from her throat, and as we stared each other down, I prayed she wasn't able to use some ghostly energy to attack me in the physical world somehow. She probably was totally capable of it, but I wasn't going to let the thought enter her mind.

My eyes were watering from not blinking, and just as I was sure I was going to let her win this staring contest, something behind me grabbed her attention, and her gaze shifted away.

"Uhm," Gryphin said, unsure what to do as he stood behind me. "I'm really wishing we'd brought some shorts out. I mean, I don't care about being nude since it's like a totally common and comfortable thing for us wolves, but I can't imagine it being super comfortable for you or Phoenix."

"Oh, honey," Phoenix said with a wave of their hand. "You don't have anything I haven't seen before. Although, not everyone can make it look as good."

I smirked, relieved that Sarah seemed to not want to eat me for the moment, but I refused to turn around. Both because I didn't want to give her the wrong idea, and because I wasn't sure I wanted to see Gryphin in the nude. That image would probably be hard to get out of my head.

"What do you want me to do?" Gryphin asked, his voice sounding only a few feet behind me.

"Hang out for a second. I'm going to summon Stephanie and see if we can get Sarah to drink the potion. I might need your help with the second part," I said and closed my eyes, hoping that Sarah didn't take that as a sign to attack me.

So far, she seemed content to watch and wait, keeping her eyes on Gryphin as if she recognized him. Mr. Tyler was nearby, but she hadn't even spared him a glance. I had no idea how close they had been in real life, but it was clear she felt more connected to Gryphin, which made sense since she was his stepmom and all.

It was much easier to summon Stephanie, compared to Sarah, to the clearing, though I had been worried that it hadn't been enough time for her spirit to appear at the bridge. Thankfully, the transition from human to ghost hadn't taken long, at least in this instance. I'm sure it wasn't an exact science.

"It worked!" Stephanie said with a little hop of excitement, holding the potion vial above her head that was now ghostly and incorporeal just as she was. Then her eyes fell on the wolf still not but a foot away from my face. "Woah."

"Hey, Steph. We need to get her to drink that now. This might seem scary, but I'm pretty sure that even though she's able to touch you, she can't really hurt you. I think?" I said, keeping my gaze level on the wolf.

"I don't feel reassured," Steph said, but she did take a couple of steps toward the wolf. "Hey there, pretty girl. Do you feel up for a tasty drink? It's probably been a while since you've had something to drink. I bet your throat is very dry."

Sarah kept her eyes on Gryphin, but a low growl told us she was aware of Stephanie's proximity.

Steph froze and glanced at me in concern as if I knew what to do.

Well, maybe this time, I did.

One trick I could have tried was merely commanding her to drink the potion, but I wasn't sure that it would work on a ghost wolf, and I was hoping to save that as a last resort. Commanding her could have provoked her in a way we didn't need. She might have refused and bit my head off instead.

No, there was another thing I wanted to try first, even if that was also risky.

"Gryphin, there are some glasses in my pocket. I need you to take them out and put them on," I said, keeping my gaze on the wolf. It wasn't too hard to keep staring at her majestic beauty.

"Glasses?" Gryphin asked as he followed my directions. His breath tickled my hair as he spoke, and I froze as I felt his hand go into my jacket pocket.

"Yes," I swallowed nervously, "glasses. You'll see why in a second."

I felt his warm hand pull the glasses case out of my pocket, heard the hinges squeak as he opened the case, and heard Phoenix draw in a gasping breath.

"Are those...?" Phoenix didn't finish their sentence, but it was enough to make my heart clench.

Had I just made a deadly mistake letting them know I was in possession of such an item? They clearly knew what the glasses were. I might have to check in with Caleb later and see if the vampire forgetting magic would work on a magic user.

I knew the moment Gryphin put the glasses on because he said, "Woah."

"Yes, okay, now try to calm Sarah down so she'll drink that potion," I said, a blush creeping up my cheeks as Gryphin moved into my peripheral vision.

Steph didn't help either when she said, "Wait, are you naked? Is he naked? Hanna, he's naked, and I'm not hating what I see."

"As lovely as this specimen is, I'm going to remind you that we have seven minutes left before Steph needs to be back into her body," Phoenix said, helping us to focus on what we needed to do.

"So, she can hear me, right?" Gryphin asked, standing next to Sarah and reaching a hand out as if to stroke her fur.

"Yes, and you can hear her now too."

"This is amazing!" he said and put his hand through her head.

As for Sarah, her full attention was on her stepson, one ear cocked to the side as if understanding something different was happening.

"Sarah, it's me, Gryphin. Do you remember me?" he asked, dropping his hand from her head, and taking a step back so they could look at each other better.

Grateful that I didn't have to appear dominant to Sarah anymore, I took a step back and raised my hand to a strategic place to block my sight of anything scandalous I might have glimpsed. Using my hand was much easier and more reliable than trusting my eyes not to wander, even if I probably looked weird holding my hand up like that.

Sarah regarded Gryphin with much of the same intense stare she'd been leveling at me. He seemed used to it more than I had been because he only smiled kindly.

"We've missed you, but I think you know that. Dad's been out here running with you, hasn't he?" Gryphin said.

Sarah nodded slowly while still maintaining her stare.

"Yeah, we've been worried about him. I'm sure you've been worried too."

She nodded again.

"We think there's a way to help him, but you've got to change back into a human so we can talk. Do you know how to do that?"

She shook her head and growled deeply from the throat.

"We suspected as much. That's why we've brought this." Gryphin turned to Steph and waved her to come stand next to him.

Steph's expressions were all over the place as she moved to stand next to the naked, muscled guy who was sculpted so finely it was as if he'd been a Renaissance statue brought to life. She kept struggling to keep her gaze on the wolf while wearing an amused smile, but her eyes kept widening when they finally focused on the giant animal in front of her.

If we'd been under different, less tense, circumstances, I probably would have laughed with her about the situation, but as it was, I kept quiet, hoping to lend them as much concentration and peace as they could muster.

"This is Steph." Gryphin gestured to her also-ghostly form. "She's got a potion that we're hoping will help you change back into a human. We had to get this arcanist here to fashion it just for you. Isn't that neat?"

Sarah looked at Steph for a moment and then turned her head to Phoenix who was watching the half of the exchange they could hear and see with a calculated focus I wasn't sure I liked. As the wolf appraised the magic user, she sniffed the air in their direction, and a small growl rumbled inside her throat. Her ears went flat against her head as she lowered her stance.

Glancing between her and Phoenix, Gryphin extended a reassuring hand toward Sarah. "Do you know them?"

She kept up her low growl and didn't move. We took that as a yes and that she didn't like them, however she knew them.

Gryphin frowned and turned to me, his eyebrows upraised in question.

I shrugged, feeling more helpless than I liked. "The only way we'll figure out what is going on is if she'll drink the potion, but now I'm thinking that will be even harder to get her to do."

Gryphin agreed with a nod and turned back to Sarah. "They're only here to help. This is the only way to get you to turn back. We believe in this so much that poor Stephanie's body is laying in the grass behind us so she can come into the spirit world and give this to you."

Steph held up the potion for Sarah to see. The wolf glanced at it, kept growling, and went back to staring at Phoenix.

"What's happening?" Phoenix asked, taking a few steps in my direction. Sarah's gaze followed their movements, and I found myself not wanting to stand close to the magic user.

"We don't know," I said, unsure how much to tell them.

It probably had been stupid of us to trust them so quickly and with so many secrets. We didn't even know anything about this person. I reminded myself that we'd been so desperate for help that we hadn't had a lot of options, but it didn't help assuage the guilt brewing in my stomach.

Despite all I'd been through, I still trusted too easily. Poor Caleb had been trying to teach me this lesson for weeks and I still hadn't learned it.

I was a terrible student.

"Has she recognized me from somewhere?" Phoenix guessed, trying to get context clues from Gryphin's and my behavior.

"It looks like it, and from the growl rumbling in her chest, it's not something she's happy about." I gave them a side-eye and wondered how rude it would be if I took a few steps in the opposite direction.

Mr. Tyler's tan wolf stood silently on his murder-capable paws and turned toward Phoenix. Then he started nudging his head toward the trees as if trying to tell them to leave.

Phoenix glanced at me before looking back at Mr. Tyler. "Is he telling me to go?"

"It might help us in the current situation," I said with an apologetic and wincing smile, wondering how rude I should be getting with the magic user. If they'd done something evil, or if Sarah knew of something bad in their past, perhaps I shouldn't have been smiling at them at all. But I didn't know, so was erring on the side of politeness.

Phoenix glanced back into the deeper darkness behind us and swallowed. "I'm not sure I want to go in there alone."

Mr. Tyler took a few steps toward them and kept nodding his head toward the trees.

"You won't be alone. He'll keep an eye on you," I said, stepping back so Mr. Tyler could keep herding Phoenix away.

They took a few steps back and looked at me in concern. "I haven't done anything wrong! I don't understand how she would know me. It's probably just some misunderstanding."

"Maybe. But we can't get her to change while you're here. Just give her some space, and we'll get to the bottom of everything," I said, hoping they didn't get angry enough to hex us all into newts or something.

Phoenix frowned but let Mr. Tyler guide them past the tree line and out of sight. It felt a bit exposing to lose Mr. Tyler's protective presence, but I knew Kage was still nearby, even if I couldn't see his inky form in the blackness.

Sarah kept glancing off toward where they had gone, but she stopped her continuous growl and only rumbled occasionally. Her ears also perked up some but kept twisting in their direction, alert and listening.

"Okay, so the magic user is gone now. Is that better?" Gryphin said.

My hand was getting tired, so I took a few steps to the left, putting most of Gryphin's exposed body out of my direct sight. If I did lose the battle of where to look, I'd only be looking at a backside instead of anything else. It did help that he was so comfortable being in his birthday suit that it didn't seem that big a deal to him, so it shouldn't have been that big of a deal to anyone else.

The line of thought almost worked to help alleviate the blush on my cheeks.

Sarah didn't respond except to keep a watchful eye on the potion that Steph was holding. Her focus pulled Gryphin's gaze, and he frowned.

"You still don't trust the potion because they made it, do you?" he asked.

Sarah growled in response.

Steph frowned and dropped her arms. "This is not working. I've got one job, and I'm failing."

"We're running out of time, too," I said, glancing Phoenix's way and hoping they were still keeping track of the minutes.

Gryphin leaned in closer to Sarah and pleaded, "This is all we know to do. Please drink the potion! Steph is running out of time before she has to go back to her body, and she's the only one who can give you the potion. Please drink it?"

Sarah shook her head and growled, still shooting glances to where the arcanist had gone.

Without Phoenix to update me on the time and cursing myself for not setting a timer with my phone, I started to feel panicked. It was clear Sarah wasn't going to drink the potion on her own, and if she knew something about Phoenix that we didn't, I was having a hard time blaming her. How did we even know the potion was going to do what it was supposed to do?

One thing I did know was I couldn't let Stephanie die again.

There was one more thing that I could try, and, even though I really didn't want to exercise control like that, the other options weren't feasible either.

I took a deep breath, told myself I was doing the right thing, and said as powerfully as I could, "Drink the potion, Sarah! I command you as a Seer and you as a ghost that you must drink the potion!"

Gryphin, Sarah, and Stephanie all looked at me in alarm, and I pressed my lips together in resolution. Yes, what I was doing wasn't right, but I didn't know what else to do. I wasn't going to let something bad happen when I could prevent it.

Steph took a few brave steps until she was close enough to the wolf that the potion could reach her. As she unstopped the top, the vial made a small popping sound. Steph's fingers trembled as she held the potion near the wolf. I had to give the girl credit for being so brave. One snap and the wolf could take off her hand, if ghosts could do that, that is. Hopefully not.

Sarah's growling became more constant and deeper, but that was the only change. Her will was strong, but mine was stronger.

"Are you sure about this?" Gryphin asked, his eyes wide with worry and concern.

I shook my head and threw my arms up helplessly. "I don't know what else to do! I'm not letting Steph die again." Forcing the panic and fear I was feeling into words, I screamed, "Drink! The! Potion!"

Snarling, her teeth on full display, Sarah's head tipped back as if being pulled by some invisible force. Steph took the chance and poured the suspect contents into the wolf's mouth and then jumped away as fast as she could.

I stood, breathing heavily, feeling terrible, and watched for what the potion did. Frankly, it was a surprise to all of us that it did exactly what Phoenix said it would do.

Sarah's fur rippled in waves, and I braced myself for snapping bones and snarling growls, but there must have been something about that potion, or perhaps the fact that Sarah had no corporeal body, because in the matter of a blink, a human fell to her knees in the grass where a wolf had been.

She looked like what I'd remembered from the picture, her sleek hair cut smartly at her chin, her body small and lithe, and her fiery eyes looking right at me in rage.

"I'm sorry! I'm so sorry!" I fell onto my knees as well, looking at her on an even level. "But look! You're human again!"

Gryphin, still wearing the glasses, although they were slightly askew, slunk onto the ground as well.

Steph grinned at me triumphantly. I had only time to grin back at her before her gaze shifted into the distance and my heart sunk, knowing exactly what that meant.

Sarah and Gryphin, oblivious to what was happening to my friend, started talking, but I was too distracted to listen to their conversation.

"Hanna? I feel weird," Steph said, staring at something I couldn't see.

Chapter 25

"Wait! Steph! Don't go toward the light!" I said, knowing that I was echoing a cliché, but not knowing what else to say.

She blinked slowly and turned to look at me. "I feel lighter and freer than I've felt in my whole life."

"Phoenix!" I yelled, glancing toward the trees where Mr. Tyler had taken them. They might have made Sarah mad, but at this point, we needed them.

Gryphin finally looked at me. "Hanna? What's wrong?"

Sarah, who was also naked of course, sat back into the grass and frowned, probably super confused about what was going on but content to let us deal with our other situation first.

And, of course, Brandon popped in next to me at the same time. "Hanna! What's going on? I could feel your distress!"

Steph's eyes grew unfocused again. "Hanna, I don't think I want to go back."

Brandon slowly turned to look at Stephanie. "Oh no."

"Phoenix!" I screamed again, tears welling in my eyes, making the dark trees blur. "Wake Stephanie right now!"

Movement came from the darkness, but I had to blink several times before I could see Phoenix and Mr. Tyler rushing toward us. Phoenix's bag was bouncing up and down with their long gait, and they clutched at the top tightly so it didn't spill its contents.

"All she needs is this antidote!" Phoenix said, holding up something I couldn't see in the dark.

"Then hurry up and give it to her!" Brandon yelled unhelpfully.

Gryphin, still wearing the glasses, gave me an odd look which I ignored, frankly not having time to explain why another ghost popped up out of nowhere.

I turned back to Steph who was starting to let off little bits of blue dust while staring into the place that even *I* couldn't see. "Hang in there, Steph! We're bringing your body back!"

Then she looked at me with the clearest focus I'd seen from her in a while. "Hanna, I don't want to go back. I had a lot of time to think about things while at the bridge, and now that I've been able to do something important to help someone else, I want to go on to see what's next. There's a peace there that's so calming...and indescribable. It's like a promise and reassurance that I'll never have to worry about anything else ever again."

As she spoke, Phoenix reached her body's side. Gryphin helped lift her head and shoulders so the arcanist could put whatever the antidote was into her mouth.

"No, Steph." I shook my head. "You can't go back. You've got your whole life to live. What about doing something to help others as a career? You could become a nurse or a doctor or even a teacher. Wouldn't that be great to stay and help others?"

"I suppose I'll have to leave that to you. Please, Hanna, let me go."

It was the "please" that really got me. Who was I to keep her trapped in life when she had a chance to cross over? Wasn't that my whole mission in life?

"Steph, I'm so sorry. I didn't mean for any of this to happen."

She smiled as she faded into emptiness. "I know, Hanna. Keep up the good work."

Phoenix was shaking Stephanie's body as her blonde hair flailed around her head. "Wake up, girl. Wake up!"

"It's pointless, guys," I said, turning away from where Steph had been standing in the grass. "She's gone. She's crossed over."

"She's crossed over? Didn't we pick this girl solely because we knew she wouldn't cross over?" Phoenix asked, stopping their attempts to revive her and gently put her back into the grass. "We were cutting it close on time, but I'm pretty sure we got the antidote to her quick enough."

As if to mock us, the timer sounded on Phoenix's smartwatch, declaring to all around that Stephanie's time was up.

I slumped into the grass, falling back into its cushioned crunch, and stared up at the stars while tears streamed down my face. It was hard to understand what hurt the most—guilt from being unable to help her live a full and happy life, or the fact that I'd miss the sweet girl who I'd known for a while but was now becoming a real friend.

I heard Gryphin explaining some of what had happened to Sarah, who, now that she was a human again, seemed to have a calm and patient demeanor. Phoenix was out of my sight, so I had no idea what they were into. Mr. Tyler's stoic wolf came up and bumped into my face with his nose. It was a sweet gesture, but I was too worried about getting tears on his fur to appreciate it at the time.

Brandon sat down in the grass next to me. It had been trampled down with all of our walking around, but a few errant sprigs stuck up through his knees. "Hanna, it's okay. I'm certain she's in a better place, and you helped her get there. It's what we do, remember?"

I took a trembling breath, trying to ready myself to speak without blubbering. "If I hadn't asked her to do this stupid thing, she could go on living and enjoying all the things in life she didn't get to do."

"Pretty sure she's enjoyed plenty of things already. More than I did, anyway. Think of all the pain and struggles she doesn't have to endure. We all die in the end. Might as well die before we have to go through oodles of pain. I know you'll agree when you're old and sitting in a nursing home while it hurts just to sit and breathe."

"It hurts to do that right now."

Brandon smiled sympathetically. "I know, sweetie."

Slowly, I pulled myself up into a sitting position, knowing that I still had work to do, and, although my heart was hurting with every beat, I needed to push aside my pain. I could mourn later. "Did you call me sweetie?"

He shrugged. "Just trying it out. I feel like we need pet names."

I gave him a flat look and then turned to Gryphin and Sarah who were standing nearby, concerned expressions on their faces. Both were still naked and completely comfortable in their own skins. I supposed it came from being wolves and changing around others in the nude so often. I kind of envied their confidence, but of course, they had a reason for it. Their bodies were both sculpted and muscled in a striking way that indicated power running just beneath the surface.

"Maybe you should take a picture," Brandon said with a scoff. "It'll last longer."

Gryphin and Sarah turned amused looks on my ghost friend and he froze, suddenly realizing he could be heard.

Flushing, having studied Gryphin a little too long, I forced my eyes to their faces. "I'm sorry I've...well, one thing at a time. Poor Steph. Sarah? How are you feeling? I'm really sorry for having to make you take that potion. I didn't know what else to do."

Sarah eyed Phoenix warily. They had backed a few paces away from Steph, and was standing up, staring at her body sadly.

"It wasn't nice, that's true," Sarah said as she looked Phoenix up and down, "but apparently this liar here doesn't lie about everything."

"Sarah, do you know this magic user?" Gryphin asked, looking a little closer at Phoenix.

"Yes, they're the reason I'm dead, actually," Sarah said, her eyes still hard and staring.

"Well, no wonder you didn't want to take a potion from them." I pulled myself up and out of the grass, wiping a few errant tears away.

Brandon stood next to me and surveyed Phoenix.

As for the arcanist, they were lost on half the conversation, still apparently thinking about Steph's cold body.

"Is it true, Phoenix? Did you murder Sarah?" I wanted to take a step toward them in case it would help me be more intimidating, but I stayed where I was as they could have been a danger to me.

Mr. Tyler seemed to sense his powerful presence would be appreciated, so he came to stand next to me, his focused eyes staring down the magic user. He also happened to walk right through Brandon who gave the large wolf a flat glare and moved around to my other side.

Phoenix was shaking their head. "No, I didn't murder her. I would never—"

"I didn't say they murdered me, just the reason I'm dead," Sarah said with a sigh and turned to face Gryphin. "I have to tell you a story."

"—hurt anyone like that," Phoenix continued, heedless of what Sarah had said. "I didn't realize who this was we were trying to talk to. But you know what? Y'all don't need me anymore. I'll come back to collect the rest of my fee later," Phoenix said with a frown in my direction and promptly disappeared.

"Wait!" I tried to stop them, too late.

"Cool trick," Brandon said with an appreciative nod.

Mr. Tyler growled and sniffed the air as if trying to track them somehow.

Kage finally made his appearance again as he oozed out of the dark night. He also sniffed the air, growled, and looked around.

"That's a big doggie." Brandon's eyes were wide as he got a view of Kage.

Gryphin growled too, but it was slightly less ominous coming from his human throat. "Coward."

Sarah shrugged. "It's fine. Better that they're gone now, really."

I had to agree, remembering how greedily they'd looked at the glasses I had lent Gryphin. I'd have to find a much better hiding place for those now that someone knew I had them.

"We've been trying to track you down for so long," Gryphin said, turning to Sarah with a soft frown. "Dad is really messed up about this, and we hoped that getting answers from you would help give him some peace."

Sarah nodded. "Yes, I may not agree with your methods," she glanced at me warily, "but I agree that we need to help your father. He spends most nights running with the ghost wolf pack."

"How do you think he can sense where you guys are? Is that a werewolf trick?" I asked, unable to prevent myself from getting answers about life's mysteries where I could.

"More like an alpha trick," Sarah said. "All the ghosts running here are former members of this pack. The ones who died while he was alpha, he can feel. I'm sure it was distracting before I died, but afterward, it was probably almost painful for Bertram to ignore."

"That's enough to make someone a little insane," I said with a pensive frown.

Gryphin furrowed his eyebrows in thought while Sarah nodded again.

"Yes, it could do that. Plus, it pulled him away from his alive pack, and I'm certain that's been causing extra problems."

"What can we do to help get him peace?" Gryphin asked.

"I'm betting we'll need to help her cross over before he'll fully be at peace," I said, my mind already thinking of things we could try to help Sarah. "If he can sense her out here running with the other ghosts, then he'll probably never be able to focus on real life."

"That is if I can get back into wolf form," Sarah said, looking down at her fleshy human body.

I winced. "Right. Sorry. Again. We needed to talk to you."

Sarah waved it off with her ghostly hand. "It's fine. I understand. Mostly. Gryphin," she turned to her stepson, "I'm afraid I owe you and your father and the whole pack, really, an apology. I went and did something stupid, and now you're all paying for it."

"I'm sure you had your reasons," Gryphin said, giving her one of the most patient and kind smiles I'd seen.

"They felt like important reasons at the time, but after everything that's happened, I'm not so sure anymore. Let me start by saying that I've often been jealous of your mother, Gryph. She was able to have a child. She was so strong, she even carried a werewolf pup for a whole pregnancy. I didn't meet your dad until you were about five, of course, but knowing that she'd been able to handle that and give birth to a wonderful child such as yourself, it just ate me up inside with jealousy."

Kage had faded back into the darkness, but Mr. Tyler still quietly kept watch nearby. His ears kept tilted in different directions as various night sounds rang out, but I had a feeling he was trying to learn as much from our sides of the conversation as he could glean.

Gryphin pulled his eyebrows together and frowned. "I didn't know you felt this way. You don't need to feel jealous, though. She died a year later when another pack attacked us. If it had been you there instead, you could have put up much more of a fight."

Sarah smiled kindly at Gryphin as he tried to understand why a werewolf would ever be jealous of a mere mortal. "Yes, that's true, but I will never be able to have a child. It's impossible for a werewolf to resist change for an entirety of nine months. Plus, a full-blooded werewolf in the womb is bound to do some damage. It's just not possible. But as a human, your mother was able to produce you, and that was a gift that I wanted desperately to give to your father."

"But he already had me, and, these days, he barely looks at me. I know he'd rather have you a million times over than another kid." Gryphin's eyes were full of pain as his shoulders slumped downwards.

Sarah tried to place a soft hand on his cheek but couldn't make contact. "I know this now, but at the time, it seemed like too big of a burden to bear. I went in search of an arcanist that I heard of who was powerful enough to give me something to help resist the changes and hopefully allow me to carry a child to delivery."

Brandon was still standing next to me, and he made a thoughtful noise in his throat. "The more I learn about witches, the more I'm thinking they're pretty powerful."

"And this magic user was Phoenix?" I found myself asking even though I was trying to give them space to talk. Of course, as Gryphin had the glasses, they didn't honestly need me sitting there, and that realization felt kind of weird. However, I was too curious to dismiss myself, and until they told me to go away, I was sitting in the grass missing Steph and hoping I didn't get any ticks from the abundance of nature around us.

Sarah turned to me and nodded. "Yes. Somehow, they had gotten a reputation for doing difficult magic. Something about bringing back someone from the dead, so I sought them out, hoping they could do other impossible things like help a werewolf have a baby."

Gryphin sighed and put his fingers into his hair, tugging at the curls slightly. They sprang back into their usual shape as if he'd never touched them at all. "Why would you do that? Did you tell Dad any of this?"

"No, I didn't." Ghostly tears pooled in her eyes as she looked at Gryphin with soft tenderness. "I made many mistakes. The first is that I tried to change who I was. The second was not involving your father in any of this."

"We could have helped you, somehow. These difficult feelings weren't something you had to suffer for yourself." Gryphin's face and voice fell as he said, "I thought we were a family."

"Oh, baby! We are!" Sarah tried again to touch Gryphin, but her ghostly arms went right through him.

Mustering some courage to shove away the awkwardness, I decided I could be of use after all. I crawled over to where Gryphin was kneeling in the grass, and making sure to stay more behind him than in front and keeping my eyes on things they should see, I wrapped my arms around his muscled arms and leaned my head on one of his shoulders. His skin was much warmer to the touch than I had anticipated, and I was suddenly grateful for the warmth to combat the chilly night air. The lean muscles were tense at first but slowly relaxed after I kept holding on to him, putting as much love as I was sure Sarah wanted to give the child she had raised as her own.

Brandon huffed and probably rolled his eyes, but I wasn't looking at him so I couldn't be sure. He didn't like the idea of me hugging this chiseled man of a wolf, but he was just going to have to deal with it.

"Of course, we are a family," Sarah said as I kept hugging Gryphin. I couldn't see her face, but I hoped she was happy I was trying to hug her son for her instead of annoyed or creeped out that I was butting in. "I care about you just as much as I ever would care for a child I bore. I feel terrible for the choices I made, and if I could have a second chance, I would do everything differently."

Gryphin had to clear his throat a few times before he could speak again, but he was finally able to get out some words. I could hear his voice through his body where I laid my head, and it felt a bit too intimate to be so close. "So what happened then? How did you die?"

"It was so stupid, really. Phoenix said they would be able to cast a spell with the help of one of their coven members, I think her name was Rosie or Rose, and they would be able to help me resist the call of the moon. They did say there would be weird side effects, and it would be best if I didn't stay around other wolves as the thrill for the change and the hunt can be contagious. I decided it wasn't worth it, and tried to leave that night, but Rose's guardian stood in my way and wouldn't let me leave the house we were staying at. We fought, but because I hadn't been able to get enough time to change into a wolf, he overpowered me and simply snapped my neck."

"What did she just say?" Brandon's voice sounded pained.

At the first mention of the witch's name, I was frozen. I barely remembered to breathe as my brain tried to catch up to everything she'd just said. In shock, I slowly pulled away from Gryphin and fell back into the grass, my lips stuck in a surprised gape.

Gryphin recovered faster than I, but that made sense since he hadn't been searching for Rose for over a month like I had. "Why would they stop you from leaving like that? It seems odd that they were willing to help you, but then refuse to let you leave."

"Her name was Rose?" I finally said, blinking slowly.

Sarah glanced at me in curiosity as she answered Gryphin's question. "I'm not too sure, but I think it had something to do with the fact that I wasn't indebted to them yet so they couldn't be sure I would keep their secrets. Maybe? The goon didn't explain to me as we fought."

Gryphin sighed. "I'm sorry, Sarah. That had to have been scary."

She shrugged. "It wasn't terrible as deaths go. It was over before I even realized it. You will tell your father that I'm sorrier than I can say, won't you?"

"Of course."

"Did this Rose have like perfectly-styled blonde hair and legs for days?" I asked, my voice rough.

Mr. Tyler had stood sometime in the last few minutes and was studying my face thoughtfully. He was aware of my issues with Rose and possibly had one himself since she was tied to a curse that had been put on him several months ago.

Sarah's focus turned to me. "Yes, that sounds like her. Why? Do you know her?"

"Do we know her? She's only the person that's been haunting us way more than any ghost could," Brandon grumbled.

"Why?" Sarah asked, glancing between me and Brandon.

"She just owes us many things, including an explanation." Brandon shook his head as he talked.

"I've got to free those ghosts," I said, still dazed. "Do you know where she is? Do you think you could tell me how to get to the place where you saw her last?"

Mr. Tyler's rumbling growl warned me that something was wrong before I heard her voice ring out across the clearing.

"That won't be necessary, honey. I'm right here. It's a shame I won't be around long enough for you to ask questions, though. I'm terribly busy," a haughty, clear voice said from behind me.

Chapter 26

S lowly, my heart hammering inside my ribcage, I turned to find Rose, Phoenix, a tall hulking man, and several ghosts standing in the tall grass near the trees. I didn't recognize the man with them, but I did remember a couple of the ghosts, including that kid from the 70s that had come to chat up Brandon while he'd been getting rid of Mr. Tyler's curse. It also happened to be that that same kid had been trapped with Rose solely because of my help. She probably wouldn't have been able to capture him without me.

Brandon cursed, Gryphin jumped up and immediately started to change into a wolf as if sensing it would be needed, while Sarah glared as she pulled herself into a standing position.

As for me, as graceful as I always am, I scrambled on the slick grass, struggling to get on solid footing for at least a few seconds. I only almost fell back down twice.

"What—What are you doing here?" I said, breathless.

Before she could answer, a snarl sounded from the left. I only had a second to see Kage's sleek black form before he clobbered the tall man, and they both went rolling into the grass and through several of Rose's ghosts who only look mildly disturbed by the confrontation.

Mr. Tyler didn't take any longer than that to join in the fray, but he didn't get far before Phoenix did something with their hands and trapped the powerful tan wolf inside a floating bubble complete with rainbows roaming around its edges.

Gryphin was still mid-change, his bones popping and skin stretching in grotesque ways. I was glad for something else to focus on rather than the sickening rearrangement of body parts. His snarls and groans told me he was rushing his change as fast as he could, but that he was only able to go so fast.

"I've come to reclaim what is mine," Rose said, apparently not worried about the wolf who was battling the male companion behind her. Her confidence told me that he was at least more than human, but what that was, I didn't know.

Both of the fighters were growling and snarling in animalistic ways, but it was too dark to make out how either of them was doing.

"What are you talking about?" I asked, glancing at Brandon, afraid for some reason that she was talking about his ghostly soul.

Brandon figured it out before I did, his gaze locking onto mine urgently as he cursed. "The glasses! Where are they?"

Sometime during Gryphin's change, they'd fallen off his face. I wasn't sure if I was more worried about them getting smashed under his painful change, or that they didn't get smashed, and Rose would get her hands on them. I didn't have any idea what Rose might have wanted them for, but I did know that whatever it was, it couldn't have been for good reasons.

Frantically, Brandon and I went searching through the grass where Gryphin had been standing and wearing them last. Sarah jumped in to help us search even though she didn't fully understand what was going on. I dropped to my hands and knees, my palms and fingers feeling desperately through the grass and hoping I didn't get trampled by Gryphin who was almost fully wolf. Thankfully, he seemed aware enough to move more out of the way.

Rose's haughty laugh echoed around us as we looked. "Did you really expect me to come here unprepared? Get her and whatever ghosts are there with her."

I glanced through the hair falling into my face long enough to see Rose gesture to the many ghosts behind her. To my horror, they started moving with purposeful steps toward us. It would be dangerous for them to use energy and make contact with the physical world, but I had a feeling that Rose wasn't worried about that. The health of her ghosts didn't matter nearly as much as her goals did. She probably figured she could just capture more, and I knew better than anybody that there were plenty of ghosts in the world if she needed them.

Mr. Tyler was still stuck in the bubble, floating in mid-air, and he struggled to break free, but Phoenix held him fast. The good thing about that is it seemed Phoenix was completely focused on keeping the wolf trapped so they wouldn't be able to do other damage.

Kage and the hulking man that was more than likely some vampire friend of Rose's and probably the same goon who had killed Sarah, were still wrestling out of sight. Every so often a snarl or yip sounded, but they must have been nearly evenly matched for the fight to have gone on for so long.

I could feel the ghosts descending upon us without having to be able to see them as I kept my eyes focused on the dark grass, hoping for a glimpse of golden metal. There was more than enough time for me to curse myself, angry that I had brought the glasses out for such a small task as this. I could have easily been a liaison for Gryphin and Sarah. It didn't look like enabling Sarah to talk right to Gryphin had been her unfinished business, as slim of the chances as that had been, so the risk hadn't nearly been worth it. Not to mention, I'd had to compel her to drink the potion anyway.

"I do not want to be trapped with her!" Brandon said, frantically searching on his hands and knees next to me.

"Yes! You should leave! Go back to your haunt!" I raised my head, hoping the tears streaming down my face weren't visible in the dark. The last thing I wanted was for him to leave me, but my heart would shatter if Rose caught him.

"No way! I'm not leaving you!"

They were silent as they came for us. It only took three ghosts using up energy to become physical since I wasn't anything but a weak-from-hunger teenage girl without any combat training. As their cold fingers wrapped around my arms and pulled me up, I kept screaming at Brandon. "Get out of here! I command you to leave! Go back to your haunt!"

Rose's laughter taunted me in the background as Brandon kept refusing my commands, using quite the amount of willpower to fight. "Never! I'll never leave you!"

It took four ghosts to drag Brandon away as he kicked and punched and yelled at them. Three more grabbed Sarah who was more confused than angry.

Even as my captors began to drag me toward Rose, I kept trying to feel for the glasses, convinced in a manic, panicked state that if I could only grab them, we could be free of this insanity. Of course, that was absurd, but I was scrounging around for some kind of hope.

I turned away from the grass in despair as the ghosts dragged me out further than the glasses could have been. Rose had pulled out some candles, lit them, and was chanting while holding a pink quartz crystal. There was a lock of my own hair dangling between her fingers, and fear lent me a whole new level of anger.

"No! No! No!" I kept screaming the word over and over again as I kicked out. One of my kicks connected with an older man ghost wearing some kind of mechanic jumpsuit, and he went down with a cry.

They were using energy to touch me, but that also meant I could hurt their physical bodies. Emboldened by my progress, I lashed out again, but another ghost took the mechanic's place, and her muscled arms clamped my legs together while yet another ghost, the one I had helped capture, ironically enough, grabbed my feet. I was practically hog-tied by the arms of five different people, screaming until my voice was hoarse and searing as I watched Rose work to capture Sarah and Brandon.

At least that answered one of my questions, a logical side of my brain noted while still refusing to believe what was happening. Rose hadn't needed my help to catch ghosts anymore because she could force her pets to bring them to the circle and push them right in. It explained why she hadn't stuck around and tried to trick me into helping her out more.

Phoenix's eyes were wide as they watched Rose's chanting. "Wait. What's going on? This isn't in the plan. Where did those people come from? Are you using *ghosts*?"

Their hands were still outstretched, keeping the spell solid on Mr. Tyler, but the bubble wobbled slightly with Phoenix's words.

Rose ignored her magic-partner-in-crime and kept chanting as her minions worked.

Sarah went into the circle first, growling and putting up a fight once she saw where they were taking her, even if she didn't exactly know what it was supposed to do. The potion must have still been in effect because she wasn't able to turn back into the wolf form.

Again, another thing I had done to doom us all.

Brandon had started talking as they forced Sarah into the circle and the pale pink tendrils of the crystal wrapped around her lithe shoulders. "Hanna, this is not your fault. Do not despair. You'll free me. I know you'll find a way. Remember that you're loved. So many people love you. You've got such a good heart, and it's amazing how hard you work to help strange ghosts you just met. You're amazing, Hanna. I'm so glad I know you, and I wouldn't trade that for anything, no matter what happens."

Sarah was gone, with one last snarl and a pleading look in my direction. The ghosts started shoving Brandon toward the circle just as Gryphin's silver form tackled Rose from the side.

I'd almost forgotten about him after the bone-crunching and howling had stopped, but I blessed his name as he stopped Rose from continuing to chant even as her ghosts finally pushed Brandon into the circle.

As their leader went down, the ghosts froze, as if waiting for directions. The ones holding me kept their hold rigidly but had stopped trying to move me closer for whatever plan Rose had had with me.

Rose screamed in anger as she went down, and Phoenix cursed, darting a glance behind them as if they could somehow help her. Unfortunately, they kept their focus and didn't let Mr. Tyler escape.

"Onyx!" Rose screamed while Gryphin held her down in the grass and snarled into her face. It would have been easy for him to clamp down onto her head with his powerful jaws and end the witch's life, but he hesitated, probably too pure of a soul to kill her so quickly.

And that cost us everything.

The bulky man/goon/vampire guy came out of nowhere and rushed toward Gryphin and tackled him roughly, dragging his heavy weight off Rose. There appeared to be something wrong with his leg because it was angled funny, but he either didn't care or couldn't feel the pain.

Once Gryphin's weight was off her chest, Rose hopped up, pushed her arms out toward her goon, and started pouring purple-lightning magic into his body. Whatever she was doing, it was lending strength to Onyx, allowing him to overpower Gryphin, despite his giant jaws and huge paws.

Muscles pulsing, eyes dancing with purple lightning, the goon grabbed Gryphin's mouth, his fingers in between the sharp teeth, and began to pull, forcing Gryphin's mouth open more and more.

Horror flooded my chest as I realized we were about to see my friend's jaw ripped open. As Gryphin whined, his eyes wide with fear, Kage came back from the darkness, favoring one of his hindlegs, and attacked Onyx from behind.

The three of them went down in a pile of raging snarls and flying fur.

Rose added her own snarl to the cacophony and scrunched her face in rage as she poured more power into Onyx. As she expended energy for the spell, her skin started to sag and a few wrinkles creased into her forehead, as if she was aging before our eyes.

Then I remembered where I'd seen that purple lightning before. It had only been a few hours earlier, but it felt like a lifetime ago. Rose was not only a witch but, somehow, trained in necromancy or perhaps even a full necromancer herself.

Which meant that the goon she controlled was probably most certainly a vampire, based on his strength and speed. The spell she was using was giving him more strength to stand his ground against two angry werewolves.

It was difficult to make out what exactly was happening with the two wolves and the goon fighting. All three of them moved so quickly. Onyx threw punches that were hard enough to daze the already-wounded Kage, but Gryphin was fresh and quick, darting in with bloody slashes, clawing through leather jackets and soft skin alike. Despite taking several hits, Onyx plowed on as if nothing had hit him except a soft summer breeze.

Rose kept aging as she poured all her magic and energy into Onyx, and it seemed like it was going to come down to who could hold out the longest. If the wolves were able to keep going then hopefully Rose would age herself to death, and she'd collapse in a pile of dust, taking Onyx with her.

Except then she did something that surprised even Phoenix. Without a word or signal from her, probably some kind of mental command, one of the extra ghosts standing nearby was pulled toward Rose in a sharp tug. There wasn't even enough time for the poor soul to cry out as Rose opened her mouth so wide that it looked creepily unhinged and *sucked*. The whole ghost poured into her mouth like a wispy wad of cotton candy.

The effects were visible immediately as Rose's wrinkles smoothed out, the grey in her hair became blonde again, and her shoulders stood taller as she poured even more energy into Onyx.

The goon roared with the extra power, and Kage went flying, hitting a tree, and slumping into an unmoving pile of shadow. Gryphin growled and snapped at Onyx only to find his powerful jaw muscles once again struggling to close over the goon's arms.

With a great inhale, Rose pulled three more ghosts into herself, causing both Phoenix and the kid holding my feet to curse.

Separating one of her hands from where it was pouring energy into Onyx, Rose aimed it toward the candle circle. Apparently eating the ghosts, or whatever she was doing, not only helped stop the effects of the aging but also gifted her with a boost in magic. With an angry grimace on her face, she began chanting again. My heart stopped as I watched the quartz tendrils wrap around my best friend.

Brandon's eyes were wide, and his hand stretched out toward me as he was pulled into the crystal still clutched in Rose's fingers.

Terrified, half-worried that I'd have a heart attack, I felt panic rush my body. Breaths zipped in and out of my chest. I was getting so dizzy with the emotion and fear gobbling me up that had I been standing I would have collapsed into the grass. As it was, the ghosts holding me had to adjust their grip slightly, but mostly kept their expressions blank, waiting for more instructions from their leader.

Except one. The kid from the 70s dropped my legs with an angry look in Rose's direction, apparently displaying a bit more willpower than the other ghosts had. When I'd helped capture him in the first place, he'd had given me quite a power struggle, and it appeared that spending time with Rose had only strengthened his rage.

Leaving Onyx to fare on his own for a second, Rose dropped the purple lightning, and hastily tied my hair around the crystal holding Brandon's soul and sealed it with a drop of wax.

The goon wavered slightly as the influx of energy died. Gryphin's growl rumbled in his throat as he was able to gain some leverage back on his jaw, forcing Onyx's arms to give in a few inches.

Then a howl rang through the night so loud it echoed through my bones. It was followed by several eerie calls in answer. Everyone inside the clearing froze for a few seconds before Phoenix jumped into action.

"Screw this," they said, dropping their arms, the bubble with Mr. Tyler in it falling with them. "I just wanted the glasses. I did not sign up to enable a plasma eater!"

They popped out with a snap, and Rose found herself being charged at by an angry tan wolf.

Grimacing, Rose waved her hand and disappeared as well.

At first, I thought she'd left her loyal servants to perish at our hands, but then her voice sounded from somewhere behind me. "Thanks for the glasses and the souls, dear. You're always good for an assist."

Snarling, I fought against the ghosts still holding onto me, and since the 70s kid had dropped my feet, I was able to get in a few more good kicks. Too bad it still wasn't enough to free me.

Mr. Tyler skidded where Rose had just been standing and pivoted. Another wolf bounded out of the trees behind him and howled again, the ghost wolves charging in closely behind the alpha as they all bar-reled toward Rose.

"See you around, Seer," Rose made the last word sound like a swear word before teleporting herself out of the clearing as it flooded with enraged wolves, both alive and dead.

Onyx and the ghosts disappeared right along with her, except for one. The 70s kid stood in front of me as I fell harshly into the grass, my captors melting into thin air. His physical body faded as he turned the ghostly blue again just as Mr. Tyler dove toward him, causing the wolf to plow into the ground in a way that had to have hurt.

Gryphin, suddenly free of the vampire's grip, turned and snarled, searching for his prey and finding nothing.

Full of rage and nothing to spend it on, the alpha and his ghost wolves howled and snarled in frustration, running all around the clearing as if they could find their enemies hiding in the grass some-where.

But we knew they were all long gone.

"Why don't you get back to your master? I'm sure she'd like to eat your soul up too," I lashed out at the 70s kid still staring at me.

It wasn't a fair thing to say as he was only trapped because of my stupidity and not any actions of his own, but my whole body was hurting. Anger, fear, and loss were beating down on my soul, and I didn't know which one of us was going to win.

It certainly didn't feel like it was going to be me.

"Free me," the kid said while wolves roamed around us, occasionally running into each other and rolling away in snarling heaps.

I probably should have been worried they'd shove into me, the alive ones easily breaking my fragile human bones, but I was too upset to care.

"Free you? But how can I? Can't you free yourself? All the other ghosts got pulled back there already." My words came out in short puffs of air, and I still wasn't sure I wasn't going to pass out at any second.

"She's a bit distracted at the moment. Your powers are helping me stay here. Now use them to set me free. I know you can do it."

As I struggled to simply breathe, words floated into my head that I'd read long ago from inside a certain book of curses that I'd used to help free Mr. Tyler. Instead of focusing on what was impossible about it, I focused on what needed to be done. There was no way I would have even bothered to try if Brandon's scared eyes weren't seared into my brain and an unyielding *need* to rescue my friend wasn't brewing inside my core.

If I could help this kid, I could help Brandon.

Grunting with effort, I pulled myself up onto wavering feet, took three steps toward the ghost, stuck my hand into his chest, and closed my eyes. As far as I knew, nothing like this had ever been done before because it had simply not been possible. But as far as my gran had known, neither could a Seer summon nor command ghosts, and I could do both.

What else was I capable of?

Imagining my hand as that ghostly blue hue, I searched around inside the ghost kid for what I knew would be a thick, plasma chain surrounding his chest. Once my fingers felt the cool metal, I wrapped it around my hand and wrist tightly, and then I *pulled*.

I didn't just pull with my hand and arm, but I also pulled with my heart and soul, putting all my grief, fear, and anger into the action.

Somewhere far away, I felt Rose's concerned attention turn to me in dawning horror as she realized what I was doing. I figured if I could feel her, she could feel me, and I sent her a mental smirk with the words, *Run away, little girl. I'm coming to set them free, and you're not going to like it.*

Chapter 27

As I pulled the chains from the ghost's chest, my ears popped, and the whole world seemed to stutter for a second. Then it all rushed back in quickly, and both the ghost and I fell back into the grass.

I groaned and massaged my hand as it tingled like it'd lost all its supply of blood.

"Far out," the ghost said, rubbing at the spot in his chest. "I think it worked. How did you do that?"

The werewolves had begun to settle down some, but I wasn't paying them much attention. All I knew was that they had stopped howling and running around like a bunch of disturbed, angry ants.

"You're asking me that after demanding I do it? Seems kind of backward," I mumbled, gingerly resting my hand on my lap until the feeling came back into it.

He shrugged. "It was worth a try. I could only resist her because she was so distracted, and I didn't know when we'd get another chance to try that out. I had to get away from that freaky deaky lady. Man, the way she was eating those other ghosts. There was no way I was going to let her eat me."

Panic settled into my chest as if finding a new permanent home. It was familiar, and I felt alarmed at the thought that I'd just recently began to get over the vampire panic attacks. I knew I was going to be in for a much higher level and…well, I wasn't ready to admit it to myself, but there wasn't going to be anyone there to help me.

It felt like the air was being sucked out of the air, and that I couldn't pull it into my chest fast enough. Through ragged huffs, I managed to say, "Does she eat her ghost slaves a lot? How many has she eaten before?"

The 70s ghost lowered his eyebrows and frowned at me. "What's wrong with you? You keep acting like that, and we'll both be ghosts."

I forced myself to draw in air, trying to do the trick of inhaling through my nose. It helped a tiny bit. "Just answer my question."

He shrugged. "Honestly, that's the first time I've seen her do that. Before today, the worst thing she'd ask of us is to use energy to turn physical for a task of some kind." He shook his head and chuckled. "And here I was thinking *that* was bad. I had no idea. Anyway, I gotta skitty. Thanks for your help! If you see that insane lady again, make sure you tell her Frank sent ya."

He disappeared as I blinked and kept trying to breathe. I could feel my heart pounding all the way down to my toes, and my stomach twisted. Stars began to dance in front of my eyes as I laid back into the grass.

A comforting weight settled onto my stomach and chest. It took great effort to pull my head up enough to see Gryphin's furry head lay on me as his worried eyes watched me warily. He put a giant paw across my legs. With another groan, I put my head back down into the grass, and my hand into the soft fur around his ears.

I didn't know if wolves purred. Pretty sure dogs didn't but, apparently, werewolves could emit a deep growling, grumble that Gryphin was giving me as I stroked him. It seemed odd, at first, that the pressure on my chest added comfort instead of more difficulty, but the more we rested and the more the soothing cool wind played in the high grass, the more I found I could breathe.

Four days later, I hugged myself against the cold wind of a cloudy fall afternoon. The weather was fitting for a funeral even without the rain.

The wolves had helped me get Steph's body back to the river where they'd arranged it to look like she'd washed up further down from the accident. Then they'd called the police, making up some story about hiking along the banks and finding her body. They'd even managed to get some water into her lungs somehow, so, that while her body looked creepily fresh, at least it appeared that she'd drowned.

Caleb had used some of his vampire voodoo to help her parents be convinced she had simply been washed away by the accident and drowned sometime later, stopping them from asking too many questions about why she still looked so fresh.

It was way past time for poor, sweet Steph to be put to rest.

Gryphin stood next to me as we gazed down on Steph's polished coffin. His front legs had both been broken and some of the bones in his neck had gotten cracked fissures, but thankfully, werewolves were no strangers to abused body parts. He'd healed easily after the pack had surrounded him and howled into the night air, lending him strength and unity.

Kage had been a bit worse off, but Gryphin had assured me he had almost completely mended already. One of the best things about being a werewolf was the quick healing.

Flowers had been heaped onto the outside of the casket as it sat on the lowering device that would put Steph's body into the dirt for good. Everyone else had left the scene except for Steph's parents who stood off to the side, hugging each other and talking to the funeral director. It had seemed like the whole school had shown up at her wake the night before and then again at the funeral. It'd been so full that they had to open the doors and let people spill out into the parking lot.

Noah had tried to grab a second with me to chat, but all I had done was given Gryphin a pointed look, and he'd moved strategically to block the football player as we fought our way out of the crowd.

I hadn't gone back to school Thursday and Friday, claiming I was just too exhausted. I hadn't answered any of his text messages either, mostly too full of apathy to even lift my phone.

Mom and Trina had given me a hard time, and I'd let them, staring listlessly from the couch while they paced in front of me, going on about how stupid I'd been to have gone to the wolf territory so late at night.

I hadn't even told them the whole story. All they knew was that I'd been out there to help a ghost for the wolves, we'd had a breakthrough, and that for some time afterward I'd been drained and so depressed I couldn't even force myself to drink my diet soda.

As good as it had felt to include them in my ghostly escapades, I wasn't yet ready to disclose the full story about what had happened that night.

Or who I had lost.

Mom had barely allowed me to come to the funeral, but Caleb and Gryphin had assured her they would be nearby to keep an eye on me.

"She was really amazing. The sad thing is that I didn't even know how much so until after she died," I said quietly.

Gryphin shifted toward me and wrapped a long arm around my shoulders. No one commented on how my "boyfriend" was moving in on me or huffed in frustrated annoyance, and my heart ached with the loss of those snarky comments.

We stood quietly for a few more minutes and let the wind flow around us.

"How is your dad?" I asked Gryphin as we turned away from my friend's grave and walked through the headstones.

He pulled his arm away as we walked, and I immediately missed his radiating warmth. "He's better. It'll take time for things to recover, of course, but he seems mostly better."

We'd decided not to tell the alpha about where Sarah's ghost was currently trapped, but they'd filled him in on what had happened to his wife and how she had died. Gryphin and Mr. Tyler had also decided not to tell him that they knew who had killed her, but that they were working on some leads and that they'd get back with everyone when they knew more information.

None of what we'd learned that night had been good news, but, so far, it appeared it was doing its job to alleviate the fears Mr. Tyler and Gryphin had for Bertram and the pack.

"That's good," I said.

We walked in silence for a few minutes before Gryphin spoke again. "What are you going to do now?"

"Oh, me? Let's just say it's a good thing I've been hanging out with werewolves so much lately."

"Why's that?" He smiled flirtatiously.

"Because I'm going hunting."

To Be Continued...

Don't Summon Necromancers

H anna's story continues in book 4, *Don't Summon Necro-mancers*. Available Now!

After Rose takes something deeply important to Hanna, the Seer is determined to hunt the tricky magic user down, no matter what. Hanna pools all her resources together, tugging on any string she can think of, including going to the necromancers and employing the help of a surly ghost named Frank.

When Hanna discovers the necros are also hunting Rose and if they kill her all the enslaved spirits will be trapped forever, she must find the witch first or else risk losing everything that means anything.

Unable to get reliable help from a suspiciously busy Caleb, Hanna turns to the arcanist Phoenix for answers, hoping that the magic user will be able to give at least a hint of where she should go next. Instead, she ends up trapped with the matron of the coven in a bleak spell while Rose is being hunted by necros and free to eat any other ghosts she deems necessary—including a certain sarcastic skater boy.

About the Author

Jeni Conrad is a wife, mother, teacher, writer, reader, and a human (honest, she can pass those robot tests almost every time!). She usually writes YA fantasy or paranormal stories . Since fifteen years old, she worked in the restaurant business while getting through high school, a BA in English, and then an MA in sociology. Now she works from home while wrangling two small girls, a dog, and two crazy cats.

www.jeniconrad.com

Also By Jeni Conrad

The Lost Guardian Series
Part 1- Game On
Part 2- IRL

The Hanna Sanchez Series
Don't Haunt Ghosts
Don't Bite Vampires
Don't Hunt Werewolves
Don't Summon Necromancers
Don't Hex Witches

The Mirror Islands Series
Peter in Wonderland
Alice in Neverland